COVER-UP

IRONS AND WORKS: KEY LARGO

E.M. LINDSEY

Cover-Up
E.M. Lindsey
Copyright © 2023

All rights reserved.

This book or any portion thereof may not be reproduced or used in any manner whatsoever without the express written permission of the publisher except for the use of brief quotations in a book review. This book is a work of fiction.
Any resemblance to persons, places, jobs, or events is purely coincidental.

Editing: Sandra with One Love Editing
Cover: Ozark Witch Cover Design
Photographer: Wander Aguiar

Content warnings: past attempted medical abuse, forced conservatorship threats, past narcissistic parental abuse, parent with dementia, parent in hospice care, grandparent loss, past major injuries from military service, past traumatic brain injury, on-page epileptic seizure, on-page mild violence (not between main characters), graphic descriptions of relationship abuse (not between main characters), and sibling with substance addiction.

COVER-UP

Felix has a major problem.

He's pining.

Well, pining might not be the right word for how he feels about the absurdly hot, one-armed chef who works next door, but it's close enough.

Felix doesn't have high hopes for romance, though. Not with the fact that his face blindness means every time he looks at Deimos, it's like he's seeing him for the first time. After all, who would want a relationship with a man who couldn't pick him out of a crowd?

But that's not his actual problem. Felix learns he needs to see his terrible family for his grammy's funeral, and Dei has offered to go along to act like his boyfriend.

And God help him, but Felix can't bring himself to say no.

But hey, what's a little emotional torture when he gets to pretend Dei is his for a little while?

It seems that Dei has softer, kinder plans for Felix's heart than to torture it, however—and Felix quickly learns there's no way to cover up being in love. Dei's words of affection are powerful, and Felix realizes the only thing in the world he wants is to let Dei in.

1

"I think I'm old. This qualifies me for being old, right?"

Felix offered Jamie a crooked smile. "Aren't you barely twenty?"

Jamie huffed. "Twenty-four, thank you. And feeling old as hell. One beer and I can't drive."

The guys laughed, and Harley leaned over, clapping his massive hand over Jamie's shoulder, giving him a tender shake. "You're alright, bud. Even fetuses have low tolerance sometimes."

Jamie flushed a deeper red than the beer had already caused and flipped him off before curling his hand around his pint glass. With a massive grin, he tipped it back and finished off what was left. "Who's driving me?"

In spite of the fact that he wasn't drinking, it was a no from Felix. He hadn't had the luxury of owning a driver's license in years. Hell, he could barely remember what it was like getting behind the wheel of a car.

Then again, he could hardly remember most things from his past anymore.

That was life before the *Incident*, as he called it in his head. Back in LA, the man he was before the seizure took him out at the knees felt like a fever dream. Like an old movie he'd watched while stoned out of his mind instead of a life he'd once lived.

His brain was still healing—at least, that's what his neurologist insisted—and he was making occasional progress whenever he went in for his checkups. His medication was helping with his seizures, and he hadn't had another one like the seizure that had sent him hurtling into another universe.

But he'd never be the same again. He'd never be able to walk into a room and immediately recognize the people in it without help. He'd always have to leave himself little notes around his house so he remembered to take his meds, and do his laundry, and eat, and shower.

And he would always live with the fear that the next grand mal would leave him nothing more than an empty shell.

He never said that aloud, of course. Not to himself, and especially not to his tattoo family, though he knew damn well they wouldn't be cruel about it. No, they'd sit and listen to him vent. Someone would offer to give him pain therapy in the form of new ink, and Linc would probably try to pierce something. They'd get food from Jeremiah's restaurant next door. Zeke would force him to eat too much cake, and they'd all start telling him embarrassing stories so he wouldn't feel like such a freak.

The thought was nice, but the kindness felt strangely unrealistic. And in all honesty, he wasn't sure he was ready to let his guard down, no matter how much they insisted they cared about him.

Felix sipped on his tonic again, grimacing at the bitter taste of underripe lime, which was a real goddamn shame, considering they lived in the Keys. But it was Jeremiah's bar, so it felt wrong to complain, considering how well he'd managed to fit in with them.

And how happy he made Felix's best friend, especially now that the two were shacking up together and Felix was finally starting to trust himself to live alone. Mostly.

There was a knock on the counter, and Felix looked over at Theo, the Deaf pilot who had also integrated himself into their group in ways Felix hadn't been expecting. He waved his hand, trying to get everyone's attention. 'I can give rides. I'm not drinking.'

Felix followed the signs slowly, his brain processing them at a speed that he knew probably pissed the guy off, but Theo never judged him for his shitty progress. He insisted that he didn't give care so long as everyone was trying, and Felix was. But his brain struggled with the most simple things, and learning a new language was starting to feel beyond him.

It took him a second to realize that most of the guys were getting up, and he stared at his drink again, unsure if he was ready to go. He loved hanging out with his friends, but he was just starting to enjoy a real and honest sense of independence, and he wanted to prove to himself he didn't need to rely on the guys for everything.

A hand fell on his arm, and Felix jumped, turning his gaze up to see Max smiling down at him.

"Come on. There's room in Theo's car."

Felix shook his head. "I'm gonna hang."

Max's brow furrowed the way it did when he was worried about him—which was still too often for Felix's liking. "Want me to stay? I don't mind if you want company."

"No," Felix said in a rush, then tried to soften his tone. "Seriously, I'm good. I'll call a Lyft or something when I'm done."

Max nodded, then wrapped fingers around the back of Felix's neck, squeezing in a quick goodbye. The guys filtered out slowly after that, and Felix was eventually on his own with Jeremiah at the very end of the bar, doing some work on his laptop. Felix had no idea if Jeremiah even knew he was there, but if he did, he said nothing and continued on with his work.

Felix appreciated the space and the silence. It was a rarity in the shop since everyone was in each other's business all the damn time. Felix knew he wasn't being singled out, which did help, but he still felt a little…lost and uncertain about where he belonged.

Everything in his life was good, but it was so damn different since moving to Key Largo. Working in LA had been hectic and loud—everything was all go all the time. Bonsai was one of those old neighborhood shops with constant music blasting and locals filtering in and out all day long.

They had a pool table and darts, and friends of friends would just hang around for hours, their voices filling up all the empty corners.

Felix didn't hate it, but he never quite felt like he fit in. He'd apprenticed under Paris for a bit and then under Max, and those two made him feel more at home than anyone else. And when Felix had been taken down by the seizure, they were the two people who showed up for him and got him back on his feet. When he was so damn sure he was going to lose everything, they made sure he never gave up.

But it was still a lot. He was still the shy kid from a busted-ass home with no real concept of how to care about other people. The only thing he knew for sure was that he wasn't going to last in a place like that. It was too much, and he wasn't strong enough to keep going for much longer. He hadn't told anyone at the shop what was going on with his mom—that she was constantly threatening to have him locked up for the rest of his life—but he was starting to believe her.

When Zeke appeared like some sort of biblical angel with a message from God, Felix knew it was a sign. This was his chance, and even if Max and Paris had declined, he wasn't going to turn it down. He knew jack shit about the South except that it was thousands and thousands of miles away. And nothing was going to stop him from putting that distance between him and his family.

He left like a thief in the night. He rode beside Paris in his truck, and it wasn't until they'd crossed into Texas that he sent a message to his mom and sisters, letting them know what he'd done.

He was definitely expecting the call that came through seconds after he hit Send, and a small part of him had whispered not to answer it, but the deeply ingrained guilt he'd been trained to feel after disobeying her forced his hand.

"Felix. Where are you?" He could barely process his mom's shrill demand, and it sent shivers down his spine. She'd been like that since he was a kid, and it had taken years of prying her claws out of him, one by one, to realize just how much control she tried to have over his life.

"It doesn't matter," he'd told her. Paris reached out to hold him by the shoulder, and he almost burst into tears. His voice trembled. "I just wanted to let you know that I left."

"You can't just leave. You're sick, Felix. You've got problems. You can't take care of yourself on your own."

His eyes went hot. "I'm fine."

"I'm going to court over this, do you hear me? You need a conservatorship. You cannot be trusted. There's no way you can…"

He never did get to hear the rest of her rant. Paris plucked the phone out of his hands and held it to his own ear. She went on for ten minutes before she realized Felix wasn't there anymore, and he could hear her screech after Paris said, "Don't worry, lady. He's not on his own. Catch you later."

Paris made him block her number, which left him feeling nauseous, and it took weeks of Max checking in with him and reminding him it was for the best before he ultimately deleted her contact so he couldn't unblock her even if he wanted to.

And then…life moved on.

He settled. He made more friends with the new artists that were trickling in. He met the guys from the sister shop in Denver, who treated him like they'd known him his entire life. He found people he could relate to.

And no one at all, not once, gave a single fuck that he could rarely remember them at first sight.

He started to feel like a person again.

He started to…

"I need'a gimlet." The sharp, slurring voice drilled past the wall of fog created by Felix's rusted old memories, and he snapped back to reality. Turning his head, he saw a woman dressed in tight jeans and a crop top leaning over the counter, trying to grab one of the bottles from the well.

"Whoa," Felix said, hopping up. He grabbed her by the elbow and eased her back. "That's a bad idea."

She turned and gave him a shove so hard he toppled into the stool. "Fuck you, man. Fuck your fuckin' face." She was still slurring, but he could hear one of those Deep South, Appalachian accents under it—just like Jeremiah's head chef, Deimos. "I need a drink a'fore that son of a bitch comes in here. If he's gonna beat the fuck out of me, I don't wanna feel it."

Felix was halfway to his feet when Jeremiah slid over toward her, and Felix glanced out of the corner of his eye to see the fury on his friend's face.

"Who's coming in here to beat the fuck out of you?"

"Some asshole," the woman said, waving her hand. "Don't worry about it." Her hair was thick and curly and very black, tied at the nape of her neck in a messy bun. She had lipstick on, but it was smeared, and in the dim bar light, Felix could make out a bruise forming on her jaw.

It definitely looked fresh.

"Someone definitely hit her," Felix murmured, leaning toward Jeremiah. "Recently."

"Fucking hell," he groaned. "Do me a favor and get her out of here. Take her out the back and call a car. Just have them put it on the restaurant tab."

Felix nodded and took a step closer to the woman. "Hey. You okay?"

She froze halfway to reaching for the liquor again and gave him an up-and-down stare. "Yeah, I'm fine, baby. We can fuck if you want, but not up the ass."

Felix almost choked on his own tongue. "Oh, honey. You're not my type."

She hummed in thought. "Okay, *fiiiine*. You can put it in my ass. But you gotta buy me a gin first because I don't wanna feel that neither."

Felix wasn't sure if he wanted to laugh in her face or wrap her in a blanket and feed her soup until she sobered up. Instead, he offered his hand. "Wanna go for a walk?"

She scoffed, but she linked their fingers together anyway. "I ain't a hooker."

"Okay," Felix said, glancing back at Jeremiah who, rolled his eyes behind his thick lenses. "That's fine."

Jeremiah reached into a small cabinet at the end of the bar and came up with a water bottle. "Try to get her name and where she lives," he said. "If I have to call the cops, I want to be able to tell them where to go."

Felix really didn't want to get that involved, but Jeremiah was protective over the peace of their community. The least Felix could do was lend him a hand.

He tugged on the woman's arm, and she followed him down the dark hall and outside. The lights in the back parking lot were a weird, hazy sort of yellow, and along with the weird feeling he got from looking at anyone's face, it made her seem gaunt and skeletal. But maybe she was just that thin. She looked strung out, and she had an acrid scent clinging to her underneath heavy cigarette smoke that told him she wasn't deep into just booze that night.

"I'm Felix," he said, pulling out his phone.

She wolf whistled quietly as she balanced on the backs of her heels. "Hot. You're really hot."

"Thanks," he said with a laugh. "You gonna tell me your name?"

"Soph."

"Nice to meet you, Soph."

"Naw," she said, snapping her fingers in his face. "Never mind. I hate that. It's Sofia. *He* calls me Soph."

"The guy who put that bruise on you?" Felix asked as he ordered the Lyft.

Her face fell, and she wrapped her arms around her middle. "He doesn't mean to. I mean, he does. He's a dick. But I just get him so riled up sometimes."

Felix's gut clenched and twisted. "Fuck that guy, Sofia."

She laughed so hard she almost toppled over, and Felix only just managed to catch her. "I did. Thaaa'sss the problem, Fido."

"Felix."

She cocked her head. "Felix is a way better name. But it's for a cat."

He fought the urge to roll his eyes as he steadied her up near the curb. "Do you know your address?"

Sofia threw her head back, laughing again, though this time, she stayed on her feet. "Yeah. M'staying with my brother. He's gonna be so mad. He's a dick too, but he don't hit me."

"Thank god for small favors," Felix muttered. He glanced around, feeling a little surge of anxiety that she might have been followed, but so far, there was no drama.

And a moment later, his phone pinged at the same time as a car pulled up. "Here," he told her, opening the car door. "Get in, and we can get the address thing figured out."

"Uhg. I don't want to go to your house," Sofia said, leaning on the window of the car.

"Hey, man," the driver called. "I'm not interested in having some drunk chick puke all over my car."

"She's not going to puke," Felix promised, hoping to god he wasn't lying. "This is kind of an emergency." Sofia started to tug at his shirt, and Felix let out a frustrated growl, pushing her off. "Seriously, please sit down."

"Get your ass out of that car right fuckin' now!" a voice bellowed a short distance away.

Felix froze, and his fight or flight went with option A as he turned to see a man with a shaved head and wild eyes storming toward them. Felix immediately put himself between the guy and Sofia and shoved her back into the seat. She let out a loud protest, but Felix dropped in after her, shut the door, and it locked.

The guy's fist connected with the window, and the driver let out a shout. "What the *fuck?*"

"I will tip you five hundred in cash if you get us the fuck out of here," Felix told him. Sofia was trying to reach the door handle, but Felix held her with one hand as he dug for his wallet with the other.

"Dude, this is exactly the shit I was trying to avoid!" the driver told him.

"I know, but that dude beat on her." Felix held his wallet between his teeth and managed to extract a wad of cash. He tossed it up into the passenger seat, ignoring the asshole who was still punching the window. "Seriously. Please."

The driver looked down, then sighed and hit the gas. The guy started to chase them on foot, but eventually, the driver managed to hit the main road, heading toward Felix's address, and the raged-out fucker disappeared into the shadows.

He sat back with a sigh, covering his face with one hand until he felt something wet poking his ear. He sat up and shoved at Sofia, who cackled.

"Wet Willy!"

"Fuck me," he muttered. "What's your address, Sofia?"

"Fuck knows."

His lips thinned, and his headache was putting him at the very edge of his patience. He hadn't been through stress like this in way too long, and he was terrified he was going to start seizing. He didn't feel any warning signs, but the one that had taken him out had crept up on him too.

He took a few slow breaths.

"Sofia. Where do you live? I'm not taking you home with me, and you need to get somewhere safe."

She scoffed. "I don't know," she said slowly. "Just call my brother. He knows his stupid address."

"Who's your brother?" Felix pressed. "Is he in your phone?"

Sofia stared at him, then burst into laughter before slumping against the door and closing her eyes.

Felix wanted to scream or maybe cry. He hadn't signed up for this, and he definitely wasn't taking her home. Now that he was close to her, he could see her arms were covered in sores, and she smelled like she hadn't seen the inside of a shower in months.

"Just, uh…keep going," he told the driver. At the very least, he could set her up in his driveway until she sobered up enough to tell him who her brother was.

The guy shrugged and said nothing, likely pissed as hell, and Felix couldn't blame him. This wasn't how he pictured his night going either. Jeremiah seriously goddamn owed him.

"Hey!" Sofia shouted, sitting up suddenly and smacking her forehead on the window so hard it made Felix wince. "I don't live here. Are you trying to human traffic me?"

Felix pinched the bridge of his nose as the car rolled to a stop in front of his place, and he quickly opened the door. "Uh. Keep my contact info if you need me to talk to anyone about the guy who punched your car. And sorry about this. Also…thanks."

The guy said nothing, but he gave a single, sharp nod and waited for Felix to drag Sofia out. He was gone before Felix registered the door slamming shut, which was just as well. He didn't want to do this alone, but he sure as hell didn't want to involve some stranger.

"I think I live here," Sophia said after a beat.

Felix blinked at her. "Are you serious?"

She laughed. "Yeah, fucker. Fifty-eight oh eight, Coral…something. Cora something?"

Coral Avenue—where he lived. They were neighbors? Fuck his life.

Under the dim streetlamp, Felix stared at the ascending addresses, counting them off before spotting what had to be her house.

He hoped. He'd feel like shit if he dropped her on some neighbor's door, but he was pretty sure her drugged-out mind wasn't making this up. The only thing that would make life easier was if Felix could remember who lived where on his street.

But thanks to his busted brain, the most he could do was read the numbers painted on mailboxes and hope the person who answered the door didn't want to punch him in the face for disturbing their peace.

His temples started to throb, and if he wasn't careful, he was going to lose his words soon.

"Come on," Felix said, and he led the way to 5808. There was a nice yard and a single porch light, but it didn't look like anyone was home. "That guy who hit you doesn't live here, does he?"

"Who? Clark? Fuuuuck no," she drawled, then tripped over her feet, catching herself on Felix's arm. She grinned, then laughed. "Hey! Wanna fuck?"

Felix carefully pried her hand off him. "No, thank you." He kept a single pace in front of her, and he was grateful she didn't try to run. "Is your brother home?"

"Yeah." She laughed so hard she almost fell over. "Dickhead's always home."

Felix said a small prayer that the guy wasn't an actual dickhead as he pushed the bell and waited. He'd had enough bullshit for the night.

It took a while, but eventually, he heard a rhythmic stomping sound, and his gut started to twist until the door opened. He gazed into a face he had a feeling he should know—the way everyone looked, like a word stuck on the tip of his tongue.

Then he noticed the arm—or the lack of one. And the missing leg.

"Deimos," he blurted.

Just like with everyone, Felix never recognized Dei on sight but did remember the chef was hot. Like, absurdly so. Like Felix wanted to sell his soul for a taste of his full lips every time he saw him.

And then it hit him. Sofia was his sister?

"So, um. This is Sofia. She says she lives here," Felix said, then glanced behind him to see Sofia a few feet away, spinning in circles.

"Woo! Woo! Oh, I'm gonna puke, fuuuuck," she cried.

Felix dove for her and grabbed her arm, and she tumbled to his feet. He held her hand, but she refused to get back up, and he gave Dei a helpless look. "She came into the restaurant tonight, and she couldn't remember her address, so I brought her to my place so I could try and figure out where she belongs. But now she's insisting it's here. Please tell me you know her."

"I know her." Dei held up a finger. "Gimme a sec. Don't let her run," he added. The door shut, and around thirty seconds later, it opened again and Dei limped out, his prosthetic leg now jutting out from the hem of his boxers.

It was only then Felix noticed how little he was wearing. A black tank top barely covered his thick chest, and his bicep was bulging as he reached down and yanked Sofia to her feet. He stared at her in the porch light, his face going stormier and stormier.

"He fuckin' hit you again?"

Sofia shoved him off. "None of your business, dickhead." She moved past him quicker than Felix thought she should be capable of moving, and then she was inside.

It felt like someone cut a string, and a line of tension drained from his spine. "Sorry."

Dei blinked at him. "Sugar, what the hell are *you* sorry for?"

Felix felt his cheeks warm at the term of endearment, though he was pretty sure Dei called everyone that. "Bringing her home like this. There was…a slight incident in the restaurant parking lot with some guy."

Dei slapped his hand over his face and dragged it down with a heavy groan. "Jesus. Jer's gonna kill me. Or fire me."

"I'm not sure he knows about it yet," Felix said. "Well…he knows she was trying to steal a bottle of gin," Felix admitted. "And he knows someone hit her. But he had me call a Lyft for her, and he was inside when it all went down."

Dei closed his eyes and tipped his head up like he was praying. "Great." Dei's eyes opened. They looked like endless pools of black in the late-night haze. "Did she fuck up the car?"

Felix shook his head. "No. But, um, her boyfriend or whatever? He did. He punched the fuck out of it while I was bribing the driver to get us out of there."

Dei muttered a long string of something that Felix was pretty sure wasn't English, and then he offered Felix a tense smile. "Come on in, sugar. You look like you need a drink."

Felix hesitated. "I can't drink on my meds. So, thanks, but—"

"I got tea. Sweet, iced and hot," Dei added like he wasn't going to take no for an answer.

And frankly, Felix had wanted to have a one-on-one conversation with Dei since the day he set eyes on him, so it was one of the easiest yeses he'd ever given. Dei held the door for him, and as Felix breathed in his scent, he realized if he wasn't careful, the man could be big, big trouble.

In all the best ways.

2

The inside of Dei's house smelled nice. Weirdly nice. Like the sweet cinnamon of horchata, which Felix hadn't come across since leaving the West Coast for the islands. It was also very sparsely furnished with a single couch by the window, a chair, and a wooden wall with a ton of oddly placed pegs and hooks all over it.

Felix couldn't work out what the hell any of it was for, so he followed Dei past a narrow sliding door and into a very well-stocked kitchen. It looked like it had come straight out of a magazine with its marble counters and hanging pots and pans, and it was sparkling clean.

"You okay?"

Felix blinked, then realized his hands were shaking and his head was pounding. "I don't actually know."

"Existentially or physically?" Dei asked as he gestured toward a barstool.

Everything started to go a little foggy, but he was missing the familiar aura that generally came with a seizure, so he didn't panic too much. He slid his ass onto the stool and put his face in his hands, his elbows pressing into the cool stone.

"Hey. Look, if my sister—"

"It's not her fault," Felix interrupted. "Even on good days, my brain's kind of like a can of condensed chicken noodle soup."

Dei let out a small laugh. "That might be the grossest, most descriptive term I've ever heard. You got a brain injury, sugar?"

Felix's cheeks burned at the endearment again, and he looked up through his fingers. "Sort of? I have epilepsy. I, uh…I guess I had it as a kid, but I stopped seizing when I was in elementary school. I don't even really remember it."

Dei leaned his arm on the counter. "Yeah?"

Felix nodded and licked his lips. "I'm sure the guys all told you about my…" He wriggled his fingers in the air between them. "Issues."

Dei laughed and shook his head. "Issues. I guess we can call it that. Jer told me not to get too offended if you don't recognize me in public."

Felix felt his mouth curve into a grin and heard himself say, "You're difficult to forget," before he could stop himself. His jaw shut with a snap, but Dei just laughed again.

"Yeah, I get that a lot." He stared for a minute longer. "But you know who I am, right?"

Felix nodded and laughed. "Yeah, I know you." He cleared his throat as his tongue started to get all twisted in his mouth, and he thought through his words first. "A few years ago, I had a bad one." He tapped his temple. "Grand mal. Lasted ten minutes. Then, I had a cluster of smaller ones for three days. The brain damage was pretty extensive. I have this…thing. Face blindness."

Dei nodded. "Gotcha. So you really didn't know who the hell I was standin' at the door."

Felix laughed and blushed. "Does it make me a shithead to say that I was able to recognize you from your, uh. Your missing…um…"

Dei's face went stormy, and Felix started to panic before he boomed a laugh and reached out, clapping him on the wrist. "I'm messin' with you, shug. This fuckin' thing's gotta be useful for something, right?" He gave the end of his very short stump a loud slap, and Felix flinched. Dei didn't seem to notice or care as he dropped his hand, then pushed away from the counter. "Now, you look like you need tea."

Felix didn't know what someone looked like when they needed tea. He wasn't a huge fan of leaf water. Just like he wasn't a huge fan of bean water. "Nothing caffeinated, please."

Dei winked at him, then turned and flipped the switch on a mint-green, very expensive-looking electric kettle in the corner by his stove. "Gettin' serious for a minute, I really owe you one for tonight. Sofia's got a lot going on right now, and most of it's her fault, but that fuckin' piece of shit…"

"Oh, I know," Felix said. "I was pretty sure that guy was going to beat the shit out of me. The worst *she* did was try to proposition me."

Dei spun around and almost lost his balance, catching himself on the counter before Felix could jump up to try and help. "She did what, now?"

Felix shrugged. "Uh. Well, she got a little handsy. She kind of… asked me if I wanted to—" He stopped and coughed. "You know. Have sex? I politely told her she's not my type. I didn't want to hurt her feelings."

"Jay-zus," Dei breathed out.

Felix stared down at his hands. "I know. I'm sorry. I should have—"

"Darlin', no. Don't you dare apologize for anything that happened tonight. Most men would'a left her to deal with her shit on her own."

Felix didn't want to tell him he'd considered it for a few seconds. Not long enough that he felt guilty, but a small part of him had wanted to just wash his hands of her and go home. After seeing her boyfriend—or whatever he was—he was grateful he hadn't.

"Is she going to be alright?" he asked as Dei turned back to the tea. "That guy obviously hit her earlier. She's got a nasty bruise on her face."

Dei bowed his head, his shoulders hunched. "I'm tryin'a stay out of lockup right now. Got a nice, clean record, and I don't wanna fuck with my benefits or any of that shit. But I'm fixin' to rearrange his face when he gets the nerve to show up here lookin' for her."

Felix tried to bite back his next question, but his filter had been bad even before the Incident, and now it didn't much exist. "Why is she with him?"

Dei turned slowly, holding two mugs with his one hand. He slid them both onto the counter, then pushed one with a floral scent toward Felix. "She's got some…" He stopped and shook his head. "Don't seem fair to call them issues, you know. Wasn't her fault. Our momma struggled when we was growin' up. We spent a good few years as kids in the middle of bum-fuck nowhere West Virginia, where my papou immigrated and bought a farm. Then he died, so we moved to Georgia, and eventually, our momma got a job down here at a resort. She made enough to buy this place, but…" Dei blew out a puff of air and shook his head. "Shit happened."

That didn't answer Felix's question, so he kept quiet because he'd come to realize that sometimes people needed to just talk. And the very least he could do for Dei was listen.

"Our momma got sick. She'd been sick for a while, but no one really noticed. I thought she was just forgetful—kind of quirky, you know?"

Felix did know. A little too well. "I'm familiar with it."

Dei shot him an apologetic look. "Guess you do." He passed his hand down his face, then snatched up his tea and took a long sip. "Turned out she had this version of Alzheimer's that hits you real young, but she didn't find out until I was deployed."

Felix winced. "*Oh.*"

Dei let out a slow breath. "Sofia's had mental health stuff goin' on since she was a kid. I had ten years on her, so by the time we realized anything was really wrong, I was long gone, and my momma just…she was strugglin' to keep herself together, so she couldn't help. Sofia was gettin' worse and worse, and Momma was needing lookin' after. I was two months away from bein' discharged when this happened," Dei said, gesturing from his scarred shoulder down his body and toward his leg.

"Well, *fuck.*"

Dei laughed softly. "Got it in one. I was real fucked-up when I woke up in the hospital. Had debris in both eyes and lost this one." He gestured to the one on the left. "Sixteen surgeries on my arm and leg…" He stopped abruptly, then laughed again, shaking his head. "*Shit*. You know, I never tell anyone that story. Ever?"

Felix sat upright. "Oh god. Am I being—"

"No, sugar. Hell no," Dei said, interrupting Felix's attempt at an apology. You've done nothin' wrong."

Felix felt something warm in his chest. "Will it help if I tell you I won't remember half of this tomorrow?"

Dei's face softened, and he reached his hand across the table. Felix hesitated, but only for a second. He was desperate to know what Dei's touch was like, and it was as rough and warm as he expected. He was calloused with burns from his work, and even with the gentle brush of fingers, Felix could feel the power in him.

"It don't help knowin' you're suffering too. And I'm sorry to dump all that shit on you," Dei murmured, running his thumb over the side of Felix's.

"god, don't be. That's a lot to hold in."

"Maybe. But you got a front-row seat to the Sofia circus tonight, and I hate that," Dei said. "Whatever she said to you…"

"Hey, no. It was nothing," Felix insisted. "I'm just glad I was there to get her away from that guy. If you want to go hunt him down and make him sorry for ever laying a finger on her, I've got your back. I can't be a getaway driver, but I can definitely hold him down while you go to town on his face."

Dei's smile went a little dark. "You got fire in you, huh?"

"Maybe not all the time, but the fact that he put his hands on her?" Felix glanced over his shoulder at the front door. "Will he actually show up here?"

Dei let out a soft growl and nodded. "He knows better'n that. I just need to convince her to stay put long enough to get out whatever garbage is in her system. She, uh…she stopped taking her meds a few months ago after my mom's condition got worse and started takin' other shit."

Felix's eyes went wide. "Does your mom live here with you?"

"Too much of a liability for her," Dei said, shaking his head. "I work too much. I can't afford the mortgage on this place with part-time hours, and Jeremiah's been real nice about keeping me busy. But Sofia can't even take care of herself, so I had to find a place for her. Feels like shit, you know?"

Felix didn't know. He could tell Dei had done it out of love, not because he didn't want the responsibility of taking care of a parent who clearly loved him and had done her best. That was something Felix would never be able to understand.

Hell, he was still waiting for some sort of subpoena or something calling him to court to defend his competency, though he didn't think his parents would have a case after this long. But occasionally, the thought kept him up at night.

"I say something wrong, shug?" Dei asked.

Felix shook his head quickly. "It's just been a long night."

Dei seemed to snap back to reality and pulled his hand away, leaving Felix aching for more. "I should let you go. You didn't need all this tonight."

"It meant I got to finally talk to you, so I really don't mind," Felix blurted, then bit the inside of his cheek. Fuck, Dei was going to think he was a total creep.

But Dei just smiled and walked around the counter, offering Felix his hand to help him down, though he very clearly didn't need it. "Been wantin' the same thing. Y'all are always so busy, though. Never felt like the time was right."

Felix didn't really know what that meant. He could almost always be found hiding in the corner, trying not to talk in case his words came out wrong or backward. Dei was probably just trying to be nice, but Felix wasn't going to turn his nose up at it.

"Let me walk you home?"

Felix blinked up at him. "Oh. I mean, it's like four houses down."

"All the same. It's late as hell, and it would make me feel better. Ask Jeremiah how fuckin' annoying I am about this stuff."

Felix gave a small laugh and shrugged. "Fine. If it'll make you happy."

Dei met his gaze—powerful and intense. "It definitely will."

Hell, who was Felix to stop him after that?

3

Felix all but jumped out of his skin when his front door slammed open and a person appeared like some sort of avenging superhero. Felix moved a frantic gaze over the man until he fell on the blue beads around the man's neck.

Max.

His best friend stalked over and dropped his ass onto the coffee table, taking Felix's face between his palms.

"Um. Bud," Felix said very slowly, "I feel like this might be crossing lines with your boyfriend."

Max's gaze stayed narrow and searching. "Did he hurt you?"

Felix blinked rapidly, wondering if this was some sort of fever dream, or maybe he'd had a seizure and had been out of it for days. "Uh…*what?*"

"Jeremiah is freaking the fuck out. Apparently, the security tapes showed some guy attacking you last night."

Felix sighed and gently pushed Max away, shifting over to make room for him on his little love seat. "Oh, god. No, he didn't touch me," Felix said. "He tried to punch through the Lyft's window. And I'm pretty sure he hit that woman from last night before she showed up at the bar, but the tape should have only shown me jumping into the car and getting the fuck out of there."

"Well, Jeremiah reviewed it," Max said a little sheepishly.

Felix stared, then burst into laughter. "Your blind boyfriend was reviewing security tapes?"

"He didn't have a choice. Dei called out today, and I had a client at nine this morning," Max said, crossing his arms over his chest. "But a cop showed up to take a statement after the Lyft driver filed a report, so he had to take a look. No one's been by to get a statement from you?"

Felix felt a small surge of panic. He'd been pretty out of it all morning, and one of his medications made him sleepy anyway, so there was every chance a cop had shown up and he'd missed them. Or, hell, he might have talked to them and then immediately forgot.

"I don't remember," he confessed.

Max softened. "Well, it's no big, but they might show up at the shop tonight to get your side."

Felix started to nod, then froze. "Did you say Dei called in sick?"

"Uh, yeah. But he does that from time to time. And he was already off work way before that guy showed up, so he definitely wasn't involved in—"

"The woman was his sister," Felix blurted.

Max's brows shot high up on his forehead. "*Sofia?*" He jumped to his feet. "Some guy hit Sofia?"

"That guy's *been* hitting her," Felix answered, his stomach twisting in on itself. "Dei's going to murder him if he ever has the balls to show his face. But she was a wreck, dude. And not just from him. She was wasted and definitely on drugs."

Max rubbed at his eyes and sighed. "That's fucking great. Uh… okay. Would you be cool going into work a little early? I need to stop by Midnight and look at those tapes for Jer."

Felix was definitely not interested in going in early. His appointments were all later, and he was closing that night, so he'd be there 'til two. "I'll catch a lift with Paris. And if he's gone already, I'll just get a car."

Max gave him a helpless look. "But—"

Felix stopped him, reaching out to grab his wrist. "Max. The whole point of us breaking up as roommates was for me to do this shit on my own. Remember?"

"Yeah," Max said with a scowl. "But I'd be just as freaked-out if this happened to any of the guys. Jeremiah said the guy was a fucking nutbag."

Felix gave him a gentle pat on the arm. "Dei probably has a handle on it. He was more pissed that we were involved than anything."

Max lifted a brow at him. "You talked to him?"

"Yeah, I walked Sofia home," Felix told him. "Then he made me come in and drink herbal tea."

Max's lips started to curl into a grin. "Oh, *really*?"

"Don't. It wasn't like that," Felix protested. He was too weak, and his lack of filter gave him away if he was pressed for even a second. Luckily, Max was kind enough not to take advantage.

"We'll talk later, yeah?" He took a few steps backward and headed for the door. "If you see that dickhead again, though, let me know. I'd like to help take care of this shit."

Felix snorted and waved him off. "Okay, Batman."

Max grinned and flipped him off, then bounced out the door.

A minute later, Felix heard the sound of his bike, and then he was wrapped in silence again. His heartbeat was racing a mile a minute, but as the quiet room wrapped around him, he started to breathe a little easier. He grabbed his sketch pad and went back to his drawing and lost time until his alarm sounded.

Felix's entire life was now defined by his phone alarms, Post-it notes everywhere, and a little pocket notebook with details about all of his friends in case his memory completely lapsed and he couldn't recognize anyone. His physical therapist and his neurologist told him that was very unlikely unless he had another *Incident*, but Felix lived in constant fear of losing it all.

Pushing up from the sofa, he hopped in the shower, then spent a little extra time on his hair. He told himself it had nothing to do at all with hoping he'd run into Dei, but he was terrible at lying to himself.

He stared at his face in the mirror, none of it ever familiar, and he pulled his lower lids down.

Objectively, he thought he was pretty good-looking. He had light hair, a five-o'clock shadow that never went away, sharp cheekbones, and a good, solid nose. He had a scar under his lower lip from when it had been pierced, which used to hold a massive spike.

He was halfway to putting his boots on when there was a knock at his door, and he trudged over, opening it to find a red beaded bracelet shoved in his face. Paris was gruff and straightforward, and Felix appreciated that about him.

"Max said you need a ride."

Felix rolled his eyes. "Your brother's a meddling dick."

Paris's mouth curved into a rare smile. "Yeah. Trust me, I tried to cook it out of him when he was a kid, but he's stubborn. Anyway, I'm heading in, so you might as well tag along."

Paris never made him feel like a burden, and he didn't ever make him feel like he was running low on favors. He was easy to get along with, and sharing property with him and Ben was one of the best things that had happened to Felix since moving to Key Largo and attempting to regain his independence.

They were there on bad nights when his brain was like a big ball of static electricity. They were there when he had small seizures and couldn't get his legs to move right for long minutes afterward. And they were there for good nights when he was feeling more like himself and just wanted someone to share that with.

"So," Paris said when they hit the road, and Felix startled because he wasn't used to him making small talk. "Max told me about Dei's sister."

Felix groaned and pinched the bridge of his nose. "He's going to kill me."

"Max?"

"Dei. I shouldn't have said anything, and Max can't keep his damn mouth shut."

Paris choked on a laugh. "Yeah. He's like a one-person knitting circle. Just tell Dei he's like some Southern granny. He'll get it."

Felix smiled, but he felt like shit for not being able to keep it to himself. It hadn't been on purpose, but he knew the last thing Dei needed was their whole community knowing his drama with Sofia and the whack-a-doo, abusive asshole who needed to be thrown into an abyss.

"What did he tell you?" Felix asked. He wanted to know how much damage control he needed to do.

Paris's jaw clenched the way it did when he was holding back anger. "About how that guy needs to learn why it's not cool to put his fuckin' hands on his partner."

Felix bowed his head and nodded. "The whole thing was so fucked. I should have stayed and beat the fuck out of him."

"What?" Paris asked. "Dude, fuck that. You got her out of there, which was the only thing that mattered. Let other people take care of that mess. It ain't your fuckin' circus."

Felix shrugged, and while he agreed with Paris, he felt…different about it. Maybe because of Dei. Or maybe because he always felt so goddamn useless, and it was the first time in a long time he'd been able to do something besides just stand there like an impotent tool.

When they got to the shop, Felix braced himself for a barrage of questions. But instead—once he was able to pinpoint who was who—he found Zeke, Amelia, Raf, and Jamie all sitting around the lobby table playing Clue. Zeke looked like he was on the verge of doing a murder while Amelia was smiling to herself, and Raf and Jamie were clearly working on their poker faces.

"This is the shit you want us to come in early for?" Paris asked, dropping onto the couch and kicking his foot up on the table next to Jamie.

"You're just saying that because you're always a poor fuckin' loser," Zeke said with a small sniff, then finally shook his hand and rolled the dice. "Mother fucking *fuck*," he said as he stopped halfway between rooms.

"You were saying?" Paris asked.

"I liked you better when you were broody and silent," Zeke told him as he passed the dice over to Jamie.

Felix smiled to himself, watching for a bit before heading to his stall. He still had a couple of hours before his first appointment, so he settled into his tattoo chair, kicking his feet up and spreading his sketchbook over his thighs.

He was working on his sketches for the Flash Friday event that Tony wanted them to start running, and he was itching to get a few more designs up on Instagram. He had a decent following—nothing like Max, Paris, or Jamie, but he also wasn't great with social media. Still, every time he posted a design, he had a bidding war on it, and that made him feel like maybe he was worthy of being at their shop.

"…drinks. Felix? Babe?"

His head snapped up, and it took him a second to recognize Eve's pink hair as she leaned against his partition. "When did you get here?" he asked.

She laughed and came around the stall to drop a kiss to his cheek. "Twenty minutes ago."

Shit, had he been out of it for that long? He glanced at the clock, and his face went pink. Longer, apparently. "What were you saying?"

"Jamie and I are going out to get food and drinks. You want?"

He didn't, but he had two long sessions coming up, so he'd regret not getting something now. "Grab me something light. Like salad with chicken on it. And unsweet tea."

She booped him on the nose before walking off, and he settled back into his drawing just long enough to realize the shop had gone totally quiet. He hopped off his chair and looked around, finding only one person left who was managing the desk.

Felix's gaze scanned him until he spotted the massive orca tattoo on his bicep. Rafe, then. Someone he was just starting to recognize.

He offered Felix a small grin full of all the caution of the newest member on the team. "You good?"

Felix nodded, leaning on the partition. "Got quiet. It's always so weird when it's quiet."

Rafe nodded. "You, uh…you know who I am, right?"

Felix grinned and pointed to his arm. "That guy gives you away."

Looking down, Rafe ran his fingers over his arm and sighed. "Good for something, I guess."

"Sounds like there's a story there," Felix pointed out.

Rafe swallowed heavily. "Uh. Yeah. But it's like a ten beers kind of story. I…sorry, it's just—"

"No," Felix said in a rush. "You're good, man. We don't need this place to be therapy every time we come into work."

Rafe gave a slightly relieved laugh as he sat back. "It's different here. It's harder to want to keep all this shit to myself, you know? Because people actually care. My old shop…" He trailed off, and his eyes got a little hazy.

"You're in good company," Felix said, and he meant it with every fiber of his being. Today felt like it could either be amazing or turn into a total shit-show, but in the quiet shop just then, he had the distinct feeling of safety.

And of home.

4

Drumming his fingers on the steering wheel, Dei stared ahead at the line of trees. There was a smaller iguana making a slow trek over thick roots, and he watched its progress for a while. Anything to avoid going in. He had to get back to work since Jeremiah was paying him more than he probably deserved to keep the kitchen running, and Dei couldn't put his whole life on hold for Sofia.

The only good thing about that morning was that his mom wasn't going to ask him where his sister was. She never did. She only seemed to remember Dei every few visits, but her brain had already deleted her youngest child. Dei's time was coming, of course, and he knew that the progression of their mother's disease had caused Sofia's most recent meltdown.

Dei had been so goddamn sure she was actually done with that piece-of-shit boyfriend of hers, so while he'd kept his cool outwardly, hearing Felix talk about what Clark had done had been a blow. He kept it together until Felix was tucked safely into his little house at Ben and Paris's, and then he'd gone home and lost it.

Sofia had passed out, so she hadn't heard him wailing on his heavy bag until his bicep felt like it was going to fall off. And even when he screamed into his pillow until his throat hurt, she stayed dead to the world.

Dei resolved to talk to her the next morning, but when he woke up, she was gone. He called everyone they knew, but no one had seen her, and her social media accounts were all quiet. When she moved in with him, she'd agreed to keep her location on so he could at least have some idea about where she was, but when he opened up her contact, she'd turned it off.

A small part of him wanted to wash his hands of it—of her. He'd done everything in his power to get her the help she both needed and occasionally asked for, but it only ever bought him a handful of months before she was back on her bullshit.

And he was tired. He was so fucking tired.

The last time she'd taken off, she'd stolen six grand in cash from his safe and went MIA for three months. She didn't call again until she was in fucking Brooklyn without a car, strung out on god only knew what and crying for his help. He told himself he was just enabling her, but he couldn't help himself.

Every time this happened, he felt like a goddamn failure.

He wasn't her parent, but he was as close as she was ever gonna get to a dad. He didn't really remember the guy his mom had been sleeping with when she got pregnant with Sofia. Only that as her belly got bigger, he stopped coming around. He wasn't even sure Sofia knew the guy's name, and it wasn't like they could ask their mom anymore.

Dei had promised both himself and his mom that he'd do whatever it took to keep her safe, and he thought joining the military was the right thing to do. The Marines offered him pay and education and the promise of a future if he could just tough it out.

And maybe under different circumstances, that would have been the case.

But now he was down two limbs, an eye, most of his dick, and one of his balls. He was living off his salary from Midnight and his VA benefits, which was enough to keep his mortgage paid, the lights on, and food in his belly.

Life could have been a lot worse, but he wasn't sure it would get any better.

He had more than he was expecting to, though. His recovery had taken the better part of two years, and when he was finally set free to figure shit out on his own, he couldn't for the life of him figure out how anyone would want him now that his body was a mess.

It didn't matter what his therapist said or his Zoom support group of guys a lot like him who had moved on with their spouses or even into the dating world. He was struggling to see his own worth.

But it wasn't just his body. It was also his failed attempt to keep what was left of his family from falling to pieces. And because of that, he didn't trust the same curse wouldn't touch the people in Key Largo who were starting to fill all the empty spaces in his life that his mom, grandfather, and sister had left behind.

Jeremiah and the guys from Irons and Works were quickly becoming more than just casual friends, and Dei was already to the point he would die for them. He just wasn't sure he deserved them.

Especially with his sister's recent antics sneaking in and ruining their peace.

Dei had been crushing on Felix for a good, long while now, and seeing Felix at his door with his drunk sister had damn near been a bridge too far. Dei wanted to hold him close and feed him soup and tea and beg for forgiveness. But instead of that, he'd just unloaded on him and then walked him home like he was a neighborhood teenager who'd gotten lost.

He felt like a complete *ass*. He probably should have checked in with him the next morning, but instead, he just…checked out. He took three days off work, put in as much effort as he could to find Sofia, then wallowed facedown on his bed until he was forced to rejoin the living.

Now it was Thursday, and he was sitting in front of the building where his mom would live out the rest of her life, trying to find the courage to go in and pretend like everything was normal.

Dei turned off the engine after twenty full minutes, and he ignored the rush of humid heat as he pocketed his keys, then reached for his cane. His fingers slipped on the handle, and he caught it right before it hit the ground. He had to brace himself on his prosthetic, and he hissed through his teeth when it made contact with the pavement.

His leg was aching something fierce, and he was worried another trip to the VA hospital was in his future. Those days were a lesson in both patience and control because a 9:00 a.m. appointment meant he'd be seen somewhere around noon after dealing with reception over lost paperwork, and ID verification, and all the other shit that came with a busted system.

He was grateful that his therapy and prosthetics were covered and weren't going to leave him bankrupt like his mom's care was threatening to, but it still wasn't something he enjoyed going through. Hell, the madness at the VA made him wonder some days if it wouldn't be worth it to just plop his ass in his old wheelchair and give up trying.

The thought was almost laughable, though. Dei had never been that kind of guy, and he wasn't going to start acting up now.

He kept as much weight off his stump as he could manage, making his way to the doors, and he gave the woman at the desk a little wave as he headed for the elevators. His mom was now in full-time care, which was on the third floor. She didn't leave her room much most days, and last week, the doctors had reduced her meals by half since she wasn't eating and digesting a lot of it.

He'd been there to see the nurse giving her some sort of chicken broth gelatin that made him want to puke, but he kept it together and tried not to see this whole thing as her careening toward the end. He didn't want her to be suffering anymore, but he also didn't quite know how to live in a world she wasn't in either.

The hallway was silent, so his heavy gait and the click of his cane sounded louder than usual. He hurried up as much as his sore hip would allow, and eventually, he pushed into her room. Dei let out a small breath of relief when he spotted her by the window, sitting up in a chair with a sketch pad on her lap and a box of crayons on the table beside her.

She was scribbling a brick-red one over a blank page, and she didn't look up when he grabbed a chair and sank into it.

Dei took his time looking at her—at the way her hair was mostly grey now, though there were still streaks of midnight black in her coarse curls. Her hands were skeletal—all the fat gone—and her skin was thin and broken in some places.

Then she looked up at him with her big brown eyes, and for just a second, he caught a glimpse of the mom who had worked her ass off for so long to try and take care of them.

"Hey, Momma."

She blinked at him, then dropped the red crayon on the floor and reached for a yellow one. Dei stared at it, then bent over and plucked it off the ground, sliding it back into the box. Before he could sit all the way back, she made a growling noise and slapped the crayons, sending them flying across the room.

"You know that's a pain in the ass for me to pick up," he told her. He gripped the arm of the chair and attempted to stand, but his hip gave out, and he dropped back down. He was more than willing to accept who he was in the body he now occupied, but there were days he missed being able to function with ease. "Your nurse isn't going to like that very much either."

She just blinked at him, then began to color with the yellow crayon. He had a feeling she was going to get pissed once she realized she couldn't grab the other colors, so he used the tip of his cane to roll a few closer to his chair. He set them on the table and held his breath, but she left them alone.

"I don't know if karma's the right word for this, but I'm assuming you did this a lot for me and Sofia when we were little."

Again, more silence. Not that he expected different. God, he missed the sound of her voice.

"I haven't seen her in a few days. I don't know if she's coming back this time." It felt wrong to unload this on the woman who wouldn't remember it from moment to moment, but he was just so damn exhausted with doing all of it alone. "I'm pretty tired of chasing after her. I don't know if I'm making it better or worse."

Dei remembered seeing some quote somewhere about the definition of insanity being doing the same thing over and over and expecting different results. He couldn't for the life of him remember who said it, but he understood it now. Every time he saw her, he couldn't help but hope that something would click. That her brain would stop the deterioration and she would be herself again. Or that she'd have just one more lucid moment that he could take with him.

But it never happened. She hadn't said a word to him in months, and he hated himself because he couldn't remember the last thing she'd said.

He felt so fucking careless. How could he not have paid better attention?

Dei's gaze snapped up when there was a knock on the door, and one of her afternoon nurses poked her head in. "Uh-oh."

Dei sighed. "She wasn't thrilled with me helping her put her crayons away."

The nurse smiled softly and stepped over them, brushing back a lock of his mom's hair. "Alexandra? Did you say hi to your son?"

His mom didn't take her eyes off the page.

"It's fine," Dei said after a long beat. "I can't stay. I got a late start, but I didn't want to go to work without popping in."

"I think Dr. Fuller wants to chat with you soon," the nurse told him. "Do you think you could come in early sometime? I'll leave him a message if you can pick a day."

Dei wanted to bury himself under his covers and not face whatever conversation that was going to be. It was probably going to be hospice and end-of-life care and all that other shit he was terrified to face. He was not the man who should be making those kinds of choices for anyone, but he was the only one his mom had left.

"I should be good next Thursday."

The nurse smiled at him. "I'll let him know. And you try to have a good afternoon."

He nodded, hoping he was smiling back, but he couldn't really tell what his face was doing. He debated about helping the young woman get the room tidy, but he had to save what strength he had for his long shift, and in all honesty, he just wanted to get out. The less time he spent thinking about all this, the better he slept at night.

At least, the better it was for now. It wouldn't last, but he'd take what he could get.

5

Since the Keys were almost always in season, except when some storm was looming off the horizon threatening to sink them into the Gulf, Dei was unsurprised to pull into the Midnight parking lot and see that it was almost full. There were three cars he didn't recognize parked in the employee spots, and he sighed to himself as he went in through the back door and paused by Jeremiah's office.

"Tell me it hasn't been this bad the whole time I was gone."

Jeremiah glanced up from his computer, his eyes looking large and owlish behind his massive lenses. He didn't talk about his vision loss anymore, but Dei knew the guy couldn't see much of anything these days. "How was your time off?"

Dei laughed. "Is that your way of avoiding the question?"

Jeremiah snorted and leaned back in his chair, kicking one foot up on the edge of his desk. "We had some drama. Turns out your sister…"

Dei knocked his head on the doorframe loud enough to cut Jeremiah off. "I swear I'm not avoiding this topic, boss, but it's a madhouse out there, and she is a very long story. Can we pick this up after close?"

"I'll buy you a drink later," Jeremiah promised. "You good, though?"

"Been better, but I need to work." He hurried off before Jeremiah could offer him something absurd, like a month's paid vacation. He'd struggle to say no, but he knew the moment he was alone with his thoughts for longer than a day, he'd regret it.

He made his way past a few of his line cooks, keeping his head down as he ducked into his own little office that Jeremiah had set up for him in the unused storage pantry. It was barely large enough for him to turn around, but Jeremiah had ordered a small dressing tree to hang on the wall, and it made getting into his chef's whites a fuck of a lot easier.

He'd mastered a lot of things one-handed and a few things with one hand and one foot, but it took ten times longer than it used to. Dei didn't quite belong to the generation of instant gratification, but he was close enough that needing to take everything slowly was a quick way to piss him off.

Life after his injury was a lesson in patience he'd never wanted to learn.

He used his button hook to close his jacket, then took a quick look in the wall mirror before stepping out and into the kitchen. They were fully staffed to deal with the lingering lunch crowd, and it took Dei a second to spot Marcus, his sous, who was leaning over the prep table with what looked like the dessert menu.

Dei walked over and lifted a brow at him. "Tell me there's not a crisis."

"Some influencer went viral last night talking about the cake," Marcus said.

Dei pinched the bridge of his nose. "Fucking great."

"Yesterday, we were sold out by one o'clock, and we've already had three dozen calls asking if we're still serving it."

Dei did a few mental calculations in his head. "Put Anthony and RJ on it. Tell them to put the first sheets in the blast chiller for forty-five seconds, then do a couple of test pieces to make sure it's not too dried out. If it works, try to get at least fifty portions done. I'm not gonna pretend like we can feed all of Southern Florida and their fuckin' brothers who decided cake was worth a two-hour drive, but if we can keep from eight-sixing it until dinner rush, I'll call it a win."

"Heard, Chef."

Dei pinched the bridge of his nose. "Just so's you know, I was not in the mood to come in to hear about some fuckin' dessert problem today."

Marcus gave him a crooked, unrepentant grin. "Then you're not gonna be thrilled to hear about your hot, sweaty balls."

Be careful what the fuck you wish for, Dei thought to himself. He'd wanted to be distracted, and he supposed this was one way for the universe to answer his prayer.

THE NIGHT ENDED ABOUT AS WELL as it could have with a nonstop wait from open to close. Jeremiah took to the restaurant's Instagram and Facebook pages to thank everyone for showing and apologized for running out of half the menu before seven while Dei helped him field a bunch of pissed-off, entitled asshole complaints threatening to have them shut down.

Jeremiah was entirely unbothered by the threats, and Dei had run himself so ragged by ten he would have *welcomed* some lawyer forcing them to shut the doors. By closing hours, the last server on shift bullied the final table out without dessert, which meant Dei could sink onto a barstool and pretend like it didn't feel as though his prosthetic had worn a hole into the bottom of his stump.

And that was not him being paranoid. He felt a small pulse of anxiety about going home and undressing to see the damage the long shift had done to him.

For now, though, he could ignore the throbbing ache as Jeremiah shoved a massive sandwich at him. It was stuffed to the brim with salami and mozzarella, and he took down half before he even looked over at his friend.

"Promise me you're not composing your two weeks' notice." Jeremiah had his glasses off, and he was rubbing at his eyes.

Dei laughed. "You couldn't pay me to leave, boss. I'm here 'til the bitter end."

"Then I feel less worried about sending your ass home to get some rest."

Dei shook his head. "Naw. I have a fuckload of prep to finish for tomorrow."

Jeremiah blinked, his eyes unfocused and slightly crossed, which just spoke to his own exhaustion. "Actually, you don't. Marcus and I are gonna stay late and prep for the rush. I need you in top form. Did he take a tally about what we sold out of and what time?"

Dei grabbed a cocktail napkin to wipe sauce off his face. "You know it. I got my boys trained well."

Jeremiah chuckled, and he felt around the counter until he found his glass of what Dei assumed was ginger ale. And he wouldn't have been surprised if it was spiked with something strong. After a long sip, Jeremiah took a fortifying breath, and Dei had a feeling he knew what was coming.

"So, I know we got our asses kicked tonight, but I need to ask you a few questions about Sofia and that guy." Jeremiah had met Sofia a handful of times, but only ever in passing, which was what Dei preferred. Now, there was no hiding her chaos.

"Yeah. And I'm real fuckin' sorry, boss. I didn't think she'd show up here like that. She knows better than to fuck with the place where I work."

"Truthfully, I'm not convinced she knew where she was. She was wasted, and I think she might have just wandered into the first place on the street that was open."

He wasn't sure if that was better or worse. "If you want me to pay for that gin she got her hands all over…"

"Oh my god, no," Jeremiah said, sounding exasperated. "Dude, I don't give a shit about a bottle of gin. I'm just worried about her. *And you.* Max helped me go through the security footage, and that guy…"

"Clark," Dei said. "His name is Clark Dawson. He's a piece of shit, and she's been back and forth with him for years."

Jeremiah's face went stormy. "Felix said she was banged up."

"Yeah." Dei felt that familiar sick feeling in the pit of his stomach again, and he tried to push it away. "She's, uh…" He glanced around, but all the servers were off doing their side work, or they'd managed to escape and go home. "She's been off her meds for a while, and she ain't listening to me about…hell, anything, really. She took off the other morning before I was up, and now I can't find her."

"Jesus," Jeremiah breathed. "Can I help?"

Dei shook his head. "Nah. Not a thing any of us can do until she wants help. I got a lotta shit on my plate right now as it is."

"I know," Jeremiah said softly.

He was one of the few people who knew about Alexandra. Dei had always kept his cards close to his chest, and it wasn't because he didn't trust the people around him. It was everything to do with the fact that he never, ever wanted his friends to look at him with that gut-wrenching pity he hated so damn much.

But it hadn't taken long for Jeremiah to crack Dei's outer shell, and for the short period of time his mom could enjoy it, Jeremiah would go with him and bring Alexandra food from the restaurant. She seemed to enjoy Jeremiah's company, and it killed them both a little bit more every day how quickly she was slipping now.

"If Sofia comes in again, just give me a call," Dei told him tiredly. "I'll take care of it."

Jeremiah's jaw worked like he was either working out what to say or trying to hold back. Then, he reached out and found Dei's arm. He gave the end of his stump a careful squeeze, and Dei felt something powerful in his chest because most people avoided touching him there like the plague.

But Jeremiah never seemed to give a shit.

"Why don't you go ahead and take off for the night."

Dei grimaced. "Come on, boss. I can stick around for some prep. You and Marcus don't need to handle all that shit on your own."

"You and I both know you need to get off your leg," Jeremiah warned. "We're fucked this weekend if you're out of commission."

Dei wanted to argue because he wanted to feel useful, but he knew damn well it would only set him back if he started being a stubborn bastard about it. "Fine. But I'll come in a couple hours early to prep more meatballs."

"I'll take it," Jeremiah said with a grin. He hopped up and walked around the bar, leaning down for a second. "You wanna do me a big favor, though?" he asked, then stood back up with an armful of takeout bags.

"Dinner for the boys?"

Jeremiah grinned. "Irons and Works is open late tonight, so I told Max I'd send food for him and the guys. It shouldn't be too busy this late. I ran some wings over there last night after we closed, and they were having a fucking Game of Life tournament."

Dei laughed, feeling a strange pulse of fondness rush through him. He felt odd about going—about seeing Felix because he had no doubt the guy was probably judging the hell out of him for his messy family, but…he wanted to see him again. He more than wanted to see him again.

He could never have Max, but he didn't mind being able to look whenever he got the chance.

"No problem, boss."

Jeremiah let out a breath of relief. "Tell Max I'll make it up to him when I get home."

Dei shook his head as he eased off the stool, ignoring the pain shooting up his spine. "Sorry, but hell no. I'm definitely not gonna send sexy messages to your fuckin' boyfriend."

Jeremiah laughed loudly and waved him off as Dei dragged the handle of the bags over toward him and hooked them over his wrist. He was moving slowly, so it took him twice as long to get to his office so he could grab his cane and keys, but soon enough, he was slipping out the back and into the night air.

The roads were slick and wet, and the air was heavy with the storm that had just passed. Across the street in the dim lights, Dei could see a collection of crabs crossing the road, and their only saving grace was that it was late enough that traffic had died down.

He pushed himself a little faster than he meant to as he made his way over to the next building, and his hand was shaking from exertion as he opened the door and stepped in.

Dei immediately flinched at the bright lights bouncing off the black-and-white tiles. He'd been to quite a few tattoo shops, having plenty of ink himself, but the difference was that Irons and Works smelled a bit like flowers, and music wasn't blasting out his eardrums.

In fact, the place was so quiet he was immediately worried that everyone had left and forgot to lock the door.

A beat passed, then two, and Dei was considering leaving when the swinging door on the far side of the room smacked the wall and a familiar face appeared. Felix's gaze scanned him, and Dei felt a little thrill when he saw the look of recognition in his eyes.

"Hey, you."

Dei smiled and lifted his cane in an attempt to wave. "Hey."

Felix walked over to him, his pace quicker than Dei had seen him usually move. "Do you have an appointment?"

Dei set the bags on the counter. "Actually, I come bearing food from a very exhausted restaurant owner."

Felix's brows rose high on his forehead. "Oh shit. More drama?"

"Some social media influencer ate at the restaurant last night, and apparently, her post about the cake went viral," Dei said, shuddering. "It was balls to the fuckin' wall all night."

Felix gave him an exaggerated shudder. "I guess that explains the random walk-ins."

Grinning, Dei leaned on the counter, trying to take a bit of weight off his leg. "What were they all askin' for?"

Felix rolled his eyes. "Minimalist crap. No, I shouldn't say crap. Stick figure cats are just not any fun for me."

"Sorry, sugar," Dei told him. "Maybe I should have you put me down on the books for somethin' big and pretty with a bunch'a color." When Felix blushed, Dei felt a surge of triumph. He was so fucking pretty with pink cheeks, and calling him sugar did that to him every time.

Maybe it wasn't fair to flirt when Dei knew nothing could happen between them, but he couldn't seem to help himself when it came to the shy artist.

"What would you get?" Felix eventually asked.

Dei looked at him for a long time. "Don't really have a design in mind. You wanna come up with somethin' for me?"

Felix's flush deepened. "Are you serious? Like, you're not toying with my emotions?"

Dei frowned. "I'd *never*, darlin'. You can go nuts with your design. I trust you, and I'm pretty sure I'll love whatever you come up with."

Oh, and there was a little shy smile to go with the pretty, soft color in his cheeks. Jesus, Dei wanted to take him in his arms and tell Felix what a good boy he was. He stiffened between his legs, and he'd never been more grateful in his life that no one could see a boner when he got one because Felix was the stuff of wet dreams. Dei took in a breath, then let it out slowly, hoping Felix didn't notice how flustered he was.

Felix pulled the bags of food close like he was trying to find something to do with his hands. "I'll see what I can do. Are you staying for dinner?"

Dei shook his head, feeling honest regret over his answer. "I'd love nothin' more, but if I don't get my leg off, I think what's left of my femur's just gonna walk right off my body whether I like it or not."

Felix grimaced. "Yeah, go home. Um. Everything's okay there, right?"

Dei opened his mouth, then shut it again, then changed his mind. "Could be better, could be worse. When you got some time off, shug? You're just across the street. You should stop in and taste test some of the stuff I've been cooking up for Jer."

"Yeah? Can I text you when I'm free?"

Dei started to say yes, then realized they hadn't exchanged numbers, so he pulled his phone out and passed it over. "Text yourself for me so we both got each other's contact."

Felix smiled, a sweet, private little grin Dei didn't see on him very often. "Done," he said, passing it back. "If you need anything, please let me know. And if you think of anything you want in your design…"

Dei smiled as he tucked his phone away. "Like I said, darlin', I trust you. Y'all have a safe night, okay?"

Felix nodded and backed up, and Dei forced himself to leave before he lost all resolve to do it and instead asked Felix if he could curl up in his arms and just sleep.

6

Felix woke with a familiar feeling in his temples, and as much as he wanted to be stubborn and ignore it, he knew better. A seizure was coming. Just one, if he was lucky, but he knew a cluster could easily happen. He sent a text off to Max and Paris, letting them both know he didn't need a ride, and then he texted Zeke and told him that he was under the weather and was taking the day off.

Zeke, of course, called immediately, panicking and trying to Door-Dash him soup, but Felix quickly talked him down because there was no telling if he'd be in a state to actually get food from the door.

"Seriously, I have food here," Felix told him. "And this isn't a chicken soup kind of under the weather."

Zeke went quiet for a long moment. "Have you already had it? Do you need someone to sit with you?"

Felix felt an instant stab of annoyance, mostly because he needed to be observed in some capacity, and it was the last fucking thing he wanted. He took several breaths before he answered and swallowed pieces of his pride. "No, not yet, but it's coming. I have aura, and I feel really funky." His words sounded a little hollow, and he had to breathe to keep from panicking. He fucking hated this. "And I'm okay alone. You don't need to worry."

"Bullshit," Zeke told him. "We're all going to worry."

Felix closed his eyes, knowing that Zeke wasn't going to let it go. And rightfully so. He shouldn't be doing this entirely alone. But he was tired of feeling dependent. "Compromise?"

"Go on."

"I'll do my best to send you a text before it happens. If you don't hear from me in half an hour after that, send someone by."

"I don't like this," Zeke said quietly. "What if you—"

"I can't live my whole life babysat," Felix told him. "I'm on good meds, and there's a chance I'm just feeling like shit and nothing will happen. Please just…let me have it this way?"

"Fine," Zeke breathed out. "I don't like it, but I get it. And I trust you to tell me when you actually need someone."

It was the best Felix was going to get, so he agreed, then hung up before grabbing a heavy quilt. He decided to chill on the couch for most of the day since it would be easy to take care of himself from there, and it was weirdly more comfortable than his bed.

The afternoon seemed to crawl by, and Felix started to feel worse. His aura got stronger, and it was when he started seeing waving rainbows of light in his periphery and his mouth tasted like it was full of pennies he realized he wasn't going to avoid this one.

He took several breaths and waited.

And waited.

And nothing happened.

Ten minutes later, there was a half-frantic knock on his door, and Felix climbed to his feet. He felt unsteady and shaky, but he made it to the door and threw it open but couldn't for the life of him recognize the person standing there. His gaze roamed all over the person, and something about the guy's strange-looking arm started to make sense.

"…gone," the guy was babbling when Felix managed to focus. "My house was torn to damn shreds, and a bunch of my stuff is missing. I hate to ask, sugar, but you seen her?"

Seen who? What was he talking about? Who even was this? Felix stared up into the man's eyes, and he was overcome with the sudden need to be tucked in his embrace. He took one step closer, then another.

"Felix? Hey, darlin', you okay?"

Felix's eyes started to close, and then he made contact with the very broad, very strong chest. Everything went fuzzy. "I—uh. Oh no," he heard himself say.

And then it all went black.

FELIX'S AWARENESS returned in fits and bursts. He couldn't remember where he was, but he was lying on something very soft, and he was very warm. There was also pressure on his ankle, and it took his brain a second to realize he was being held by a strong, calloused hand.

He attempted to lick his lips, but his tongue didn't want to listen to his brain. He blinked a few times, and the blur in front of his eyes got a bit clearer.

Home, he thought to himself when he saw a painting above his TV.

He turned his head to see a man staring down at him. Felix tried to reach for the memory of who he was, but there was nothing left to grab. It was just empty space. His eyes started to well with tears, and a second later, he was sobbing.

The man had him up quickly, and Felix clung on as emotions poured from his chest. He had a vague memory that this was normal —that he'd been in a similar position like this with…

With…

"Max?"

"Naw, sugar. But I can give him a call if you want."

Sugar.

God, why did that feel so good?

He cried a little harder, then sniffed. As he wiped his hand under his nose, it all came back, like a crashing weight against his temple. Humiliation accompanied the recognition, and he attempted to pull away. "Deimos?"

Dei smiled at him. "I like when you say my whole name. Sounds real sweet."

Felix's cheeks heated, and he glanced down at himself. Had he been wearing these clothes before? He would sometimes piss himself when he seized if it was bad enough, but he didn't have the telltale signs of being cleaned up. He smelled like his shower from the morning and a bit like sweat.

"Did I…" He stopped, his brow furrowed. Had he left the house? Was that how Dei found him? "Were you here this whole time?"

"It's only been three minutes since I came to your door, honey."

Felix hated the sensation that an entire day had passed instead of just minutes. He felt like he'd been asleep for hours. His head began to hurt, and he carefully extracted himself from Dei's grip, easing back down to his little nest of blankets and pillows.

"Sorry," he muttered after a beat.

"Dunno what you're sorry for," Dei said, resuming his grip on Felix's ankle. "Seems like you're having a hard day."

It wasn't the worst day, Felix thought with a wry smile that he buried into his pillow. He'd woken up in a lot worse places than the arms of his crush. Or arm, in this case. Felix turned his head to get a better look at Dei, and it was then he noticed the man looked exhausted.

He had dark circles under his eyes, and his lips were chapped like he'd been dehydrated for hours. Felix pushed up on his elbow and took a few breaths to collect himself.

"Something happened."

"Well, I think you had a seizure," Dei said.

Felix snorted and shook his head. "No, to *you*. You look upset."

"Well, you scared the piss outta me, I have to admit."

Felix took a few seconds to finish composing his thoughts, rubbing at his eyes, which felt gummy from the tears that had dried while he was coming out of his seizure. After a beat, he pushed himself up a little more and took his pulse. His heart rate was a little fast, but it was steady.

"Are paramedics on the way?" he remembered to ask.

"You have a bracelet on," Dei said.

Felix's brow furrowed, confused by the answer. "Um."

Dei reached over and took his wrist gently, lifting it up. The metal medical alert bracelet glinted in a ray of sun coming through the blinds. "It says not to call 9-1-1, so I didn't."

Felix swallowed against a dry throat. "Yeah. Yeah, that's right. I remember."

Dei smiled softly and shook his head. "Glad you had it. I wasn't sure what to do except put you on the couch and wait it out."

Felix felt a strange and unfamiliar warmth pooling in his belly. "Thanks. Um." He cleared his throat. "Please don't take this the wrong way, but why are you here?" He had a vague memory of opening the door to Dei, but the rest was a mess of static.

Dei shook his head and stared down at his fingers, which were resting on his thigh. "I came by to ask if you'd seen Sofia."

Felix frowned, his brain not quite processing who she was. Sofia. It sounded incredibly familiar, and while he hated the feeling of not being able to remember, he appreciated Dei let him take the time to get there.

Sofia. Dei's sister. Dei's sister who'd been in trouble. "She's missing?" he finally asked. "Do you think that guy—?"

Dei's groan stopped his words, and he passed his hand down his face, then let his head fall back against the couch cushions. "I wish I could say it was, but I doubt it. I had to work late last night. Jer and I were in the kitchen until about two. I got home, and my place was trashed. She got into my safe and stole a bunch of cash, and two of my emergency credit cards were missin'. I'm pretty sure it was her. She'd done this before."

Felix sat up further in spite of the sudden and intense fatigue settling in his bones. "Jesus." The word was slightly slurred as he held back a yawn.

Dei shrugged. "I've called just about everyone we both know, but she's in the damn wind. I don't know why I thought she might've stopped over here. I feel bad about draggin' this further into your life."

Felix waved him off, yawning again. His arms felt like lead. "I don't care about that. Are you going to be okay?"

Dei frowned at him. "She didn't hurt me."

"No, I mean...do you need cash? I could—"

"Oh, sugar," Dei interrupted very softly. His fingers twitched like maybe he wanted to reach for Felix, but he didn't. "You're so sweet, but I'm not hard up for cash. I mean, it sucks losing my savings and all, but I ain't broke."

Felix wanted to press the issue—to tell Dei that in spite of his medical bills, he had more money now than he ever had in his life and it would make him feel euphoric to be able to actually help someone. But he could see the stubborn look of pride on Dei's face, and he knew there was no point.

"If anything changes…"

His words were cut off when Dei reached over and cupped his cheek. "It won't. But you could do something for me."

Felix fought every single instinct in his body telling him to lean into Dei's palm. He licked his lips, then took a breath. "Anything."

"I can tell you're exhausted. Let me sit here with you while you take a nap, and later, let me make you some dinner."

"That's not a favor for you," Felix pointed out with a frown.

Dei chuckled under his breath. "You have no idea, do you? Let's just say it'll help me feel better knowin' you're safe and taken care of. So what do you say?"

Felix wanted to dig his heels in and refuse because he was just as stubborn, but his exhaustion was overwhelming, and he found it impossible to do anything except slowly nod his head, settle back into his pillows, and let himself drift.

FELIX WOKE LATER FEELING a lot more revitalized and with a gnawing hunger in his gut. His house was filled with the smell of something cooking—like rich spices and something fresh and citrusy. He tested himself for vertigo, but his eyes were steady, and his legs didn't buckle as he stood.

After making his way to the bathroom to take a piss, he splashed water on his face to chase away the last bit of sleep. Seizures—even small ones—always made him feel loopy for the rest of the day, but the nap had helped.

And so had knowing Dei was just a few inches away from him on the couch. Felix wished more than anything he could close his eyes and picture Dei's face, but his imagination had gone almost entirely blank since the *Incident*. Now, all he was left with were odd impressions of what used to be and memories full of holes like swiss cheese.

When Felix got to the kitchen, he found Dei standing with his back to Felix, his body massive and broad. He was wearing a white T-shirt and shorts, a robotic-looking prosthetic extending from somewhere above his mid-thigh. Felix took in Dei's short, dark curls, and the ink on the back of his neck, and the place where his arm ended in a very short, very scarred stump.

Felix knew a little bit about what had happened to Dei, but he hadn't ever pressed him for more details. In reality, it didn't matter. Dei existed in this body, and he seemed at ease with himself. Felix could only be so lucky. He was still coping with the way his brain had changed, and he'd lost hope that it would ever get better.

"Hey," he said, startled at how raspy he sounded.

Dei spun and grinned. "Hey there, sunshine. How you feeling?"

Felix shrugged, rubbing away a bit more sleep from his eyes. "I've been a lot worse. Thanks for staying."

"Sugar, you couldn't have paid me to keep away," Dei told him, winking before jerking his chin toward the small kitchen table in the corner. "Get yourself a seat. I made street tacos."

Felix tried to peer over his shoulder, but the bigger man waved the spatula at him, so he held up his hands in surrender and took a seat. He could barely see over the counter from the low chair, but he had a great view of Dei bobbing around the stove, humming to himself in his low, low baritone.

It was goddamn delicious.

"Were you in a choir?"

Dei glanced up, his blush only just visible under his dark beard. "Yeah. I, uh…I was in chamber choir in high school."

Felix smiled, shaking his head. "Sorry. I'm an uncultured fuck who grew up on DIY punk music. I don't even know what a chamber choir is."

Dei laughed softly as he stooped low, and when he stood back up again, he had one plate balanced on his forearm, the other ten inches below on his palm. He set them both down on the table with a little shimmy, and Felix was impressed by the look of the food.

"God, it's no wonder Jeremiah said he'd sell his soul to keep you in his kitchen."

Dei blinked at him. "That fucker. He could do a lot better than some washed-up, one-armed geezer like me."

"Washed-up geezer?" Felix scoffed as Dei went to the fridge and came back with a couple of bottles of sparkling lemonade. Felix tried not to stare, but it was impossible to look away as Dei sat, holding the bottles between his impressive thighs so he could twist off the caps. His mouth felt oddly dry, and he took a long drink before speaking again. "You and I both know you're young *and* amazing. False humility is boring."

Dei studied him for a beat. "Humility, huh? You sayin' you're willing to brag up your talent as an artist?"

Felix took a big bite of the first taco, the carne asada all but melting in his mouth. He was pretty sure none of that had come from his kitchen, but he was too afraid to ask how Dei had just made magic in his home. "I'm saying that I have more money than I know what to do with, and it all comes from my hands putting my art on people's skin. So…yeah. Maybe I am."

Dei's eyes gleamed as he pulled his plate close and swept one taco into his massive grip. It was dwarfed by his palm, and Felix found himself getting lost in a new sort of hunger. "I like you, darlin'. You're somethin' special."

"You keep saying that, but I'm really not," Felix muttered.

Dei just shook his head and took down the taco in two bites before taking a long drink. "Honey, do *not* get me started. I might never stop, and then where would we be?"

Felix had no idea what to say to that, so he busied himself with his lunch. The food was amazing, and it settled his uneasy stomach, so by the time he was finished, he felt full and lazy and happy. He couldn't stop his smile, which Dei caught and gave him a crooked grin right back.

"Did I see a bit of metal in your mouth?"

Felix frowned, then realized what he was talking about and stuck out his tongue. He had two barbells—one large in the center and one smaller one near the tip. "Technically, I shouldn't have this. My neurologist is always freaking out about what if I swallow it or something, but I don't know." He trailed off with a shrug. "I've already given up so much to my condition."

"I get that," Dei said very softly, and Felix knew he was one of the few people who actually did. "And for what it's worth, I think it's pretty wild-lookin'."

Felix laughed. "*That's* not wild. There's a guy who works at the Colorado shop who's got a split tongue."

Dei almost choked on his drink. "He's got a what now?"

"Like a forked tongue?" Felix said. He stuck his out and used his finger to drag a line down the middle.

Dei pulled a face. "What's the point of that?"

Felix felt a little hot under the collar. "Both sides can move independently. I've heard it feels amazing when he…uh, you know…"

Dei's eyes widened when he realized what Felix was trying to imply. "Goes downtown?"

Felix shrugged and glanced away. "Yeah. I mean, not that I would know," he said in a sudden rush. "Miguel's got a husband, and their relationship isn't open."

"Oh shit," Dei said. "Miguel? I met that guy. We declared each other stump bros for life. I didn't know he had his tongue all…whatever."

Felix laughed and shook his head. "Split. And yeah. A couple of the guys at the shop were…interested in it after Amit told them how much he liked it."

"You?" Dei pressed.

Felix shook his head. "I guess for a guy who works in a tattoo and piercing shop, I'm kind of a wimp about pain. When I got my tongue piercings done, I wanted to die for the two weeks it took for me to eat solids again."

"Poor baby," Dei said with a grin. Felix flipped him off, and Dei laughed. "Wish I'd'a known you back then, darlin'. I would have fed you soup."

Felix didn't know what to say to that. He wished a lot of things these days, but as the guys at the shop liked to say, wish in one hand and shit in the other—see which one fills up faster.

"Alright, you," Dei said, dragging Felix from his thoughts. "Let's get you back into that blanket nest."

Felix wanted to protest, but he knew the best way for him to get back to normal was more sleep. He stood up, feeling a little sluggish, and he let out a startled noise when Dei's arm came around him. He leaned in and breathed in the scent of him—woodsy with cologne and spicy from the food.

"I don't want to keep you," Felix said as he settled back against his pillows. "If you've got somewhere to be."

Dei hesitated, glancing at the door. "If I go back out, I'm just gonna be running myself ragged tryin'a find Sofia, who's probably in the middle of nowhere, bum-fuck Georgia by now. But if I'm in your hair…"

"No," Felix said quickly, then bit the inside of his cheek to try and give himself some semblance of a filter. "No. You're not. I like the company. I get extra emotional after a seizure, and it really sucks to be alone. I'm just trying to feel like less of a burden on all my friends."

Dei's face went stormy as he sat. "Those guys makin' you feel that way?"

Felix sat halfway up. "*God* no. If anything, they're a little too far up my ass. But I…I don't know. I hate having to rely on people. Like, Zeke always makes me promise that I text him right after I have a seizure or sends someone down here to check on me. And I know I should do it every time, but it makes me feel like I can't take care of myself."

Dei glanced at the door. "We expecting cavalry?"

Felix frowned. "Hmm? Oh, no. I didn't get the chance to let him know because my really, really nice neighbor came over and distracted me with food and cuddles."

"Aw, hon…" Dei breathed out.

"Trust me," Felix told him, feeling just a little bold, "I don't mind."

Their gazes connected for a long time, and then Dei's hand reached for Felix's, and their fingers linked together. Once again, Felix told himself not to read into it, but it was getting harder and harder each time Dei seemed to pull him closer.

Silence settled between them, and Felix let himself drift with a warm pulse beating gently against his own.

7

"Hey, boss," Dei said, walking into Jeremiah's office. He didn't know why his heart was thumping in his chest. He had a tattoo appointment in ten minutes, and it sure as hell wasn't his first time sitting under needles, but for some reason, he felt like jumping out of his skin.

Jeremiah peered from around his computer, but his glasses were off, so Dei knew there was no chance the man could see him. "What's up?"

"I'm gonna take a break before I get on dinner prep."

Jeremiah lifted a brow. "Home for a nap? Or is something else going on?"

Dei opened his mouth to tell him the truth, but for some reason, his tongue stuck to the back of his teeth, and the words refused to come. After a beat, he cleared his throat. "Nothin' important. You need anything while I'm out?" It wasn't exactly a lie, even if it sounded like one. The tattoo wasn't important, but somehow, it held that sort of weight in his chest.

Jeremiah sat back, gently rubbing at his eyes. "Uh, not that I can think of. It would be super awesome if you could—"

"Run that big-ass to-go order to your boy?" Dei asked with a small grin.

Jeremiah had the courtesy to look a little sheepish. "I've got a meeting with that new produce vendor, otherwise I wouldn't ask. I swear."

Dei snorted. "I know. You never miss a chance to suck face with him if you can help it." He thumped his cane twice on the floor. "I'll be back in a couple hours. Call me if you need me."

Jeremiah shot him a wave just before Dei turned, and he snagged the three bags sitting on the edge of the to-go line and wrapped them around his wrist. It was awkward trying to manage everything with just the one arm, but while he'd mastered the fuck out of his prosthetic leg, his upper limb had been a real bitch.

A lot of it was due to the tendon and nerve damage that made it difficult for him to work the mechanics of the robotic arm, even as sensitive as the new technology was. He'd done a few weeks of PT with it, but in the end, he ended up more frustrated with the damn thing, and it had been hanging by the strap in his closet for almost a year now.

In reality, he preferred to just let his stump hang out. People were going to ask questions anyway, and the prosthetic made him feel like a newborn baby giraffe trying to walk. He struggled with his spatial awareness thanks to his missing eye, and knocking shit over just drew even more attention to him, which was the last thing he was ever in the mood for.

But days like today, when he was hoofing his ass to the shop with ten pounds of food, he wouldn't have minded the extra limb. Even if it was just to hang grocery bags from the mechanical wrist.

When he got to the shop, a couple of the guys were out front. Jamie spotted him first and lit up, and Dei felt his belly warm. He loved that little fucker. He was short and loud and unapologetic about who he was. He was the little sibling Dei had always wanted to have, and he'd warmed to the guy in ways he hadn't expected to.

"Hey! Is that food? You love me that much?"

Dei laughed. "Uh, this would be the work of Max taking full advantage of having a boyfriend with a restaurant."

"God, I love that," Jamie said. "Did you cook it?"

Dei shook his head. "Nah, man. I've been stuck on inventory most of the morning."

"Gross. No, thank you," Jamie said. He darted forward and opened the door for Dei. "You gonna stick around?"

He'd been planning on going home to take a nap, but he shrugged anyway. "For a bit." He brushed past Jamie and walked inside, unable to help scanning the immediate bodies for Felix's face. He was nowhere to be found, even after he turned his head to compensate for his left-side blindness, so he tried to temper his disappointment when Max jumped up and rushed to the counter.

"I hope he's paying you overtime for this."

Dei rolled his eyes. "My ass is on salary. But I do get afternoon naps, so I can't complain too much."

Max pulled the bags toward him. "Tell him he'd better be working on your Christmas bonus. I'm starving, and you're literally saving my life."

"He's just being dramatic," came the voice Dei really wanted to hear, and Felix appeared a second later, wearing a big grin. His gaze moved to Dei's stump, then to his hand, which was still clutching his cane. "Aren't you sick of being their errand boy?"

"Not when it means I get to visit with you. Uh. Y'all," he amended, a bit too late by the look on Max's face. But no one said a word, and he was grateful for it.

Felix's smile went a little shy, and he leaned his arm against the edge of the counter, his hand covered in a black latex glove. "Ready to get inked?"

"Yep," Dei said, trying to hide his nerves.

Felix raised a brow at him. "Not going to chicken out on me, are you? You seem a little green."

"Never," Dei said, and he knew he sounded a bit too fierce when Felix took a step back.

"Hey, I was joking," Felix said at the same time as Dei blurted, "Do you have the design finished?"

There was an awkward silence, and then Max slowly took a step back. "I'mmmmm gonna go put the food in the drawing room."

Dei wanted to burrow under the floor. "God, I'm such a fucking awkward piece of shit."

"Yeah, no. That was definitely me," Felix corrected. "Sorry. I'm a social disaster."

Dei's brows furrowed, and he turned his head to see Felix just a bit better. "Oh, sugar, you're not at all. I told you I was more than ready. It's just been a while, and I think I'm a little nervous."

"But you're sure?" Felix asked.

Dei's heart thumped at the sweet hopefulness in his voice. "Hundred percent. I gotta get back to work in a couple hours, so as long as you can be done by then, I can't think of a better way to spend my break."

Which wasn't a lie. Napping would be more logical, and he could think of a thousand different things he could suggest Felix do with his hands than give Dei another tattoo, but he'd take any time with Felix, and this was what the man was offering.

Felix reached over and pulled the swinging door to the side, and Dei walked through, gently clipping his hip on the counter. He let out a sigh as he followed Felix past a low wall of partitions and through a small opening.

"Did that hurt?" Felix asked.

Dei scoffed as he sat down on the edge of Felix's tattoo chair. "I don't even notice it anymore. I just forget to turn my head since I lost the eye."

Felix pulled a face, and Dei wasn't sure he even realized he was doing it. Everything about him lacked most social filters. It was so honest—so genuine—and he couldn't seem to get enough of him.

"So, I have three designs," Felix said, holding a photo book close to his chest. "I mean, I have a lot more than three, but I have three I picked out for you, and they shouldn't take more than an hour and a half at most."

When Felix tried to hand Dei the book, Dei shook his head. "Mind holdin' it open there for me, darlin'? Just so I can flip the pages."

"Oh. Shit. Yeah, of course," Felix said.

He flipped open the cover, then thumbed four pages until he stopped on a sketch of a snake curling around a sundial. It was nice, but it wasn't quite speaking to him. Dei reached out and flipped the page to the next one. It was an eye with a clock where the pupil and iris should be, and it was wild.

It was something he'd love to have, but it still wasn't right.

He flipped the page again, and his breath caught in his chest. It was a crashing wave with a bird coming up out of the water like it had been birthed from the sea. Or, as he saw it, a rebirth. He swallowed heavily.

"You can do this in less than two hours?"

Felix glanced down, and his cheeks pinked. "If we keep it greyscale and less than the size of my palm, yeah. I can do this in under two."

"Sweet thing, you are so goddamn talented," Dei murmured. He watched as the color in Felix's cheeks darkened, and he filed that away for later. "Would it be hard to put on the side of my neck?"

Felix's brows furrowed in thought as he set the book down. Then, without warning, he took Dei by the chin and tilted his head up. The touch was tender, the caress of a lover without being allowed to do more than touch. His heart hammered in his chest under the weight of Felix's gaze.

He tried not to jump when Felix then traced a few shapes over his pulse point. "Here?"

Dei swallowed heavily, and it felt like there was a stone lodged in his chest. "Yeah."

"I can do that," Felix said very softly.

Dei closed his eyes for a long moment, nodding so long he probably looked like a fool. But it was getting harder and harder to care the longer he was around Felix. "I'm all in, sugar."

He wished to god he was allowed to mean that in a totally different way.

Felix let out a soft breath that fanned over Dei's face. He smelled like mint gum and coffee. "You okay to lie back?"

Dei tried not to shudder at the thought of being under Felix in any capacity, and he nodded. "Yep. However you want me."

He did not miss the look on Felix's face at those words, and he refused to clarify or take them back. *Jesus*, he was in so much trouble. He quickly pulled himself away, heaving his prosthetic up on the leg rest before settling in, and he turned his head so he could watch Felix ready his station.

"Please tell me you didn't cancel anyone for me when I called the shop," Dei said after a long silence.

Felix looked up from where he was wrapping cling film over a metal tray, and he laughed. "No, but trust me, the people I've had this week? I'd do it just to give myself some damn peace."

Dei pushed up on his elbow. "Bad?"

"Entitled," Felix said with a small sigh. He laid out several small cups, adhered to the tray with globs of Vaseline. "You know that saying, don't fuck with people who handle your food?'

Dei grinned a little wolfishly. "You know I do."

Felix glanced over and grinned at him. "I feel like that should also apply to people who are using a high-speed machine full of needles to permanently ink your skin."

Dei choked on a laugh. "Yeah, no shit. I thought that would be common sense."

"Common sense is definitely misnamed," Felix said with a huff as he walked over. He had fresh gloves on and a disposable razor in his hand, and he used his thumb to tip Dei's chin up again. "People seem to think that because they're paying me for my art, they can talk to me however they want. And it's…" Felix went quiet as he spritzed something astringent on Dei's skin, and then he felt the dry scrape of the blade. "Sometimes I get flustered, and I lose my words. And I can't…I hate looking weak."

Dei felt his gut twist, and he curled his fingers around Felix's wrist without realizing he was doing it. He started to pull back, but he felt

Felix press into him, and he froze. "People are dicks, and your reactions to shit like that doesn't make you weak, sugar."

Felix shrugged and glanced downward. "I guess. It's just hard not to feel like it. This woman came in—she's had two pieces done by me, and she walked in and just started talking and…uh. Well, I didn't recognize her. And when she realized that, she started cursing at me like I was doing it on purpose. Zeke had to kick her out."

"Good. Fuck her," Dei said, his voice a little more heated than he meant it to be.

Felix huffed a soft laugh and shook his head. "I just wish it wasn't like this for me."

"I know what you mean," Dei said. He twitched his stump. "But it is what it is. Nothing we can do will change it."

Felix nodded, and after a beat, the moment passed. He stepped away to prep his stencil, and Dei lay back, lowering his eyelids and sinking into the dark as Felix's hands eventually lay down on him.

And in spite of the pain, it was maybe the best Dei had felt in a very, very long time.

8

Dei fought the urge to pick at the plastic shield covering his neck as he finished the last of the dinner rush. His hip was aching something fierce, and sweat had dripped between his eyelid and prosthetic so many times that he just took the damn thing out and shoved it into his pocket halfway through service.

The heat only made his mood worse, and he kept dropping shit. He burned the cream for pasta, lost half his cheese when one of the line cooks bumped into him, and when four dishes came back from the same table, he was seconds away from cracking.

One of the customers started demanding that they talk to the chef, and Jeremiah walked out there to deal with them, saving the group from Dei's temper.

Finally, when the handle on his herb knife broke, he nearly threw his apron onto the flaming grill and quit. Luckily, Marcus took over and sent him to take a breath outside, and he sat against the back of the building with his head resting on the bricks, his ears ringing from how loud the kitchen had gotten.

He loved his job, he really did. Even on nights like this when it felt like everything was going wrong. But he wasn't sure he wanted to deal with his professional life competing with the chaos of his personal one. He checked his phone for the thousandth time to see if Sofia had bothered to message him, but she was still in the goddamn wind.

He hated himself a little for not making more of an effort to find her, but he couldn't burn down his own life with the flame she lit on her way out the door. He just wished he hadn't felt so damn lost. He didn't know where to draw the line between enabling and helping her, and there wasn't some sort of book out there for older brothers who had to take over because their mom got too sick to parent.

He felt entirely lost at sea, with no lighthouse to guide him back home.

Taking a breath, Dei used his cane to climb to his feet, freezing when he heard footsteps coming toward him. He turned his head to see the walkway better, and a second later, he saw the one man he'd prayed he wouldn't see ever again.

"Just the fucker I was looking for," Clark said, his voice thick and slurring.

Dei didn't really have any qualms about beating the fuck out of a drunk guy as long as that drunk guy was this one. He set his cane against the wall and curled his hand into a fist. "If you know what's good for you, you're gonna get the fuck out of here."

Clark laughed. "Fuck you, man. The fuck is your dickless ass gonna do with your one arm and one leg?"

"Beat the absolute shit out of you," Dei said calmly.

Clark took another few steps and stumbled. "Where's your sister?"

Dei felt a small pulse of relief when he realized Clark actually didn't know. "That's not your business. And I'm dead serious, man. You got no business here."

"*You got no business here,*" Clark mocked in a faux-deep voice, then laughed again. He tumbled toward the building and caught himself on the bricks. "I'm gonna find that bitch and make you watch as I—"

He didn't get the chance to finish his sentence. He swung without thinking, and he knew the second his fist connected with flesh, Clark wasn't going to get back up. Not for a good, long while. Dei stared, his vision a little hazy as Clark's mouth and nose let out a steady trickle of blood. His chest was moving, so there was a good chance the punch, combined with whatever drugs he'd taken, was what knocked him out.

He pulled his phone out of his pocket and hit Jeremiah's work cell. It rang twice before he answered. "I'm next door at the tattoo shop. Is there a fire?"

"I'm in the alley," Dei said, feeling a little woozy. "Clark showed up."

"Sofia's—"

"Yeah," Dei interrupted. "I knocked him out. He's laying here unconscious."

"Shit. Okay, uh…don't move. Just give me a second."

The line went dead, so Dei tucked his phone back into his pocket, then tapped Clark with the tip of his cane. Clark groaned and turned his head, but he didn't open his eyes. Jesus *fuck*. Maybe he'd done some actual damage.

Dei took a few steps back, pressing two fingers to his temple, and after what felt like a short forever, he heard more than one person approaching. Whipping his head to the side, he saw Felix with Max close at his heel and Jeremiah on his arm.

"Is this him?" Max demanded, coming to a stop.

Felix kept moving until he was at Dei's side, and he put a warm hand on his arm. "You okay? Did he hurt you?"

Dei let out a tense laugh. "No, uh. No. He just ran his mouth, and I knocked him out." He felt suddenly disgusted with himself for unleashing that way. What kind of man was he? Any better than the piece of shit on the ground?

He realized he was shaking when he reached up to comb through his hair and his fingers were trembling like fall leaves. The world seemed oddly muted, and shit, was he breathing? He pressed his hand to his sternum to feel his lungs move.

"Hey, I think you're having a panic attack," Felix said very softly. He turned his head. "Jer? Can Deimos take off now?"

"Yes. Go. Max and I will take care of this."

Felix nodded. "Why don't you come with me? I can get you out of here."

Dei nodded a little numbly and realized his hand was still shaking as he picked up his cane. "I, uh…" His voice sounded far off, and he felt like he was floating outside of his body. He hadn't had a full-blown panic attack in years, but the sensation was all too familiar. "Felix?"

"I've got you," Felix said very softly. "Paris is waiting around the back in his truck."

"Wait. No," Dei tried to protest, but Felix stopped him, squeezing his fingers hard enough to keep him momentarily grounded.

"Did he do something to you?" Felix asked.

Dei shook his head. "He threatened my sister, and I snapped. I didn't even think. I just knocked him out."

Felix grimaced. "That was probably the least he deserved."

"Yeah, but I just fucking *hit* him. I—"

"Dei?"

He took a breath. "Yeah?"

"Wanna come to my place tonight?"

Dei blinked, then let out a tense laugh. "That might not be the worst idea. Don't know if I should be alone right now."

"Cool, because I don't want you to be alone right now," Felix told him. He threaded their fingers together and tugged until Dei started moving again, and he realized Felix had taken his cane before he dropped it.

The simple, careful gesture that Dei hadn't even noticed hit him right in the center of his chest.

He swallowed against heavy emotion as he met Paris's gaze through the windshield, and he appreciated the man's quiet stoicism when he got in. The truck had the AC blasting, so Dei was able to rest his head against the cool window, and in the back seat, Felix reached between the door and Dei's side, curling fingers over his wrist.

"There gonna be cops?" Paris asked when they were a few minutes from their street.

Dei took a breath. "Maybe. I knocked that fucker out, but he was high as a kite, so I don't know if he's gonna involve them."

"You telling them the truth, or do you want an alibi?" Paris asked.

Dei stared at him, surprised by the question. "I'll tell them the truth. My sister's not around to back me up about how that fucker's been beatin' on her, but there's no point in me making shit up."

Paris just nodded, then fell silent again until he pulled into his driveway. Dei carefully got out of the truck, and he took his cane when Felix offered it. He was steadier on his feet now than he was before. He felt heavy after the panic attack, but his head was clear again.

And that was all it took for the humiliation to settle in. His face was burning by the time Felix got his front door open, and when Dei stepped inside, he had to physically shove back the urge to run.

"Want some water?" Felix asked from the kitchen.

Dei blinked and realized he'd been standing in the doorway for way too long. He slammed the door shut and hoped he hadn't let in a flock of mosquitos. "I'm…actually, yeah."

Felix appeared a second later with two cups filled from his fridge spout. They were already covered in condensation from the humidity, and his fingers nearly slipped off the glass as he raised it to his lips. The water felt just shy of too cold, and he gulped it all down in a couple of swallows before swiping the back of his hand over his mouth.

"I'm really fuckin' embarrassed," he admitted as he made his way over to the couch.

Felix, who was hovering near the kitchen doorway, frowned. "What the hell for?"

"Losing my mind back there," Dei told him. "I haven't lost control like that since I was first injured and my head was a damn mess."

Felix carefully lowered himself to the edge of the love seat and stared first at Dei's stump, then at his thigh where the prosthetic socket was visible. "It must have been hell."

Dei shrugged. "Reality didn't hit me for a while. I was full of tubes and drugs for so damn long. The first time I realized how badly everything changed was when I got my cath out and the nurse told me I'd have to sit to take a piss for the rest of my life."

He watched as Felix's throat bobbed with a heavy swallow. "They couldn't, like, plastic surgery that shit?"

Dei laughed in spite of himself. "Yeah, they could. There's a ton of options. Could'a given myself a monster dick if I wanted."

Felix's lips twitched into a tiny smile. "Why didn't you?"

Dei shrugged and felt a little shy when he answered, but Felix's question seemed genuine. Like he actually gave a shit instead of wanting to know out of some morbid fascination.

"What I got left down there's got a *lot* of sensation. Feels real good, you know? All those nerves bundled in one place. But most of that would go away if they did a reconstructed cock, and I don't know. Maybe that means no man's ever gonna want to fuck me again, but it doesn't seem worth it. I already lost so much. I didn't want to give up being able to feel something. And I figured I'd eventually find someone who was okay with all the ways my body ain't the same as it was."

Felix stared down at his hands. "I think you're brave. And not in that horrible way people always say it. I haven't been able to feel like I'm worth the burden that comes with knowing me, and I don't know how to."

"Time," Dei said very softly. He wanted to hurt the people who made Felix doubt himself. "And the love of the people around you."

"Yeah," Felix said, looking up with a small laugh. "I do have a lot of that."

Dei shrugged. "It took me a good, long while to get to where I am. Now, when guys like fuckin' Clark call me dickless to my face, it's easy to laugh at him because at least I won't ever be the piece of shit he is."

"He called you that?" Felix all but whispered.

Dei shrugged. "He's called me worse."

Felix licked his lips, then said, "I wish you'd hit that fucker harder."

Dei froze, then burst into laughter. "Damn, sugar. You're vicious."

"He's a monster," Felix said, his tone dark and furious. "Men like him don't deserve the opportunity to hurt other people."

Dei felt warm all over. Fuck, he wanted to kiss this man. He reached his hand out, and Felix let him grasp his fingers, and Dei was then helpless to do anything except meet his gaze and kiss his knuckles. His lips pressed long and lingering against Felix's dry skin.

There was a moment—tense and unsure—but just before Dei could panic like he'd gotten it all wrong, Felix reached out and cupped Dei's cheek with his free hand.

"I like you."

"I like you too, darlin'." Dei couldn't bring himself to move, but Felix quickly shifted over, pressing together from thigh to knee. He felt waves of both desire and panic rushing through him, and he wasn't sure which one was going to win.

It had been so, so long since he'd let someone touch him, and he'd been unsure he ever would again.

But Felix didn't look at him like he was a *thing*—like some sort of wounded creature. He didn't look at him like he was half a person or that he could only be loved and desired in *spite* of everything that happened to him.

Dei felt his control slipping further, and he gave Felix's hand a single tug, smiling when the man came easily. They fell into each other, first sharing air as their noses nuzzled together, and then Dei turned his head just so, and their lips met.

His eyelid fell closed as he let himself feel the warmth of Felix's kiss and the light, teasing touch of his tongue as his mouth opened. Dei met him motion for motion, his body heating up under Felix's delicate, hesitant touch. He felt a strong, thick pulse of want between his legs, and it was that which scared the absolute shit out of him.

Yes, he was fine with Felix knowing that his body had been ravaged in so many ways. Yes, he fully believed that Felix would never, ever belittle him or make him feel like a freak. But he wasn't ready. He desperately wanted to be, but the panic was taking over.

"I can't," he gasped, pulling back.

Felix looked absolutely devastated as he shuffled all the way against the arm of the love seat. "I'm s-sorry. I d-didn't mean…I…," he stuttered. "I'm…I…it…"

Dei could see Felix struggling to find his words and the crushing agony that came with not being able to. "No. Sugar, it's not you. It's *not* you."

He reached for Felix, but the smaller man shook his head and put his arm up in defense. Dei curled back into himself and desperately wanted to stand up, but he wasn't sure he could hold his own balance.

How had it gone from the only thing he'd wanted in a long time to a total train wreck?

"Felix," he said very slowly.

Looking up with half-lidded eyes, Felix nodded. "I didn't mean to push you. I'm so sorry."

Dei curled his fingers into a fist and fought the urge to punch himself in the face. "It wasn't you," he said again. "Please believe me. I want you more than I can say, but I haven't…not since my injury. I don't know how to do this anymore, and I can't fuck it up. Not with you."

Felix took a breath, then met Dei's gaze. "Okay."

It felt like everything around them—time, the world, the universe—all stopped moving. "Okay?"

Felix nodded. "I believe you. It's not me."

Could it possibly be that easy? No games? No passive aggression? "Dei?"

He took a breath. "I need time," he blurted.

"Okay…"

"But I don't want you to waste your life waiting on me."

At that, Felix burst into laughter, covering his face with one hand. "Right. Because of all these guys lined up around the block to get into the pants of the crazy guy who sometimes can't talk and will never remember their faces and has seizures where he pisses his pants?"

Dei swallowed heavily and gave in to his desire to touch Felix. He kept it careful, his fingers resting over his thigh, but it was enough to make Felix drop his hand and meet his gaze. "The fact that there aren't people lining up around the block to get into the pants of one of the kindest, hottest, smartest men I have ever met will never make sense to me."

Felix's cheeks pinked, and he got that look on his face again—the one that said he was really, really into being complimented. "You're being nice."

Dei snorted. "Yeah, but I'm being nice with the truth. I want nothin' more than to pin you to this couch and make you come so hard you see god. And I mean to have my way with you someday. I just…"

"Need to take this at your pace," Felix said so softly it was almost a whisper. He laid his palm on top of Dei's and held it there, warm and calloused but soft. "I can give you that, Dei. I promise."

Dei felt like his chest was burning from the inside out. "I meant what I said, though, darlin'. You're worth the wait, but I don't want you wasting—"

"Okay, no," Felix said sharply. "If I'm worth waiting for, shouldn't you be too?"

Dei swallowed against a throat tender with emotions he hadn't felt in a long, long while. "Don't be using logic on me now, sugar."

Felix grinned at him and shrugged. "Fair's fair." He moved his hand, but he didn't back away. "Are you, uh…are you going to leave?"

"Do you want me to?" Dei asked. "I don't know if I can keep my hands to myself. I just know I can't give you what you want."

"Don't be so sure about that," Felix told him. "I want a lot of things. And the other day, when I fell asleep with you, was probably the best afternoon I've had in years. I'm never, ever going to turn that down."

Dei knew he should probably leave. He didn't trust himself not to push boundaries, but at the same time, he didn't want to be alone. He wanted a moment to be selfish and reckless and brave. He had no idea where this thing with Felix was going to go, and he wanted to be greedy while he was allowed.

Taking a slow breath, he eventually shuffled lower on the love seat, then kicked his leg up on the table and rested his arm along the back of the couch. "Come on, then, sweet thing. This big ol' body isn't gonna cuddle itself."

Felix laughed all the way into Dei's embrace, and he didn't let go for a long, long while.

9

Felix hadn't seen Dei in two weeks. At least, not as far as Felix was aware.

His memory for faces was still shit, but it felt like more and more, his brain was compensating in other ways. It had been a long while since he couldn't recognize most of the guys at the shop, and not just by the bracelets they wore. He was starting to just get a feel for their presence, and although sometimes he still had to search his brain for names—and so many things still felt like he was trying to find a word on the tip of his tongue—it was getting easier.

Not better, but he could live with it.

His mood was definitely shitty, though, wondering if he'd fucked up by kissing Dei. He hadn't told a soul about their evening together, and the guys were all distracted by the fact that Dei had knocked out his sister's ex.

Zeke came over to Midnight sometime after Paris, Felix, and Dei left, and the cops showed up not long after that. Zeke told the harrowing tale of Clark trying to get up and run off, and he and Max pinned the fucker to the wall until a deputy arrived.

Felix was unsurprised to learn that Clark had both a criminal history and a reputation with the sheriffs, and he was immediately searched and arrested for possession.

None of them had been questioned further, so Felix knew Dei wasn't facing any legal charges for knocking the fucker out. Felix had assumed that would cheer Dei up, but with his pressing absence, he supposed he was wrong.

"You'd look prettier if you smiled."

Felix's gaze darted up to a smiling Linc, who was leaning over his partition. "Keep it up, asshole, and I'm gonna pierce your lips shut."

"I met a guy at a piercing convention once who did that. He ate all of his meals out of a straw," Linc said. He let his arm hang low over the partition, his finger drawing shapes along the fabric.

Leaning back in his chair, Felix crossed his arms. "What would be the point of that?"

"Aesthetic," Linc said, then stuck out his tongue to reveal his three piercings.

Felix absently clicked his own against his teeth. "Do I really look that bad?"

Linc stood up, then walked into the stall and dropped into Felix's tattoo chair. "Babe. Take my shoes off. My feet are killing me, and I only have a couple fingers." He waved them in Felix's face.

Felix rolled his eyes but did as he asked. "You're such a toddler. Do you pull this shit with Ryder?"

Linc wriggled the two toes he had, humming happily. "No. I'm the massager at home, so I have to take what I can get here." He waved his left foot at Felix. "Please. I'll love you forever. I'll pierce your dick for free."

"I don't want a pierced dick," Felix said, but he grabbed Linc's socked foot and began to knead at the tight tendons. He was always begging for foot rubs at the shop, and everyone always gave in. "Thinking about my lip, though."

"You'd look hot as fuck," Linc told him. "Right here." He pressed the tip of his finger against the center of his bottom lip.

"I think my face is crooked," Felix mused as he dug his knuckles in, making Linc fall back and groan. "Would it look weird?"

"Never. I'd never let you walk out of here lopsided, my love." Linc wriggled happily, then took his right foot away and offered his left. "Do you wanna tell Daddy why you're pouty today?"

Felix faked a gag. "First of all, never call yourself that again. Second, no, not really."

"But you are upset," Linc said, his voice taking on a more serious tone. "What happened?"

Felix took a slow breath. "I, uh…had a weird…" He stopped. He didn't know what the hell to call the night he took Dei home and cuddled with him on the couch until they both passed out. He'd woken up alone with a blanket around his shoulders and no note, but Dei had texted him a few hours later and told him to have a good shift.

So he wasn't being ghosted.

He was just being kept at a distance.

"Weird what?" Linc pressed.

Felix dropped his foot and sat back again, hugging himself. "It wasn't a date, but we spent some time together."

"Fucking?" Linc asked.

Felix scowled. "Dude. Does that make a difference?"

"It might to him," Linc defended, then relaxed back against the seat. "Hey, sorry. I, uh…I'm way overstepping."

Felix shook his head and rubbed at his temples. His brain was struggling, feeling a bit like static again, but he couldn't tell if it was trying to warn him that a seizure was coming on. "It's not you. I'm just in kind of a shit mood. It feels like everything in the world's going wrong, and—" His words were interrupted by his phone buzzing in his pocket, and it took him a second to realize it was a call.

His heart beat in his throat as he hopped up and grabbed it, and then the world started to spin.

It was a California number.

He hadn't spoken to his family in a long time. His mom's number was blocked, and his siblings had written him off. So, the only reason someone would be calling was some kind of emergency. Someone was either in a coma, or they were dead.

"Hello?"

"Felix?"

He knew that voice. It was his sister, Fiona. "Whatever you want, just tell me. I'm working." He hoped to god he didn't sound shaken. He didn't want any of them to know they still had an effect on him.

"Nice attitude, considering we haven't talked in over a year," she snapped.

Felix squeezed his eyes shut. "Is there something wrong or not?"

Fiona gave a long, long pause. "It's Grammy."

Felix closed his eyes and sank back into his chair, his lungs deflating. He'd been close with his grandmother growing up. He'd clung to her dresses so often and for so long, his cousins used to make fun of him, calling him a homo and accusing him of wanting to be a girl. But none of that had ever bothered him. Not when he could spend long, perfect weekends at her house, just existing at the edge of the city away from his overbearing mother and his nasty brother and sister, who seemed to live to make his life miserable.

And he had no doubt that Fiona was getting some kind of joy out of being able to give him this news.

"When?" he asked.

"Last night. Mom didn't want me to call you, but…I mean, you were the only one who was really close to her, so I figured it was fair. Uncle Robert's planning her funeral for next weekend so everyone has time to fly in."

Felix rubbed at his temples, trying to chase away his stress tinnitus that was now blaring in his ears. "Okay, uh…"

"I get it if you don't want to come," Fiona said. "Like, not to be rude or anything, but I know you're mentally unstable or whatever now. And you can't drive, and I know you don't have a boyfriend, so…"

"I have a boyfriend," he blurted, then slapped his hand over his mouth. What the fuck?

Fiona just laughed. "Felix, come on. I said I wasn't trying to be rude, okay? You don't have to make shit up."

"I'm not," he snapped. He sat forward, and he could feel Linc's eyes on him. And not *just* Linc's. He'd been loud enough that he'd drawn a crowd, but he couldn't seem to focus on who was in the room.

Fiona scoffed on the other end of the line. "You're mentally challenged, Felix. Isn't that against the law or something?"

His face started burning. "I will not dignify that with an answer. Thanks for letting me know."

"I'll pass along condolences," she said to him.

"Don't bother. I'll do it myself. Let everyone know I'm bringing a guest."

"Felix—"

He hung up before she could keep going, and he sat back, pressing both hands over his face. He was trembling from head to toe now, and he felt like he was going to throw up. It was just like her to drop the bomb about the only member of his family who loved him dying while also making him feel like he might have been better off dead.

And it was awful because he loved his life. He did. Nothing pissed him off more than the fact that they still had the power to affect him this way.

"Come with me." A low, familiar rumble forced past his spiraling thoughts and drew Felix back to earth.

He opened his eyes and searched the strange face before he settled on the necklace the man wore.

Paris.

It was Paris.

Felix let him guide him to his feet, then led him through the back door and out into the alley. The sun was blazing down on him, and the humidity was thick enough he could almost see it, but the fresh air was enough to pull him out of his shock.

"I thought you blocked her," Paris said as they hunkered in a patch of shade.

Felix swallowed heavily. "That wasn't my mom. That, uh...that was my sister. I didn't think she'd ever call, so I didn't bother."

Paris grunted, shoving his hands into his pockets. "What happened?"

"My grandma died." Felix took in a deep breath, and it trembled on the way out. "I liked her. I *loved* her."

Paris nodded, leaning his shoulder against the building. "I'm sorry."

Felix nodded. His throat was kind of hot, but as much as he wanted to cry, he couldn't. "Shit. I told her I had a boyfriend. I told her I'd come to the funeral with my boyfriend." A beat passed, then another, and then he found himself doubled over, both laughing and sobbing a little. "What the hell's wrong with me?"

Warm arms righted him, then curled around him, and Felix buried his face in Paris's chest. He took in several deep breaths, feeling a little wild and unhinged. He didn't know if it was just the powerful grief of knowing he'd never see his grandmother again or if it was his brain once again betraying him.

"I don't know why I'm like this."

"None of us know why we're like this," Paris said, his voice rumbling against Felix's ear. "I think you should go home."

"I've got clients," Felix muttered.

"Are you gonna do your best work today?" Paris asked.

Felix pulled back and was forced to shake his head because he couldn't lie. "I've canceled a lot lately. My goddamn seizures, and now this…"

"Your clients get you. And if they don't get you," Paris said, his tone fierce and a little terrifying, "we don't fuckin' want them here."

Felix bowed his head and stared at his feet. He really, really didn't want to be alone, but he also knew that what Paris was saying was for the best. He swiped his hand under his nose, then stepped back until he hit the wall, sagging against it. "I'll…I'll order a car."

"Ben's on his way," Paris said. "He'll give you a ride."

Felix wanted to argue just for propriety's sake, but the last thing in the world he wanted was to be trapped in a vehicle with some stranger, even if it was only for a few minutes. So he just smiled instead, then let Paris lead him back inside.

FELIX CRASHED the second he got home. His mind was going a thousand miles a minute. He couldn't say more than a few words to Ben on the drive, so he figured he was going to go down hard the moment he was out of the car. His body just sort of shut down the minute his ass met his couch, and the next thing he knew, he was waking up to loud pounding on his door.

The light was dim in the room, which meant the sun was near setting, and Felix's stomach ached with a hollow emptiness from forgetting to eat all day. His brain struggled to come back online, and his feet didn't seem to want to walk straight as he made his way to the door.

He didn't even think to look in the peephole before answering it, and it took him a second to recognize the person staring at him with worried eyes.

"Dei?"

"Hey, sugar."

Felix's throat went all hot again, and this time, the grief in his chest felt ten times more powerful. He cleared his throat. "What are you doing here?"

"Well, the guys were all in a bit of a panic. Apparently, your phone's been going to voicemail all afternoon, and they were worried you'd had a bad seizure."

Felix scrubbed a hand down his face, then turned and left the door open as he walked back to the couch and grabbed his phone off the coffee table. Sure enough, there were fifteen missed calls and fifty messages between individual and group chats.

Jesus, these guys.

> Felix: I'm alive. Just napped all day. Dei's here. Sorry.

He set his phone down and ignored the buzzing as Dei took a tentative step in. "I thought you might be hungry."

Felix's head whipped to the side, and he stared at him. "Seriously?"

Dei shrugged, looking unsure. "Soup. Figured it would be easy on the stomach."

"Uh." Felix swallowed, his mouth painfully dry. "Uh. Okay."

Dei looked like he wanted to say more, but instead, he used his right hip to shut the door, and then he walked past Felix and into the kitchen. After a minute, Felix heard a pot hit the burner, and a second after that, he heard liquid being poured.

His head was still a mess, and now so was his heart. Was Dei seriously there to cook him soup like he hadn't kissed him, confessed he wanted him, and then disappeared for two weeks?

Was that all it took to get his attention again? The death of a family member?

He started laughing and suddenly couldn't stop. But it quickly turned ugly—the sound going sour and then moving deep into his lungs as he sobbed. He grabbed a pillow and buried his face in it, and he didn't look up, even when a warm, strong hand gripped the back of his neck.

"Is my being here makin' it worse?"

Felix shook his head, then stopped and shrugged. "I don't know," he said, words muffled against the fabric. "I wish I'd seen you before all this happened."

"I'm a shithead, I know. And I probably should'a stayed away tonight, but I knew you weren't gonna feed yourself."

Felix laughed, sniffing a little as he finally turned his head to breathe. "I kind of just…passed out, I guess. Didn't mean to."

"Yeah. I know how that goes."

Felix let himself take comfort in the fact that Dei was now drawing soft lines over the backs of his shoulders. "I knew I was never going to see her again. My grandma," he clarified when Dei's brows furrowed. "She was old when I left, and we both knew I wasn't coming back."

"Why?" Dei asked very softly.

Felix squeezed his eyes shut so tightly he saw sparks. "My mom kept threatening to get a conservatorship over me so she could collect my disability checks."

Dei suddenly looked ready to murder. "She did what now?"

Felix let out a heavy breath. That was an old pain he really didn't feel like reliving. "I wasn't even on disability, but she thought she could put me there by proving I couldn't take care of myself. My brother and sister were on her side."

"Fuck them," Dei snarled. "Who gives a shit what they think?"

Felix laughed, the sound hollow. "I shouldn't. But, uh…I think I made it worse today."

"How the hell could you have done that?" Dei asked.

Felix grimaced and buried his face in the pillow again. "Told them I had a boyfriend and he was coming to the funeral with me."

Dei stroked his fingers through the back of Felix's hair. "Can you repeat that, darlin'?"

Felix sighed and turned his head, debating about lying, but he couldn't think of a good one. His brain was too worn-out. "I told my sister I had a boyfriend who was coming to the funeral with me. Like a *moron*."

"You think having a boyfriend makes you a moron?" Dei asked.

Felix rolled his eyes. "I think lying about my hot Canadian boyfriend like I'm in middle school makes me a moron."

Dei blinked, then laughed and squeezed down on Felix's neck. "Okay, yeah. I can see how that's not so great."

Felix groaned, and he sat up, falling back against the couch cushion. "I never thought I'd end up so—"

"Don't," Dei told him very softly. "Sugar, don't you dare say whatever it is you were gonna say."

Alone, he was going to say. And pathetic. But at Dei's warning, he didn't.

Felix bit the inside of his cheek and didn't meet Dei's gaze. "It is what it is. It hurts to lose her, and it hurts to know I can't go back there to say goodbye without admitting they're all right and I'm just a giant, lonely loser."

Dei got up and walked off, and Felix couldn't help but wonder if maybe that was the last straw for him. After all, Felix knew everyone was going to have a line with him, and eventually, he'd cross it. He was needy, and no matter how independent he was, he'd always be just a little bit dependent on others for some things. Who the hell wanted to stick around forever for that?

"Legs down, darlin'."

Felix opened his eyes, startled to see Dei hovering over him with a hot pad and a bowl balanced on his palm. He quickly dropped his feet to the floor, and Dei's face did something complicated as he bent over and set the bowl in Felix's hands.

"It's real hot, so eat that slowly."

Felix stared down into an opaque reddish broth, but he didn't recognize anything else in it. "What is it?"

Dei laughed as he settled back down a bit closer than he was before. "It's called fakes," he said, pronouncing it with a Greek flourish, *fah-kes*. "It's lentils. Good for the stomach."

Felix took a tentative sip of the broth, then a bigger bite, and warmth immediately flooded through him. "Oh. It's amazing."

Dei laughed. "Not to toot my own horn, but have I ever made you something that wasn't?"

Felix shook his head as his hunger took over, and he polished off most of the bowl before he looked up again. He still felt a little like he was on the verge of losing it, but at least he wasn't hangry anymore. When Dei took the bowl from him, he let his hands fall into his lap, and he appreciated the other man didn't go further than leaning forward to set it on the coffee table.

"So, I think there's a solution to your problem," Dei said.

Felix leaned back, then rolled his head over to look at his friend. "No. There's seriously not."

Dei's brows flew up. "You won't even hear me out?"

Refusing to give a shit, Felix reached out, and Dei didn't hesitate to offer his hand. Their palms fit together too perfectly, and it made every atom of his body ache for more. "My sister was right, okay? With my condition, I'm not independent enough. Traveling alone is dangerous for me right now. And I'm not about to ask anyone I know to take time off work to go with me."

"You do know any one of them would, right?" Dei pointed out.

Felix sighed. "Yeah. I do. But that doesn't change anything."

Dei rubbed his thumb over the side of Felix's hand. "What if you didn't have to ask?"

Felix groaned and slapped his hand over his face. "I'm sure they're probably making plans and starting some boyfriend crowdfunding or something, but…it's too much. *I'm* too much."

"You're not. Sugar," he started, and then he went quiet for so long Felix finally dropped his hand to look at him. Dei was watching him with an unreadable expression, his eyes sort of heated and dark, and when their gazes connected, Dei licked his lips. "I feel like your family might shit a few solid gold bricks if you brought home a big-ass Marine veteran with no arm, a robot leg, missin' eye, and a mouth like a sailor, but…you know I'd drop everything for you in a heartbeat, don't you?"

Felix blinked, then almost choked. "Dei…"

"And I know I would draw more attention than you were wantin' from them, so please tell me no if it's too much."

Felix's heart started pounding against his chest. "You can't take that kind of time."

"I can do whatever I damn well please with my vacation time, and Jeremiah's been up my ass about usin' my days so he doesn't have to pay me out at the end of the year." Dei smiled, sweet and kind of playful, and he nudged Felix with his knee. "You also got friends who'd do the same thing if you wanted to take someone a little prettier."

"You're the prettiest man I've ever seen," Felix blurted, and he couldn't bring himself to take it back because that would be a lie. "My family's terrible, though. Trust me, you don't want to be around them."

"Neither do you. I can see it in you, darlin', and I'd die before letting you face them alone. You deserve to say goodbye to your granny, and you deserve to feel safe while you do."

"Grammy," Felix corrected absently, then huffed a laugh. "I always used to confuse my *M*s and *N*s, and she thought it was cute."

"You're the sweetest thing, I swear to god," Dei muttered, squeezing his hand, and for a second, he made a face like he was constipated. "Truth is, I'm not sure I want someone else pretending to be your guy."

"My guy?" Felix repeated with a grin.

Dei scoffed. "Mocking me already?" When Felix laughed, Dei tugged him a little closer and released him only to cup his cheek and stroke his big thumb over the edge of Felix's jaw. "You had it rough for long enough, sugar. And as long as I'm not too much of an eyesore to bring around these people—"

"No. God, please stop saying that about yourself. You're…you don't even know, do you?" Felix said. He stared between Dei's organic eye and his prosthetic one, noting the differences and just how much more unique that made him. He wanted to kiss him again, but he didn't want to ruin things again. "I just don't think you understand how much you're going to hate it there."

"If it makes it more tolerable for you, then it won't matter how much I'll hate it," Dei said.

Felix searched his face, and he wasn't sure if the man was being honest or if Felix was blanking again. But he wanted to trust Dei would stand up for himself if it was too much.

"We won't be staying near any of them. And I'm paying for the trip," Felix finally said.

Dei's lips stretched into a grin, and he grabbed Felix's hand, pressing a lingering kiss to his knuckles. "You really know how to treat your fake boyfriends, sugar."

"And you really know how to make your fake boyfriends blush, baby."

Dei suddenly went bright pink along the tops of his cheeks, the color spreading to his ears, and Felix realized that meant he liked that word. He also looked a little stunned, and he couldn't help but wonder if no one had ever been sweet with Dei before. It was obvious he liked it with all the little pet names he threw around to everyone.

Had no one ever picked up on that?

Felix swallowed heavily, then changed positions, fitting himself under Dei's arm. Even though he was on his right, he could still hear the heavy thump of his heart as he laid an ear to Dei's ribs. "Sorry I don't have a bigger couch for you."

Dei laughed. "The fact that you're here with me at all is a damn miracle, shug. You won't ever hear me complain."

Felix was pretty sure Dei meant that, and it just made him fall that much harder, and that felt like a death sentence.

The trip back home was necessary, but the truth was, giving his heart to Dei for the sake of showing off to his family might also be the thing that did him in.

10

"Did you think I was going to say no?" Jeremiah asked, looking over at Dei with his big, big eyes behind his glasses.

Dei shrugged, scratching the back of his neck. "Not really, no."

"Did you...*want* me to tell you no?" Jeremiah sounded a little confused, which made sense. He probably expected Dei to be elated about getting his time off approved.

Letting out a sigh, Dei turned his head and found a chair, grabbing it and whipping it around to straddle it next to Jeremiah's. Sitting like that was easier on his hip, and he pressed his chest to the back. "I feel like a damn fool."

Jeremiah sat back and pulled off his glasses, rubbing his eyes. "So, friend to friend, you do realize you're allowed to tell Felix he's asking for too much."

Dei bowed his head and muttered, "He wasn't the one who asked."

"What was that?"

"He wasn't the one who asked," Dei said, louder. "I kind of insisted when he was ready to throw in the towel. But I can tell he loved his grammy, and his family sounds like a real piece of work."

Jeremiah's face darkened. "I haven't heard much, but what little

Max did tell me makes me want to fly my ass down there and beat the fuck out of their calves with my cane."

Dei winced, knowing how bad that aluminum hurt when swung with enough force. "I'd be right there with you, but I don't think Felix would appreciate it."

Jeremiah rested his elbow on the desk and propped up his chin. "So, you're the one who insisted on going. You're cashing in your vacation. You actually want to spend time with him. Have I got all that?"

Dei rolled his eyes. "Yeah."

"And you're panicking now because…?"

"I'm gonna be his boyfriend," Dei said.

Jeremiah made a soft choking noise. "Again…*and?*"

"Fake boyfriend," Dei said, then covered his face and let out a loud groan. "He told his family he had a hot boyfriend, and somehow, he's choosin' me to be that guy."

Jeremiah scoffed. "Take this with a grain of salt since I can't see shit, but pretty sure it's not somehow, bud. He's choosing you for the reason any attractive, single man would choose you."

"You don't need to butter me up. My ego's fine, thanks," Dei said.

Jeremiah waved him off. "You like him."

"Guilty."

"You want to date him."

"More'n guilty."

"But you won't because…"

Dei groaned again. "My life's a damn mess, and I ain't been with anyone since I lost my dick. Which he knows about, don't get me wrong. Told him about it before I even considered pursuing him. But…" He trailed off. He didn't quite know how to explain how he felt both ready and entirely unprepared and wasn't sure that would ever be resolved.

"Did he get weird about it?" Jeremiah asked.

Dei shook his head. "Nah. He was a little curious and real sweet. And that didn't stop him from—" He snapped his jaw shut so hard he almost bit his tongue.

Jeremiah looked like it was Christmas. "From what?"

"Uhg. Kissin' me," he said, and as much as he'd told himself not to breathe a word about being able to taste Felix's lips in case it didn't work out, it felt like a sudden and intense load off his shoulders. "We kissed, and it was amazing, and I want him so damn bad my teeth ache."

"So your solution is to go on a trip across the country and *pretend* to be his boyfriend, even though you both are really, really into each other," Jeremiah said dryly. "Sounds super healthy."

Dei was close enough that he could lean forward and bang his forehead on the desk. "I fuckin' know. That's why I wasn't jumping for joy when you approved my time off."

Out of the corner of his eye, Dei saw Jeremiah's fingers reach for him, and eventually, they made their way into his short hair. The blunt nails felt good along his scalp, and Dei closed his eyes, sinking into the comfort of darkness.

"Instead of thinking of it as fake dating," Jeremiah said quietly, "why not think of it as testing the waters. You don't mind being affectionate with him, right?"

"Hell no," Dei said. He could survive on Felix's touch alone, he was pretty damn sure. And also watching him enjoy Dei's cooking.

Jeremiah laughed. "You definitely won't mind playing it up to piss off his family."

"Nothing would give me more pleasure." Except maybe giving Felix a few screaming orgasms, but that wasn't something you said to your boss, no matter how close you were.

"So do that. Bring it up to him—suggest that maybe you could use this trip to see how the both of you feel making things more serious."

Dei snorted and lifted his head, looking into Jeremiah's slightly off-center eyes. "Your talents are wasted in a kitchen, boss. You should have a couch and a notebook back here."

Jeremiah shoved him away and sat back. "You couldn't pay me to play therapist to anyone but the people I love."

"Aww," Dei said with a grin. He tapped the desk with his hand, then heaved himself out of the chair and steadied his balance as best he could without his cane. He stretched his arm above his head and flexed the muscles in his stump to relieve some of the tension in his back. "I'm gonna run next door and let Felix know about the plan."

Jeremiah smirked from his chair. "You do that. And tell Max that tonight I'm going to take his shirt off and—"

"No," Dei told him. "No matter how much I love you, darlin'."

He left the room as Jeremiah cackled behind his desk.

It only took him a couple of minutes to get to the tattoo shop, and when he walked in, he felt everyone's gaze on him. There were a few clients waiting on the couches, and while Dei didn't think he was the topic of open gossip, he still couldn't help but feel like he was under a microscope.

And it wasn't entirely comfortable.

"He's in the back washing up," came a voice from behind the partition, and then Max's head popped up, and he smiled. "Jeremiah said you have a message for me, by the way."

"I do not, and tell him I'll be plantin' roots in West Coast soil if he doesn't knock that shit off."

"And break our hearts?" the woman up front asked. Dei couldn't remember her name—she was newer and working on becoming a piercer, but she fit in perfectly with the rest of the Irons and Works family.

Dei sighed and leaned against the counter, drumming his fingers on the cool stone. "Y'all got questions, or are you just gonna stare?"

"Stare," Max said.

"Aren't you literally in the middle of a tattoo?" Paris demanded as he stood up from where he'd been bent over a drawing table.

Max flushed. "Shit. Sorry, hon," he said, dropping out of sight.

Paris rolled his eyes and jerked his head at Dei. "Come with me and get away from the damn circus."

Paris got a chorus of boos, but Dei happily followed him through a set of swinging doors and into a very quiet hallway. "Don't hate them," Paris said. "They're like a goddamn knitting circle. When Ben and I first started dating, they were ten times worse." He stopped abruptly and offered Dei a sheepish smile. "I mean, not that you and Felix are dating, but you know what I mean."

Dei's chest burned with the need to correct him. They weren't dating, but fuck him if it wasn't the one thing he wanted more than life itself. He just wasn't ready to say that aloud.

Yet.

"Thanks for this," Dei said as Paris held open a door that led to a decent-sized room filled with several tables and art supplies.

Paris nodded. "This is kind of our quiet space. I'll let Felix know you're waiting for him."

Dei appreciated that Paris wasn't one for small talk, and he settled into a chair. He barely fit, but it was nice to be off his leg for a bit as he tried his best not to count the seconds Felix kept him waiting.

The silence wasn't his friend, though.

Dei hadn't been away from his mom since she was put into care, and while he knew he deserved to take some time away, the idea of not being close enough to run to her made him feel sick. He'd already been by that morning, and every member of her team that was there said Dei was safe to take a few weeks if he wanted.

Her condition wasn't spiraling, even if it was progressing quickly.

Nothing would be the same after she was gone, but as much as he'd be freer to travel again whenever he wanted, he didn't want to wait for it. He was tired of putting his life on hold all the damn time.

The door creaked open, and Dei jumped a little as Felix stuck his head in. There was a pause—the way there always was when Felix was searching him for something to recognize—and then he smiled, sweet and sunny.

"I heard the guys were giving you shit," Felix said as he stepped in and closed the door.

Dei snorted. "No worse than I gotta hear at work, shug. How's your day goin'?"

"Good." Felix shot him an apologetic grimace. "I can't talk long, though. My client's already in my stall."

Dei stood and reached for Felix, who leaned into his touch like a cat. His cheek was scratchy and warm. "I'm not here to keep you. I got a mountain of dinner prep to finish. I just wanted to let you know I got my time off approved and got my momma's team all informed."

Felix's eyes widened. "Oh my god," he whispered. "I forgot about her. You really don't have to—"

Dei touched Felix's lower lip with his thumb, his words trailing off into a sigh. "I want to go. I want to be there with you."

Felix swallowed heavily, then nodded. "If anything happens…"

"We hop a plane and get right back," Dei said, ignoring the little curl of anxiety at the base of his spine. Shit could happen anytime, anywhere. There was no point in constantly preparing for disaster. "What time is our flight?"

"We leave Miami at four," Felix said quietly.

Dei nodded, then slowly drew his hand away, hating the space he created between them. "I'll get all packed up and ready to go tonight. And if you want some company, you come right over, okay?"

Felix looked happy about that. Happier than Dei expected him to, and it made him think about what Jeremiah had told him. Testing the waters. It was sure as shit going to test his resolve, but Dei couldn't begin to imagine what would happen if he gave in.

The truth was, he was petrified. Not of Felix, but of the hurt he could cause—of the hurt both of them could cause if they weren't careful enough. He wanted Felix more than he'd wanted anyone in a damn long time. He just wasn't sure if he trusted himself to take the risk.

DEI STACKED his travel shoes on top of his suitcase. Flying for him was a thousand times trickier than it was before his injuries. His pride wanted him to skip disability services because being wheeled in some hulking hospital-style chair by a total stranger was mortifying, but the fuss they made in the security line if he didn't was often worse.

The last time he'd left the state, he'd been dragged into one of the private security rooms and strip-searched, and the security agent had broken his collapsible cane, which made navigating the Dallas airport awful.

The stress was weighing on him, though not nearly enough to make him want to cancel on Felix. He wasn't sure anything short of the damn apocalypse could do that.

Moving to his closet, he stared inside at his dressier clothes and sighed. He hadn't been to a funeral in years, and the last two he'd attended were for Marines, which meant his Dress Blues. But he wasn't sure he wanted to draw that kind of attention to himself this time. Especially with how difficult Felix's family had been. He knew that Felix showing up with him was going to cause a stir enough as it was.

Dei felt a headache coming on, but before he could do anything about it, his doorbell rang. For a brief second, he thought maybe it was Sofia. He moved faster than usual, ignoring the pain in his hip as he hoofed it to the door.

When he peered out of the peephole, his heart sank for a split second before rising into his throat at the sight of Felix there, looking awkward and uncertain. He had one hand pressed to the back of his neck, and the other was clenched around the handle of a small suitcase.

Dei quickly let him in, taking him by the shoulder as he closed the door behind him. "You look white as a sheet, sugar."

Felix swallowed heavily. "Having second thoughts."

"About me?" Dei asked carefully. He'd bow out if Felix asked him to, even if that went against every instinct.

Felix immediately shook his head. "Fuck no. You're the only reason I'm brave enough to stand here right now. I'm…it's…" He closed his eyes in a slow blink. "Is it okay if we don't talk about it right now?"

"'Course." Dei released his shoulder and carefully took the suitcase out of his hand, bracing it against the wall. "We got the couch or my bed to snuggle up on," Dei told him carefully.

"Oh. Uh," Felix said, a tiny smile playing at his lips.

"And I might only have the one arm left, but I can still give a mean massage."

"Massage?" Felix echoed.

He shrugged. "You look like you could use it."

Dei was talking out of his ass. He'd never given a massage in his life, but he'd figure it out if it kept *that* look on Felix's face.

"Bed, then?"

Dei nodded and led the way to his bedroom, his pace slower this time. His stump was starting to fire up with nerve pain, but he breathed through it as he limped to the bed and started to move his stuff over.

"Oh shit, I interrupted your packing," Felix said.

Dei waved him off. "You interrupted a crisis of clothing. I don't know what I should be wearin' to this thing."

Felix grimaced. "I picked out some slacks and a button-up. It's got skulls on it, but they're really hard to see. My grammy would have loved it, and if my mom notices and gets pissed, it's a bonus."

Dei snorted. "Okay, so I don't need to bring my Dress Blues."

At that, Felix's cheeks went faintly pink. "Uh. No. But…well. No."

Dei cocked his head to the side. "Darlin'?"

"It's…I'm not trying to be a creep. I just think they'd look hot on you." He glanced away, covering half his face with his hand.

Dei's heart felt kind of warm and soft. He took two steps closer and grabbed Felix by the chin. "You wanna be feelin' all that stuff during Grammy's funeral?"

Felix quickly shook his head. "Maybe another time?"

Dei laughed and nodded, releasing him as much as he didn't want to. He gestured toward the bed as he backed up, then turned toward his closet to grab one of his nice, navy blue button-ups and some trousers from the shelf. "I promise you'll get the chance to see 'em." He tossed his clothes on top of his suitcase, resolving to press them when they got to their hotel, then turned back to Felix, who was now perched on the end of his bed.

Dei had wanted to see him in his room for so long now, but this wasn't what he envisioned. Felix didn't look wild and worked up with need. He looked like he was on the verge of shaking apart.

"I know you said you don't wanna talk about it, but I don't know if that's doin' you any good, sugar."

Felix rolled his eyes up toward the ceiling and let out a slow breath. "Paris was with me the last time I talked to my mom." He swallowed heavily, then flopped backward and landed with a dull thud on a pile of Dei's blankets. "When she was threatening to have me put under conservatorship."

Dei's chest burned with anger all over again. "Mhm."

"I talked to the guys about it tonight. I know it's totally irrational. I mean, I'm kind of…brain damaged or whatever. I know I am. But I'm not incapable of taking care of myself."

"I think your time here has proven that," Dei said. He walked over and sat down, giving them only a few inches of space. "You worried she's gonna try it when you get there?"

"I'm worried that she's got the ball rolling already," Felix admitted quietly.

Dei dropped back on the bed, regretting immediately that Felix was on the side of his stump instead of his arm because he wanted to hold him, but maybe it was better that way. He needed to figure out how to keep some distance between them until he knew for sure whether or not the line was worth crossing.

"This guy at the tattoo shop in Denver—he's married to a lawyer," Felix said. "I…sorry, my head is a mess, and I can't think of their names right now."

"It's okay," Dei assured him quietly.

"It's not, but…whatever. He was so nice to me. He said my mom can't just decide I'm incompetent, and I haven't done anything that would suggest she has a case. He said any lawyer worth anything wouldn't take her on as a client."

"Sounds like he knows what he's talking about," Dei said.

Felix laughed, then rolled onto his side and propped his head up on his elbow, looking down at Dei. "I hope so. I know this is totally irrational, but I'm terrified. I can't…I can't let her keep me there. I won't survive it."

Dei reached for him and cupped Felix's cheek. "That won't happen. If some shit goes down, we run."

Felix's eyes widened. "We run?"

Dei nodded sternly. "We steal away into the night and get the fuck out. Then we hire the best goddamn lawyer money can buy and get her off your back for good."

Felix let out a slow breath, turning his face to nuzzle into Dei's palm. "I'm sorry I'm such a mess."

"Darlin', you're anything but. Now, go ahead and get yourself comfy. I've got sweats and T-shirts—whatever you want. I'm gonna get us a couple drinks and maybe a snack, then I'll be in to help you unwind." Dei didn't mean it like that, but he enjoyed the way it affected Felix. Especially the way his cheek went all pink at being given orders.

And if he were a weaker man, or if he liked Felix any less, he might have given in to his desires.

But he wasn't, and he didn't, so he was going to do his damn best to behave himself. Even if it made him want to give up everything he owned for a chance to make what they had something lasting and something real.

11

Felix wasn't overly fond of flying. He hadn't gotten on a plane since before the Incident, and he was a trembling mess as Max dropped them off at the airport. Instead of staying in the car, Max got out to help them unload their bags, and he took Felix by the shoulders, holding him tight.

"If any shit goes down—and I mean *any* shit—you call me. Got it? The entire goddamn shop will fly our asses up there to take care of your bitch mom."

Felix ducked his head and laughed. If this had been two years ago, he might have tripped over himself in an attempt to defend her. He used to tell others and himself that she only acted the way she did because she loved him. It wasn't until he got enough distance that he realized just how toxic she was.

"I'll see you soon," Felix promised.

He let go of Max and found Dei by the glint of his prosthetic—not to mention the way he towered over everyone. But the rest of the crowd was a buzzing sea of strangers, like bees in a hive. His brain couldn't process their faces individually, so they faded into a blur, and he felt panic rising in his gut.

"Hey," Felix said, hoping Dei could hear him. "I don't feel so well."

Dei let go of the bag handle and pressed his massive palm to the side of Felix's neck. "What can I do?"

"Get me out of this crowd," Felix said, his voice trembling.

"That might be tricky, sugar. It's busy inside too. But I can get us through the line quicker if you can be patient with me for a few minutes."

Felix was willing to do anything to get out of the chaos, so he just nodded and grabbed his bag, following Dei through the doors to the main airport lobby. They had to wait in a long line to check their bags, and Felix's ears were buzzing with tinnitus, but he watched as Dei smiled and leaned over the desk to talk to the man behind the computer.

He shot Felix a wink after a minute, and eventually, another attendant came around the corner with a wheelchair. Felix's brow furrowed until Dei turned and lowered himself into it, but before they moved, Dei grabbed his wrist.

"Just follow along, okay? We're gonna get through this."

Felix had about a thousand questions, but he was grateful he could follow the wheelchair without his brain losing track of Dei's face. They were able to bypass the main security lane and went through a much shorter one, and it wasn't long before the row of mostly empty seats was stretched out in front of them at their gate.

"This is where I leave you," the attendant said to Dei, helping him stand.

Dei unfolded his walking cane and leaned on it, giving the guy a nod before shuffling over to a small row of seats. Felix's knees were trembling with nerves, so it was a relief to take the weight off and lean into Dei's arm.

"You good, darlin'?"

Felix nodded. "I am now. I haven't been on a plane in years, so I think I'm freaking out a little."

Dei dropped his cheek to the top of Felix's hair and let out a long sigh. "We've got ourselves a nice spot in first class. You'll have a drink and take a nap, and we'll be there before you know it."

Felix couldn't help a small laugh. "That's not as comforting as I want it to be."

"I know, but we've got a whole day before we gotta deal with your family, right?"

"Right," Felix murmured. His body was starting to feel the adrenaline crash, and his eyes were struggling to stay open.

"So think of something nice to show me. Something you really liked from back home that had nothing to do with your family. We'll make some nice memories before it all goes to shit."

Felix laughed sleepily, then yawned. "Do you mind if I nod off?"

"Go for it, sugar. I'll be right here when you wake up."

In a perfect world, that would have been a comfort, but for a man whose brain turned those he loved into strangers when he blinked, it was almost like a threat. But for the first time since his mind betrayed him, Felix heard those words and felt comfort.

THE FLIGHT WAS LONG. It felt like days had passed by the time they landed, though the West Coast sun was almost in the exact same position in the sky as when they left the east. Felix spent most of the flight either managing his panic or stress-napping against Dei's side, so he was both groggy and wired when they picked up their rental.

It was the most bizarre feeling in the world, like Felix's brain was filled with Pop Rocks.

Dei kept in close as he filled out all the paperwork, winking several times at Felix, who flushed each time he grinned, showing off little dimples in his cheeks. He was falling even harder than before, which was difficult because while Dei was more touchy than usual, it could easily be chalked up to the fact that he was practicing for his role as doting boyfriend.

Felix was damn sure the week with Dei and his family was going to kill him. He'd be in heaven when he was allowed to touch, and going home would rob him of something he was growing too accustomed to.

Then, when they got home, he'd be in hell when he couldn't reach for Dei and wouldn't find him reaching back.

"Hey, darlin'?"

Felix blinked and realized Dei was several steps away from him. "Sorry. Lost in thought."

"You tell me if you start feelin' wonky, okay? Like if we need to find somewhere for you to go prone."

Felix nodded. "Trust me. The last thing I want is to have a seizure in front of an audience." He'd only done that a few times, and it was always when the most mortifying side effects happened—like pissing himself or drooling all over.

And there was always some camera-happy asshole with his phone out.

They trudged out to the parking lot where all the cars were waiting, and an attendant walked them to the little bay, giving Dei a side-eye when it became obvious he was the driver. Felix could see the line of tension in Dei's body, but the attendant didn't ask, and Dei didn't offer an explanation.

They had a nice luxury car with soft seats and a moon roof, which Dei immediately opened, grinning at Felix as they pulled into the sun. "It's kinda nice not having afternoon clouds."

Felix laughed. "Yeah. There are far more sunny beach days in summer here than there are at home."

Dei turned his head left and right, probably compensating for his missing eye, then pulled out onto the road and started following the quiet tones of the GPS, which was leading them to their rental. Felix had chosen someplace near the water, missing the Pacific waves and sand and feeling some type of way about being able to share it with Dei. He knew the man was well traveled, but the way he was looking around, it was obvious he'd never been there before.

"So. This is LA?"

"Barely, and we're getting the fuck out," Felix told him. "The 5 is going to suck balls, but once we're away from the main city, we won't need to worry about it until we're heading back for our flight."

Dei's smile soon became a grimace when they got trapped in total gridlock, but his mood didn't seem too down in spite of all his yawning. "I forgot how much flying fucks me up," he said after the fifth time his jaw nearly cracked.

Felix laughed. "You were on a plane a lot?"

"Yeah," Dei said, and oh, there was some tension. "Got deployed more'n once. Stationed in Okinawa for three years."

Felix's eyes went wide. "How was that?"

"Pretty fuckin' cool for the collective three months I was physically there," Dei said with a small chuckle. "They didn't like to keep us in one spot. I'd like to go back one day now that I'm a civvy. Get to enjoy all the shit I didn't get the chance to see while I was there."

Felix couldn't imagine what his life was like. It would be odd to love a man who was never around, though for Dei, it would have been worth it. But Felix was coming to learn he was a pretty clingy guy, and he would have missed him painfully.

"What you thinkin', shug?"

Felix blushed and shrugged. "That dating or being married to someone in the service must be hard."

"Harder'n some, better'n others. I know CEOs who are gone a fuck of a lot longer than I was."

Felix smiled and shrugged as the car finally started picking up speed, and the GPS told them he was twenty-two miles from their exit. "I guess I wouldn't know. I wasn't good at dating before my brain injury, and my life is obviously not great for dating after."

Dei made a soft noise like he wanted to argue, but he didn't, and Felix wasn't sure if he appreciated it or not. He wanted someone to defend him, but he also wanted honesty, and there was a clear reason —more than just Dei being busy—why they were only doing this for pretend.

They settled into comfortable silence, and then eventually, the exit for Santa Bella came into view. Dei took the cloverleaf with one-handed ease, which dumped Felix onto a street that should have been familiar, but he didn't recognize much of it. He wasn't sure if it was just time or if it was his brain, but the sensation wasn't comfortable.

"You okay? You just went real pale," Dei said.

Felix took a calming breath. "I grew up here, but none of it looks like home, you know? But I can't tell if it's my brain being all fucked-up or if that's what happens when you move away."

"It might be a bit of both. I went back home a few years before my injury, and it was all strange. It's like you know the streets with muscle memory, but none of it's familiar anymore."

That was it. That was exactly it, and Felix didn't feel like he was totally nuts. He watched the roads as they passed, and as he scanned street signs, things started to make better sense.

"My sister lives down there," he said, passing a Circle K on the corner of Coral Ave. "I helped her move in when she and her husband bought the house."

"Is it nice?"

Felix laughed, shaking his head. "It might be now. It was a total piece of shit when they bought it. It was piss-yellow with two bedrooms, and someone had ripped the bathtub out, but they were too broke, so they took standing showers over a hole in the floor."

"Christ," Dei said.

Felix shrugged. "This place is kind of a nightmare, but they seem bound and determined to live and die in here."

"And you chose different," Dei said.

That wasn't the first time Felix had heard that, but it was the first time he felt proud. "I don't think the island is where I'm meant to be forever, but for now, it feels good."

Dei just smiled at him as he took a turn up a hilly road and eventually pulled into a circular driveway. The front yard was perfectly manicured with big river rock and succulents, and over the fence, he could see a ton of citrus trees that he knew surrounded the pool.

Dei let out a low whistle as he leaned against the car, half-braced on his prosthetic. "You spending big bucks, darlin'?"

"I wanted to have something nice to come home to since we have to deal with my family," Felix admitted. "Maybe I went overboard."

"Honey, I'm not gonna turn down being spoiled on this trip," Dei said, then gave the roof of the car a pat before shutting his door and leaning on his cane.

They left the bags behind as Felix led the way to the door, then scrolled through his phone for the code. "It's pretty small. It's only got two bedrooms and one and a half bathrooms, but it has a massive yard with a spa and a fully equipped kitchen in case we get sick of takeout."

"I'm already sick of it," Dei said with another laugh as he breezed past Felix into the foyer. The floors were a polished concrete, and they led right to a living room with a very slender, white leather couch, which Felix doubted would hold Dei's bulk. The windows were floor-to-ceiling, though, which let in light, and that filtered into the massive kitchen he could just make out through an archway.

"Oh, darlin', you didn't tell me the ocean was right here."

"Right," Felix said, grinning sheepishly as he followed Dei to the terrace. "And the ocean's right there."

Dei rolled his eyes and elbowed him before fumbling with the lock and getting the door to slide all the way to the left. The breeze hit him right away, waves visible through the palms and over an accessible blue walkway that was half buried in the sand.

"We ain't got waves like this," Dei said, gazing past the small pool.

Felix shook his head. "No. We really don't. I do miss it. I just don't miss anything that came with being here."

Dei turned to him and brushed a touch over his jaw. "We'll get you some better memories, sugar. I swear it."

Felix swallowed heavily, and instead of giving in to his urge to lean in, he leaned back and walked into the house. He could hear Dei right behind him, following him down the short corridor and to the first bedroom. He turned the handle, but it wouldn't budge, and he frowned.

"What's wrong?"

Felix looked back over his shoulder. "First room's locked. I'll email the property manager if you wanna throw your stuff into the other bedroom," Felix said, gesturing to the open door.

Dei walked past him and let out another whistle. "Damn, what do they call these beds? Alaskan kings?"

Felix peered around him, then burst into laughter. "At least there's room for all of your…" He waved his hand up and down Dei's body.

Dei grinned at him. "Yeah. I guess even missin' a couple limbs, I still take up a lot of space."

"I like that about you," Felix said softly. Their gazes connected, and just when he couldn't take it anymore, Dei turned away. "I'm gonna go call the rental agency and see what's up with the other room."

Without waiting for Dei's response, Felix made his way back to the kitchen and leaned on the counter where the welcome packet was sitting. He flipped open the first page and reached for his phone when something caught his eye.

Welcome guests! Thanks for choosing Blue Coastal Rentals for your luxury stay. Unfortunately, this unit is currently undergoing some renovations, so the first bedroom is currently inaccessible. Please feel free to utilize the sofa for the second sleeping area, and don't hesitate to call if there's a problem...

Felix slammed the book shut and dropped his forehead down to the counter. The sofa looked about as comfortable as sleeping on concrete. It was all rich person aesthetic—beauty over comfort—and he wasn't looking forward to spending a week with his back seizing up.

He jumped a little when fingers brushed the back of his neck, but instead of sitting up, he just turned his head. "Hey."

"What's got you in a tizzy, darlin'?"

Felix closed his eyes against the sweetness in Dei's tone. "That room is apparently closed for renovations, so I'm going to be sleeping on that shitty-ass couch for the week."

"The hell you are," Dei said.

Felix snorted and forced himself to stand upright. "Don't tell me you're going to squeeze onto that thing."

Dei grimaced. "No, shug. The both of us are gonna find room in that planet-sized bed."

"But…"

"Or I'll make myself a little pallet on the floor if you're not comfy there, but there's a ton of room for us both, and a midnight cuddle never scared me none."

Felix swallowed heavily. He wasn't worried about a cuddle. He was worried about the way they both very obviously wanted each other.

"I can be a difficult sleeper sometimes," Felix said.

Dei raised a brow at him. "What's that supposed to mean?"

"Um. I don't know. Just that I might, you know, not respect your space."

Dei stepped closer. "First of all," he replied, his voice dropping, "I've already had you sleepin' in my arms, so unless that idea bothers you…"

"It doesn't," Felix said, a little too quickly. He rubbed the back of his neck, his head starting to hurt with how he was trying to find the right words. "I just don't want you to think I'm pushing you into something you're not ready for. And I don't…I can't…"

Dei seemed to notice quickly because he reached for Felix and pulled him close. "Breathe, darlin'. You're my boyfriend for the week, right? So what's the harm in sharing some space?"

But that was the problem. That was the literal *root* of Felix's problem. They were just pretend. At least when there were separate bedrooms, he had a way to retreat from all the ways he wanted to just roll over and let Dei have him.

But there wasn't another solution unless he wanted to sleep on the tiny couch barely wide enough to hold a toddler or run down to whatever store was nearby and grab an air mattress, which was something his body felt too damn old for these days.

"As long as you don't mind," Felix said softly.

Dei tipped up his chin again and held his gaze. "No, sugar. Minding is the last thing I feel."

12

It took Felix some coaxing to relax, but Dei did everything in his power to put on a happy face. And it wasn't like he didn't want to be in bed with Felix. In fact, if his heart had its way, they wouldn't do anything *but* make use of the giant mattress that damn near spread wall to wall.

Except he was trying to do this right. For both his sake and Felix's.

He wanted to make sure that if he decided to take that step, it wasn't going to leave Felix devastated in the end. He'd rather die than let that man feel another moment of pain.

It felt like a small triumph when Felix finally agreed to unpack, and Dei lounged on the bed with his leg off, giving his stump a break from the socket as he watched Felix carefully arrange his things, then add little yellow and orange Post-its to several items.

"Can I ask what those are for?" Dei said into the silence.

Felix glanced over his shoulder, then down at his hands where he was writing something, and he laughed. "Oh. Uh, they're not very interesting. I tend to forget routine stuff, like brushing my teeth or taking my meds, so I put notes on everything." He put his pen down and held up a pill box organizer. "I feel like a ninety-year-old man sometimes."

Dei just grinned at him. "Hottest ninety-year-old man I've ever seen."

Felix flushed and looked back down at his task. "If any of this clutter annoys you—"

"Darlin', I work in a restaurant kitchen. This ain't clutter. Trust me."

At that, Felix laughed. "Okay, fair. I mean, I've never been in a restaurant kitchen. I'm barely in my own kitchen, but I also know what it's like to share a supply room with a bunch of dudes."

Dei chuckled, stretching his arm above his head before he sat up and swung his leg off the side of the mattress. They had no obligations for the rest of that day, so what he really wanted to do was cook them a nice meal, then maybe spend the evening soaking in the pool.

But it meant a trip to the store, which Dei thought might be a good way to get a little space and clear his head. "Hand me my lube right there, sugar." He looked up when Felix made a choking noise, and he realized what he said. "Aww, hell, not that kind of—I meant—it's for my socket. That little bottle right next to your elbow."

Felix slapped a hand over his face as he groped for the bottle. "Right. I…yeah. I knew that."

Dei was helplessly charmed every time Felix got embarrassed and stumbled over his words. His heart throbbed in his chest, and he wished he had his leg on so he could walk over there, pin Felix to the wall, and kiss him senseless.

So maybe it was a good thing he was stuck on the bed.

His breath caught in his throat a little as Felix finally walked over, and their fingers brushed as Dei took the bottle from him, catching his gaze as he did. "Thank you."

Felix swallowed heavily. "Anytime."

The moment hung in the air between them, offering a chance to relieve their tension, but Dei forced himself to hold back, and eventually, Felix returned to his task as Dei poured a generous dollop of the cream into his palm and slathered it over the end of his leg. He coated his socket, then stood and braced himself against the wall as he slipped his stump inside. He could feel Felix's gaze on him, but he didn't look up as he adjusted the vacuum compression.

"Are you getting ready for something?" Felix asked after a long beat of silence.

Dei shuffled back over to the bed to retrieve his shoe. He'd become an expert at tying laces one-handed, though there were days he wished he could be nine again and have those bad-ass, double Velcro Reeboks he'd loved in fourth grade.

"Did I do something wrong?"

Dei's gaze snapped up. "Not at all, darlin'. Just shakin' off this jet lag, so I thought I'd head to the store and get us something for dinner."

"I could take you out," Felix said very quietly.

Dei laughed as he pushed back up to his feet and tested his balance. He felt a little off from the long flight, but nothing he couldn't manage. He took a few steps closer to Felix, but not as many as he wanted to. "Why don't you let me take care of you for a bit."

"You're already doing—"

"Don't say I'm doin' enough," Dei interrupted, refusing to let him finish that sentence. "You just let yourself unwind while I pick us up some food, and I'll feed you up real nice."

Felix looked like he had a thousand things to say to that, but instead, he just nodded and refused to meet Dei's eyes.

He stood there another moment, but when it was clear he wasn't getting anything else out of Felix, he turned, grabbed his cane, and headed out the door.

The drive to the supermarket was close. It was some expensive corner shop that looked like it was trying to be a gourmet bodega. The produce section was tragically small, but it had enough for what Dei wanted to cook. He grabbed zucchini, squash, and a couple of different types of mushrooms before heading to the butcher. The counter only had a few items, so he went with shrimp and steak, then snagged a bottle of some nondescript, brownish marinade that the butcher recommended.

The fact that the market was so small made the few customers in there feel a little claustrophobic, and there were eyes on him no matter what aisle he turned on. A small part of him regretted not wearing his dog tags simply because it stopped total strangers from asking him what happened.

Usually, the conversation turned to the simpering "thank you for your service" or some shit, which was easier to deal with than the invasive questions. And Dei didn't mind it all the time, but there were days he wished he could just exist in his body like everyone else and not as some showcase for public consumption.

Luckily, before he ran his mouth off at some old woman who had damn near rammed her cart into him three times because she couldn't stop staring at his arm, his phone rang. He hooked his cane over the cart handle and dug into his pocket, surprised to see Jeremiah's name on the screen.

"Bud, I just left. Please tell me this ain't some crisis call," he all but begged.

Jeremiah laughed. "No. But someone forgot to tell me that they landed and got in safely. And you know me. I'm a goddamn helicopter mom."

Dei rolled his eyes and pinched the phone between his ear and shoulder as he leaned on the cart and headed for the bakery. In a perfect world, he'd throw together something from scratch and continue to woo Felix through his food, but he didn't have the energy to do more than fire up the grill and toss a few things onto an open flame.

There was a massive display of tarts that looked fresh, and he hummed as he eyed them. "Well, we landed, and I'm safe," he said into Jeremiah's continued silence. "Anything else you need?"

"To check on my friend," Jeremiah said. "To make sure you're not getting in over your head."

Dei sighed as he snagged one of the tart boxes, then eyed the lines. There were only two checkouts open, and none of them were self-serve. He made his way toward the crowd and wondered if West Coast culture was gonna invite people to yell at him for being on the phone.

"Everything's goin' exactly as it should be. Felix is back at the house getting settled in." He debated about telling Jeremiah about the bed situation, but he didn't want to. Jeremiah was a fixer—which meant he'd come up with a reasonable alternative to sharing, and Dei didn't want that.

"And how is he feeling? Max has literally worried himself sick over it."

"He probably has a right to," Dei said, his heart sinking. "His family's a real piece of work. He's tryin'a keep it together, but I feel like tomorrow might be rough."

"I'm glad you're there with him. Even if you two have your heads too far up your asses."

Dei rolled his eyes and shuffled one step further in line. "Well, thanks for the pep talk, boss. Now, I'm gonna let you go before this one-armed bastard makes a fool of himself tryin'a load up all these groceries."

"Are you cooking for him?" Jeremiah asked with obvious glee.

"Fuck you. And yes. See you when I get back. Don't let the restaurant burn down before I get home." Dei snagged the phone from his shoulder and ended the call before he finally reached the conveyor belt.

As he reached into the cart, there was a hand on his arm, tugging at him. Dei wasn't a big fan of being touched by total strangers, and he reared back, ready to strike, before he saw a middle-aged woman with a short, blonde bob.

She was smiling at him. "Let me help."

"No, thank you, ma'am. I've got it."

Her face immediately dropped. "Do I really look old enough to be a ma'am?"

Dei licked his lips. That was a trap, and he knew it. "Where I'm from, don't matter your age. It's just polite. Unless I got your gender wrong, and then I apologize from the deepest part of my heart."

Her face fell even more. "Do I look like one of *those* types?"

Dei had a feeling this was gonna go from bad to worse if he wasn't careful. "I do my best not to judge anyone by the way they look. If people did that to me, god only knows what strangers would say." Then he turned and began to load his things onto the belt.

He could hear her muttering under her breath, but he did his best to ignore it as he pushed his cart toward the end of the line. There wasn't a bagger, but he didn't put up a fight when the cashier took one look at his missing arm, then began to do it for him.

At this point, he just wanted out. He was missing his tiny community where people didn't look at him cross-eyed or like he was helpless. He missed not watching his tongue and feeling at home in his own skin.

He tried for a smile when the guy read his total, and then he swiped his card, gathered everything onto his arm, and leaned heavily on his cane as he walked out. They were probably saying a dozen awful things behind his back, but he'd leave them to their cesspool of judgment. He had an absurdly hot man back home with a wounded heart he could attempt to comfort and—hours after the sun went down—a big bed to cuddle up in.

THE POOL DECK on the rental property had an outdoor kitchen, and it only took Dei a couple of tries before he figured out how to get the propane going. After a little coaxing, he managed to get Felix to throw on some swim trunks and lie out near the grill, and as Dei slowly turned the kebab skewers over the fire, he let himself stare at the long, lithe form of the man he was falling for.

Felix wasn't very muscular, a little thick on his hips and belly, just the way Dei liked. And so much of his skin was covered in ink—different scenes in different styles, and he had both nipples and his navel pierced, which was the first time Dei had gotten a good look at them.

Felix seemed relaxed for the first time since they'd landed, which put Dei at a little more ease. He was in black trunks and matching shades, and he had one arm behind his head as he soaked up the very last of the afternoon sun. The breeze was drier than back home, which made it a little cooler, and Dei could appreciate it, even if he missed his own beach.

"We should take a walk after we're done eating," Felix said.

Dei blinked out of his thoughts and quickly looked down to make sure he wasn't burning anything. "Yeah?"

"If you're up for it," Felix added. "Is it hell to walk on sand with your leg?"

It was, but Dei would rather die than admit it. At home, he usually just went with his crutches since he didn't like taking his prosthetic into the water, but he hadn't wanted to deal with checking them or storing them on the plane. He'd heard far too many horror stories about destroyed mobility aids, and he didn't have the capital to keep replacing that shit every time someone was careless.

"It'll be fine. Just don't ask me to hike ten miles."

Felix laughed, the sound sweet and genuine. "You couldn't pay my ass to walk ten miles. I just thought it might be nice to put my toes in the water. I used to surf."

Dei got a sudden image of Felix out on the waves in a formfitting wet suit, his hair mussed from salt water, and goddamn, he popped half a chub. He shifted so Felix wouldn't be able to see him behind the little counter.

"You miss it?"

Felix nodded. "Yeah. Not enough to come back, but there are days I wish we had better waves. And maybe less sharks and man o'wars."

Dei snorted a laugh. "No shit. A guy came to Midnight a few weeks back. Some tourist from Minnesota who got stung in the face."

"Jeeeesus," Felix said, twisting so he could look over his shoulder. "I can't believe he stayed after that."

"Poor fucker looked like he wanted to die, but his wife wasn't havin' it. She just shoved a big piece of Jer's cake at him and told him to shut up."

Felix groaned and dropped the side of his forehead to the edge of the lounger. "Why do straight spouses hate each other so much?"

"When you grow up bein' told that your bullies are your admirers and that marriage is a ball and chain, that's what you expect," Dei answered. He'd always known he wasn't going to marry a woman, but for a long time, he hadn't realized why. All he knew was that everyone around him seemed to be miserable, and that was the last thing he wanted for himself.

"Did you ever meet Tony?"

"That silver fox daddy?" Dei asked.

Felix looked slightly put out. "I'd kill to age that hot."

"You remember what he looks like?" Dei asked.

Felix shook his head. "I just remember thinking he was goals."

"Darlin'..." Dei said, then stopped himself. It was too close to honest, and that would ruin the moment. "You got nothin' to worry about."

Felix waved him off. "Well, anyway, he's been married for decades, and I mean, he's not straight. He's in a polyamorous relationship, but all he did while he was at the shop was obsess about how much he loved his and missed his wife. And not in that creepy, overcompensating way. You could just tell, you know? That he was in love with her today as much as he was in their honeymoon phase."

Dei carefully removed the skewers onto a massive serving plate, then let them rest as he walked over to Felix's lounger and sat. Felix shifted to make room for him, and their skin touched—warm and soft from the late afternoon.

"I want that," Felix murmured after a long moment of silence. "I want to meet my best friend and marry him and stay best friends for the rest of our lives."

"You think you won't find that?"

Felix looked him dead in the eye, almost like a challenge, and Dei almost rose to it.

Almost.

When Felix said nothing, Dei breathed out a sigh and shrugged. "Soup's on. Or...kebabs. Whatever."

Felix cleared his throat, then swung his legs over the side of the side of the lounger and stood. "Cool. Table?"

In the end, Dei directed them both to the little bistro table covered by an umbrella. He stretched his legs out, taking as much pressure off his stump as he could, and he listened to Felix picking at his food since he was sitting on his blind side.

It was almost like a reprieve, not being able to see him, since Dei was worked up and afraid that lines were going to be crossed before he was ready.

"Did I say something wrong?" Felix asked after a long moment.

Dei turned his head, and his heart beat a little harder when Felix filled his line of sight. "What makes you think that?"

"Because you haven't said a word since we sat down. And I know my head's a little wrecked, so I'm not the best at interpreting social situations, but I feel like I know you." Felix bowed his head toward his plate, and his ears went a little pink. "Maybe I'm overthinking it."

Dei felt like a complete asshole. He was working on his own shit, but he hadn't taken into consideration how much harder things were for Felix. And that wasn't taking into account the fact that they were here for his grandmother's funeral, seeing his shitty-as-fuck family for the first time in a long time.

"Christ, I'm so sorry."

Felix's gaze snapped up. "What?"

"I *am* being weird." Dei set his kebab down and swiped his fingers over his shorts. It was time for honesty. If Felix was on the same page, then they could figure it out from there. If Felix wasn't, then Dei would take time to get over him. "I really like you."

"Yeah. I like you too," Felix started but went quiet when Dei held up his hand.

"Romantically. Sexually. Just to be clear."

Felix snorted a laugh and rolled his eyes, leaning his elbow on the table so he could prop his chin on his hand. "I know. You're not subtle. And we have talked about this a little."

Dei grimaced. "Yeah. But I *really* like you, Felix. I'm falling so hard, and it's a little terrifying because I don't know if I'm ready. And I don't want to string you along."

Felix looked a little upset, his gaze darting away from Dei. "People seem to think that I can't handle uncomfortable situations. I mean, yeah, I guess regulating my emotions can be harder for me, but I'm not a fucking child."

"I'm not saying you are," Dei said in a rush.

Felix gave him a withering look. "Would you be having this conversation with someone else?"

"Yes," Dei told him firmly. "I've never been in this position, but I like to think if I'd fallen for anyone—no matter who they were—I'd be taking care with their heart."

Felix let out a slow breath, his eyes a little wide and stunned. "Oh."

Realization hit Dei, and he wanted to simultaneously put his fist through the wall to punish a world that had allowed Felix to go so unloved and also gather him close and never let him go. "You deserve to be loved, Felix. Without reservations or fear."

Felix licked his lips. "Is there anything I can do to help?"

Dei laughed softly. "Maybe tell me how you feel. I've been mostly running on assumptions."

Felix sat back with a heavy thud. "Have I seriously never—god. I guess I am terrible at this."

"You're not—"

"I think I'm halfway in love with you." No other words had ever robbed Dei of his voice as quickly as those ones had. His throat felt like it was closing up, and he couldn't unstick his tongue from the roof of his mouth. Felix met his gaze, then shrugged. "It's new for me. This feeling is…I didn't know it could be like this. I don't want to push you, so I think that's why I've been keeping it to myself."

Dei's breath left him all in a rush. He knew, of course. Logically, he was well aware that Felix was into him. He just hadn't been able to convince himself that it was something truly worth fighting for.

Something worth the risk.

"I don't…" He trailed off. He had no idea what to say.

Luckily, Felix took pity on him. "We don't need to talk about this now, okay? We don't need to figure anything out here. I wasn't asking for that. I just needed to know it wasn't me making you miserable."

Dei wanted to kiss him. He wanted to cradle Felix's face against his rough palm, push him up against the wall, and devour him until neither of them had the strength to keep standing. "I do want to talk when this is over," he finally confessed.

Felix ducked his head, and Dei couldn't read his expression or his tone when he said, "Yeah. That's probably a good idea."

Blowing out a puff of air, Dei tapped his hand on the table before pushing up to his feet. He'd lost his appetite, and Felix didn't seem all that hungry either. "I'm gonna clean up this mess. Then we can go on that walk, if you're up for it."

"I might just hang here," Felix said very quietly. He wasn't meeting Dei's gaze. "But you can go if you want to."

Dei didn't. He offered Felix a small smile, then gathered up the plates, balancing them on his hand, before making his way inside and wondering if he'd just royally fucked everything up.

They didn't say much to each other for the rest of the evening. Felix stayed outside until the sun was down, and then he lay on the thin, uncomfortable couch with one arm flung over his eyes. Dei had half a mind to leave him there since he looked peaceful, but he couldn't condemn him to a raging backache the next day.

He took his time with his evening routine, however, bracing himself with his hand against the wall as the too-light water pressure flowed down his back. He scrubbed the airport smell off his skin, then slipped back into his prosthetic in spite of the pain shooting along his hip. What he wanted was to strip down to nothing and slide under cool sheets, but things were already weird enough with Felix.

Dei was done fooling himself. He knew when they got back home, he was going to ask Felix on a date. Hell, if it wouldn't make him a freak, he'd ask Felix to goddamn marry him, but he was actively trying not to scare the man off.

He'd fallen.

He was head over heels and beyond hope, and all he could do was pray to whatever god was willing to listen to him that Felix would feel the same way when they got home.

The thought buoyed him a little as he put on a pair of light sleep pants and a T-shirt, then made his way back into the living room. Felix had gotten up, and Dei felt a small rush of panic until he saw movement out the kitchen window. He felt a little unsteady after the long day, but he managed to get out back without falling on his face, and he found Felix sitting on the top step of the patio.

"You want the shower?"

"I used the other one," Felix said. Dei took notice of his wet hair and the way it clung to his head. His fingers itched to reach out and touch it.

"Sorry I took a hundred years."

Felix leaned his head back and rolled his eyes. "Dude. Stop apologizing for everything. It was a long day, and we're both beat."

Dei couldn't argue with that. He took a step closer, then extended his hand. "Come on, sugar. We both need to knock the fuck out."

Felix only hesitated for a second, but he eventually took Dei's hand and heaved himself up. They let go after a few lingering seconds, and Dei wondered if his body was going to let him keep to himself all night. The need to touch this man was almost overwhelming, and he knew he was going to crack sooner rather than later.

He felt a little trembly as they got to the room, and he deliberately didn't look over as Felix started to rummage around his suitcase. Instead, he sat on the edge of the bed and took his leg off, then—after some hesitation—peeled his shirt away and lay down with the overstarched sheets rough against his back.

He missed home suddenly. He missed the thick humidity of the evening air and his perfectly broken-in bed. He missed the sounds of the islands at night and the smells on the breeze. At home, at least he knew up from down.

He turned his head when he heard Felix shuffling closer and saw him approaching, his bottom lip between his teeth.

"I won't bite, but I do prefer the edge if it's all the same to you. I don't do so well tryn'a roll out of bed without two of my limbs."

Felix let out a tiny laugh, which was exactly what Dei had been going for. "I guess I can compromise on that one thing." He knee-walked over the blankets until he was able to slip under them, and there was a damn ocean of space between their bodies, which Dei hated.

He rolled onto his side, his stump pressing uncomfortably against the pillow, but it was worth it for the view of Felix's sleepy face. Silence settled between them, and Dei rolled over with a hard grunt as he fumbled for the bedside lamp, flicking it off when he found the button.

Darkness wrapped around them as Dei turned back, and he waited for his eye to adjust so he could make out Felix's profile. He was still on his back, and though Dei's vision wasn't great, he could still make out how tense he was.

"Talk to me," he whispered.

Felix let out a long, slow breath. "Tomorrow's going to suck in so many ways. I'm stressed-out that I'm going to have a seizure and give my mom a reason to try and keep me."

"She ain't comin' anywhere near you, darlin'. There's not a goddamn chance in hell." Dei's voice was a low growl, coming from the very depths of his soul. He'd give his remaining eye and limbs to make sure no one ever, *ever* made Felix feel like he was trapped again.

He wanted to tear apart anyone who made him this afraid.

"I know it's irrational. I mean, both logically and legally." Felix shuffled, and Dei watched as he rolled onto his side. "But for a long time, I believed her."

"What do you mean?"

"When I was leaving town," Felix said quietly, "I was in the car with Paris, and she called and threatened me. Paris took care of it—of me. But…I believed her. I think I've been waiting all this time for her to make good on her threat."

Dei was unable to stop himself from reaching for Felix. He found his wrist, then closed his fingers around it. "Why did you decide to come back?"

"Because I need to prove to myself that she doesn't actually have that kind of power over me or my life."

Dei wanted to tell him that torturing himself wasn't worth it, but he also understood in ways most people couldn't. Dei had done a lot of things that felt terrible to prove that he was still strong, and capable, and worthy. Hell, being on this trip and tormenting himself with the man he wasn't sure he could have was one of them.

"Just know that I'm yours," Dei finally said. "Whatever you need me to do, whatever you need me to be. Okay?"

"Okay," Felix said so softly Dei could barely hear him. "Can you just…" He stopped, then let out a sharp breath. "Never mind."

"No. There's no never minds on this trip," Dei said. "Tell me what you need."

"Can you just hold me? I know that's unfair because you're still trying to work everything out, but…"

"Like I said," Dei told him, tugging until Felix rolled into the circle of his arm, "on this trip, I'm yours."

And he'd be Felix's long after too, but now wasn't the time to say it. He wasn't going to add more. Not until all the hard parts were over. By then, maybe they'd both understand exactly what they needed from each other.

And what they wanted.

13

Felix woke pressed against a giant, warm body, and he'd never in his life felt more content. He hadn't looked at the time, but instinctively, he knew it was later in the morning, though he felt no need to move. His head was gently rising and falling with the rhythm of Dei's breath, and Felix knew that if he was given the choice, he'd just stay there forever.

But that felt like a cruel fantasy, considering he had his grandmother's funeral to attend and his family to confront, all while trying to maintain the lie with Dei and not let his stress win. It sounded like a Herculean task, but just before falling asleep, Dei had made it clear that Felix was his top priority.

It might have been the best thing he'd ever heard, especially considering that Dei had openly admitted to wanting him. He also hadn't gone running when Felix's lack of filter completely gave him away.

It was something.

It was *hope*.

He just couldn't let himself think about it until this was all over.

"Mornin'."

The soft rumble of Dei's sleep-thick voice startled him, and he jumped, trying to roll away, but Dei grabbed him and held tight.

"Not so fast. You're comfortable."

Felix rolled his eyes, but he snuggled back in, laying his hand over Dei's chest. His skin was smooth in most places, but there were swaths of knotted scar tissue from his injury. Felix wanted to lay him out on his table and create a canvas of art using them as the template.

"That sounds gorgeous, darlin'."

Felix's face erupted into heat when he realized he'd said that aloud. "Sorry. I know that's kind of fucked-up."

He managed to dislodge himself from Dei's grip, and he propped up on his forearms, sinking into the too-soft mattress. Dei's fresh, unfamiliar face was staring at him with a sleepy gaze, his prosthetic eye a little crooked, which gave him—somehow—even more character.

"I ain't the kinda man who needs to look at all his scars and missing bits and see beauty in them, but I like that you see somethin' in me that's worthy of art."

"Everyone's worthy of art," Felix told him with a shrug. "My mom used to get so freaked-out when she'd go through my sketchbook. She thought something was wrong with me, so she made me go to therapy until the therapist told her that I was just an artist. She didn't let me go back after that."

"I got a few choice words for her, but out of respect for the day, I'll keep them to myself," Dei said. The passion in his words did something to Felix —a warmth cascading through his chest. But before he could say anything about it, Dei pushed himself up to sit, then swung his leg over the bed.

His back was even more scarred than his front, especially around his shoulder where he'd lost his arm, and Felix fought the urge to touch all the hills and valleys.

"My hip's a bit out of place right now," Dei said without turning around. "I'm gonna hop to the bathroom, so promise me you won't laugh at the sight of my jiggly ass."

Felix decided not to tell Dei that the last thing he wanted to do with his ass was laugh at it. "I can cover my eyes if that will make you feel better."

Dei looked over his shoulder with a grin. "Naw, shug. I trust you."

Those three words hit Felix like a physical blow, and he was helpless to do anything except smile as Dei got to his foot and then—true to his word—hopped across the room and shut the bathroom door behind him.

The moment he was out of sight, Felix rolled onto his back, pressed his hands to his face, and groaned. What he'd give for his only problem that day was figuring out how to get Dei on board with a romantic date and a lot of making out. Instead, he'd have to drag the man to his grandmother's funeral, play pretend boyfriend in front of his shitty family, and somehow get over that enough to navigate the start of a relationship.

It felt doomed.

Rolling over, Felix climbed off the bed, then shuffled down the hall and into the kitchen. Dei had done a little shopping the day before, but he'd only picked up pastries for breakfast, which Felix was going to avoid like the plague. Sugar and caffeine weren't ever his friend when he was stressed-out, so he pulled out some of the leftover kebabs and lamented not being able to have coffee as they heated up in the microwave.

He was grabbing a plate when he heard the telltale thump of Dei's prosthetic foot, and he looked over his shoulder to find the man in question with a white button-up shirt halfway on and a sheepish look on his face.

"You know how when you go on a trip, you always forget at least one important thing?"

Felix frowned. "You're talking to the guy who can't even remember his own face in the mirror. So…yes."

Dei laughed as he took another step closer. "I have all these super badass tools to help me get dressed, but I forgot the one to do up my buttons, and my fat, stumpy fingers don't cooperate without it."

Felix grinned and beckoned him close, basking in the warmth of him when they were inches apart. Dei smelled very faintly like aftershave and soap, and Felix took a deep breath as he tugged Dei's shirt so it was even, then did up all the buttons.

"Pants?" he asked as he took a step back.

Dei shook his head as he tucked his shirt in. "There's a website that sells clothes for fuckers like me. I didn't get a chance to order a shirt in time, but got me some Velcro."

Felix's grin widened. His emotions were warring in his chest, fighting between grief, which he knew was going to feel ten times worse once they got to the funeral, and the need to just say fuck the complicated situation and hold Dei for real.

Instead, he went back to his plate, leaning against the counter as he picked at some of the meat. "So. Just to warn you, some of my family might be kind of vocal about me. And probably us."

Dei scoffed and reached past Felix for the pastry box, taking out one of the plain croissants. "There's not a whole lot I haven't heard back from when I was in the service. I don't think anything your family can say will be worse than that."

Felix dragged a hand down his face with a sigh. "Well…if they do, I need you to let it go, okay? Even if they're really fucking mean to me."

He saw something flash over Dei's expression, but it was gone before he could figure it out. Felix didn't know if it was a *him* problem or if it was the fact that Dei's poker face was amazing, but he accepted it when Dei nodded.

"Whatever you need from me, sugar."

"Thank you." Felix turned and put his plate in the sink, and when he spun back around, Dei was a few steps closer. "Did you—"

"Come here."

Felix moved like he was helpless against Dei's command, and in seconds, he was engulfed in a powerful, warm embrace that felt like actual heaven. He buried his face in the front of Dei's shirt and groaned slightly when fingers pushed into his hair.

"Had a feeling you needed that," Dei murmured.

Felix hated himself for his weakness, but it didn't feel terrible to admit it. He nodded, refusing to step back in spite of the little voice inside his head telling him he was being too greedy—taking too much.

But he couldn't bring himself to care right then. The grief he'd been ignoring since he'd gotten the phone call from his sister suddenly felt like water pressing against a failing dam.

"Hold on to me, darlin'," Dei whispered.

Felix tightened his grip, but his lungs began to burn, and his knees began to shake. Panic erupted through his body. He didn't want to fall apart. He knew pain wasn't weakness, but he didn't want anyone to see him like this.

Especially not his family.

"I can't—I'm..." he tried.

Dei walked him backward until he hit the counter in front of the sink, and the pressure from both the front and back was enough for him to crack. He felt enveloped and safe, and suddenly, his face was all hot and wet from the tears. He wanted to lift his hands and wipe them away, but he couldn't seem to unlock them from where they were curled in Dei's shirt.

"Sorry," he managed to get out. "Sorry, sorry, sorry..."

"Don't you dare," Dei whispered roughly.

Felix didn't fall apart like he was afraid he might do. He didn't start wailing or screaming. He just let himself feel the burning loss deep in his belly, softened by the fact that he wasn't alone. And not just because Dei was there, but because he had a home to go back to—a family to welcome him. He knew the day he got into the truck with Paris that he wasn't going to see his grandmother again.

That part of his life wasn't just over—it was dead and buried. He was no longer the man he'd been when he left LA. And he knew that was all his grandmother had ever wanted for him, so it softened the guilt of missing her last moments and not being able to tell her one more time how much he loved her.

"Tell me your best memory of her," Dei said once Felix had caught his breath.

He turned his face to the side and rested his cheek against the steady beat of Dei's heart. "That's not easy. She was so great. She used to make me mint tea whenever my anxiety gave me a stomachache.

And whenever my mom was being really awful, she'd take me to the toy store and let me get Play-Doh."

"Play-Doh?" Dei asked, a smile in his voice.

Felix laughed. "Yeah. I wasn't allowed to have art supplies as a kid, but when I was little—like eight, I think—I really wanted to be a sculptor."

Dei eased Felix back and looked down at him. "Did you ever try it?"

"Once. I sucked at it," Felix said with a laugh. "But I found what I was best at, and I don't have regrets."

"She sounds like she made life bearable," Dei said after a beat.

Felix's heart thumped hard. "Yeah. Uh…I mean, she wasn't perfect, but in the worst moments, she was there. She took me shopping for my first date with a guy."

Dei raised a brow. "Oh yeah? Who was he?" There was a note of warning in his tone, and Felix knew jealousy was an ugly trait, but for some reason, he kind of liked it on Dei.

"A co-worker. I was working at Domino's, and we were always flirting, but it took me like a year to work up the courage to ask if he was actually queer. I was having a self-esteem breakdown two days before we went out, so she dragged me to the mall and made me try on jeans until we found the ones that made my ass look good."

Dei dragged a look up and down Felix's body. "Can't imagine you'd look bad in anything, sugar."

Felix's cheeks burned. "Trust me, there are things I can't pull off. Chaz liked the jeans, though. The date was a total disaster, and he literally quit four days later because of it, but at least it wasn't because of the jeans."

Dei made a soft choking noise. "He *quit*? What the fuck?"

"He was a little dramatic," Felix said, then wiped the back of his hand under his nose and sniffed. "She took me out for tacos and fried ice cream once I was done crying enough to eat something."

Dei's face softened, and he reached up again, cupping Felix's cheek and swiping the last of his tears away with his giant, calloused thumb. "I'm sorry you have to miss her this way."

Felix shrugged. "That's just life. I knew she wasn't going to be around much longer when I left. I think I'm kind of glad she didn't see the worst of my recovery from all this."

Dei looked like he wanted to say something else, but instead, he pulled his hand away and shoved it into his pocket. "Might wanna go get dressed so we're not late, darlin'. I don't mind making an entrance, but I think that might be your worst nightmare."

Felix shuddered and nodded. "Give me ten."

He hurried into the bedroom, and when the door shut, the silence was almost overwhelming. He damn near called Dei back into the room just to keep him company, but his phone started to buzz on the nightstand, and he rushed over, snapping it up.

He almost started crying when he saw Max's name on the screen and fumbled before managing to swipe his thumb across. "Hey."

"What's wrong?" Max immediately demanded.

Felix laughed, dropping to the edge of the bed and hooking his foot around the edge of his open suitcase. He dragged it close and pulled out his wrinkled long-sleeved shirt and slacks. "I mean, apart from going to a funeral?"

"Is Dei being a dick?"

Felix rubbed at his left eye, which started to twitch. He found himself wishing he could remember Max's face. It would have been a small comfort, though his voice was enough. "Has he ever been a dick?"

"I…well. No. I guess not. But I know today's gonna suck, and that fucker better be sensitive about it."

Felix managed a smile as he peeled off his T-shirt and tossed it on the pile of his clean clothes. "He's probably being a lot nicer than I deserve." Standing up, he attempted to step into his slacks with one hand, and when he almost brained himself on the nightstand, he pinched his phone between his ear and shoulder. "God, how the fuck does Dei do this every day without his other arm?"

Max laughed. "Bro, he spent a long fucking time in rehab. They teach you that shit."

"Right," Felix said, feeling a little bit like a moron. "Right. Yeah, I knew that."

He'd done the same thing. Sort of. But at the time, he couldn't afford to stay longer than two weeks, and his parents refused to cover the cost. He'd been able to get an additional six outpatient sessions, but the rest had been all him.

He wondered if things would have been different if someone had actually given a shit.

"Felix. Seriously. Are you okay? You know you don't need to do this, right? You can just come home if it's too much."

Slipping his arms into the sleeves of his shirt, he walked into the bathroom while he buttoned it. "I know. But I didn't even say goodbye to her when I left. I think I need this for me."

"She knew the shit you were going through."

"Yeah, and she knew I loved her," Felix said. "But I don't think I could live with myself if I didn't at least say goodbye." He didn't tell Max the rest—how he wanted to prove to himself that he could stand up to his family no matter what they threw at him. That he needed to prove to himself that he was stronger than they ever gave him credit for.

He grabbed his pills and swallowed them down with the water from the sink, then replaced his Post-it note with a new reminder. "Did you call to second-guess me, or…"

"Shit. No," Max said, sounding immediately sorry. "I just really fucking miss you, and I think I'm a little scared that something will change and you won't want to come home."

Any irritation Felix had left in his chest disappeared at Max's confession. He knew how hard that must have been for his friend. Max and Paris had grown up even more unloved than he'd been, and it had taken them years to find a way to trust that the people around them actually gave a shit.

"I miss you too. But there's nothing on the planet that would make me want to stay. I hate it here."

Max was quiet for a moment, and then he sighed. "Yeah, I get that.

I miss it sometimes…more than sometimes. But the longer we're here, the more this feels right."

Felix understood that in more ways than he wanted to think about. And maybe it wouldn't have been as profound before he knew how Dei felt, but now that he did, it was different. "I'll probably cut the trip short, if I'm being honest. There's not a lot to see around here."

"Take your boy to Bonsai," Max told him. "Go say hi to the guys. Take him to the beach. Bring him somewhere they know how to actually wrap a burrito."

Felix choked on a laugh as he wet his hands and attempted to order his hair. Max's biggest and loudest complaint was the lack of decent Mexican food since moving to the East Coast. Two weeks before the trip, Max had pitched a fit when he ordered takeout and the burrito had been both over-stuffed and gently folded instead of wrapped tight.

"You know he's not exactly a homebody, right? *And* he's a professional chef. I'm sure he's had better food than I could ever dream of."

"Yeah, but something tells me he'll appreciate it."

Felix couldn't argue with him. He was pretty sure that would make Dei's entire week, and it seemed like the least Felix could do after dragging him into this. And, selfishly, he thought it might be a good test to see how he felt about Dei when his grandmother's funeral wasn't hovering over him like a dark cloud.

"Listen, I gotta go," Max said a second later. "My client just walked in, but if you need me…"

"I'll call," Felix finished for him, though there was very little on Earth that would get him to bother his friend during his workday. Whatever happened, he could deal with it. That was the point of the trip, after all. He was goddamn ready to show both himself and his family that he didn't need them to survive.

And he never had.

14

Dei wasn't sure what to expect when they got to the church, but it didn't look a whole lot different to the little churches he'd grown up around in the small town of his childhood. The parking lot was halfway full, and there was a strange mood in the air when Dei got out of the car and waited as Felix leaned against the passenger door, breathing slowly.

Dei gave him a moment to himself, then stepped into his space. "Alright, sugar. You gotta tell me how you're doing cuz you look like you're fixin' to bolt."

Felix blinked slowly, his cheeks a little pale, but his eyes were clear and his expression calm. "I actually think I'm okay. I just wish I could hold your hand."

Dei all but flung his cane back into the car and offered his arm. "Wish granted."

"Don't you need that?" Felix asked with wide eyes.

Dei shrugged. "Let me lean on you if I need it. But as long as we're not climbing mountains or stairs, I think I'll be alright."

Normally, Felix would have made a sarcastic joke, but Dei understood when he stayed silent and clung tightly to his hand as they headed across the parking lot. The building was small and a little drab

—all wood-browns and beige. They were nothing like the Greek Orthodox cathedrals his grandfather had taken him to when he was still around.

Those had been massive, with vaulted ceilings, rounded arches, and huge, brightly painted saints looming over them. He'd never really believed much in a deity, but there was something sort of powerful about the echoing chambers.

They were almost a direct contrast to the muted little hall they'd just stepped into. The lobby reminded him more of a dentist's office than a place of worship—complete with a reception desk, though no one was sitting at it.

"Do y'all sing here?" Dei asked very softly as Felix led the way past several people who were openly staring—a few of them even pointing.

Felix was resolutely ignoring them, though Dei could see a twitch in his jaw. "Yeah. They sing here. Why?"

Dei couldn't imagine how it would sound, the notes crashing against walls stuffed thick with insulation, voices with nowhere to go. The one thing he'd loved with his whole heart was the hymns sung by the choir. He wasn't really sure what the hell he believed in, but he never felt closer to something ethereal than surrounded by song.

Dei realized they'd come to a stop at the chapel doors and that Felix was shaking. "Darlin'…"

"That's…she's…" Felix took a trembling breath, and Dei followed his gaze to the front, where there was a small table covered in photos and a floral urn in the center.

"It ain't her," Dei murmured, leaning in close. "Not really."

"Yeah, no. I know." Felix licked his lips, and Dei—unable to help himself—lifted Felix's hand and pressed a soft kiss to his knuckles.

"I've got you."

Felix made a soft noise, then leaned harder into Dei as they stepped past the threshold. There was a profound moment when everyone noticed. A hush fell over the small crowd, and Dei watched as several people in the front row turned.

Dei recognized Felix's mother almost immediately. He shared so many features with her it was almost startling. Her eyes were icy, her lips turned down into a natural frown, and Dei wondered what it must have been like to grow up staring at that face.

"I don't know which one she is," Felix said.

Dei didn't have to ask who he was talking about. "Red flower pinned to her jacket."

Felix's eyes got watery. "You sure?"

"Looks just like you, darlin', only she's ugly in all the places you never will be. Now, where you wanna sit?"

Felix glanced around, then jerked his chin to the row third from the back. There was definitely not enough of a crowd for them to need the space so far removed from everyone, and that would probably put more attention on them than anything, but Dei was letting him take the lead.

He nodded and held Felix's hand tighter as they took their seats. There was a low, rushing murmur of voices after that, and Dei could hear Felix's mom getting upset, but the woman beside her—he assumed it was Felix's sister—was talking her down.

"I hear my sister's voice," Felix said.

Dei nodded. "Anyone gonna pitch a big fit?"

"I doubt it. They'll be more concerned with how that'll look," Felix told him. He leaned his head against Dei's shoulder and closed his eyes. "It'll be over soon, right?"

"Should be," Dei said, not sure if he was telling the truth or a lie. He'd been to funerals that lasted hours and some that even lasted days. He'd been to ones that were just moments outside—a celebration of life—and more somber ones, spending an hour remembering someone who probably wanted to be forgotten.

He was pretty sure Felix's grammy was none of those things. She was clearly a woman who had given Felix a safe space to exist, even if she hadn't made a difference with the rest of the family. And Dei wanted to be there as Felix worked through losing her.

"Hold my hand," Felix murmured.

Dei didn't hesitate. He wasn't sure if Felix was asking for himself or to put on a show, but it didn't matter. He tangled their fingers together and brought Felix's knuckles to his lips, pressing a soft kiss against his cool skin. Felix shuddered just once, then let out a long sigh before his body relaxed against him.

"She'd have liked you," Felix murmured. "She'd have asked super-inappropriate questions about your injuries and definitely about our sex life. She would have offered you whiskey and a cigar and wouldn't have let you say no."

Dei rumbled a soft laugh. "Yeah?"

Felix looked up at him, all wide-eyed and sweet. It was giving Dei very inappropriate thoughts for a damn funeral, but from what Felix said, maybe that's what his grammy would have wanted. "She'd have wanted to see you kiss me."

Dei licked his lips. "I would have let her. I wouldn't have been able to resist."

"I—" Before Felix could finish his sentence, there was a crackling sound over the PA, then organ music. It was just as muted as Dei expected it to be, but it was enough to break the spell between them. Felix settled back down against his side, and Dei tucked his disappointment away because they were at a funeral, damn it. This was no place to be coming to the realization that before the night was up, every single reservation he had about getting physical would be destroyed.

As Felix had assured him, no one made a scene. Dei relaxed when he realized that no one was going to call Felix up to talk, and no one was going to confront them in spite of all the obvious glares they were getting.

Felix cried silently at some parts and went stoic at others. He was tense all over when they played a slideshow of her life on a faded screen, which Dei could barely see with all the lights on. Halfway through, Felix started getting antsy.

"This was a bad idea," he whispered.

Dei leaned in close. "You wanna bail?"

"People will notice," Felix answered, his eyes darting from right to left.

They were still being watched, but Dei couldn't bring himself to give a shit. "Do you actually care about that?"

"I," Felix said, then laughed almost silently. "No. I really don't."

Dei stood up, and he extended his hand, which Felix took and hauled himself to his feet. All eyes were on them. Dei felt them like a pressing weight against his back, but he couldn't bring himself to care. He was all too aware of the way Felix was on the verge of a total meltdown, and while he had the right to be, Dei couldn't let it happen in front of an audience.

Especially not *this* audience.

He pressed his hand to the small of Felix's back and gently ushered him toward the doors. There were two men standing beside them—relatives, he assumed based on the way they glowered at Felix—but neither attempted to stop them from leaving.

The doors shut behind them with a loud clang, making Dei's ears ring, and he felt Felix's muscles start to spasm under his palm.

"Honey," he murmured.

"Get me outside." Felix's words were soft, thready, and desperate.

Dei quickly slung his arm around his would-be lover, and it was only a moment of heavy limping before they were past the front doors and out in the California sunshine. There were no clouds in the sky, the light was soft, and the air was briny and rich from the ocean. Dei took a deep breath of it as he glanced around, and eventually, he found a stone picnic bench under the shade of a few trees.

"Come on, darlin'," he said, urging Felix along.

For his part, Felix followed like he was moving on instinct alone. His arms were like limp noodles, and his feet were dragging enough that Dei was afraid he was about to go into a seizure. He eased Felix down onto the bench, then tipped his chin up with careful fingers, his eye roving over Felix's face, trying to see if he had any tells.

"Talk to me, sweet thing."

Felix licked his lips. "Um."

"Do we need to get you lyin' down somewhere?"

Felix blinked, then shook his head. "I want to cry."

"Okay," Dei said with a confused frown. "It's a funeral. You can go ahead and cry."

"That's what they want," Felix said. "My mom, my sister. Everyone. They invited me because they wanted to know losing her hurt me. They got all of her last moments, and I had nothing because I ran."

"No," Dei said, his tone making Felix flinch back. He felt a small surge of guilt, but not enough to stop himself. "Fuck them. They didn't get shit. You get to live, love, and eventually die knowin' that woman accepted you for who you were. Not some version she wanted you to be. They'll have to go the rest of their existence knowing they spent their lives too cowardly to be anything other than hateful and sad."

Felix's lips twitched, and then he laughed. "I don't know if any of them are that deep, babe."

Dei went warm all over at the sound of being called babe, but now wasn't the time to think about it. "Maybe not, but you can't let them control this moment. This ain't about them."

Felix shrugged. "I feel stupid for coming here. I thought I was proving something to myself, but instead, I just let them get to me."

Dei didn't know what to say to that. He hadn't questioned why Felix wanted to come—why he really wanted to come—because it wasn't his place. The only thing that had mattered to him was being there for Felix.

Because fuck, he was *so* in love.

He cupped Felix's cheek again and leaned in. "You want me to get you out of here?"

Felix's eyes slipped closed. "Yeah. I also want you to kiss me, but I know you're not there ye—"

Dei didn't let him finish the question. He *was* there. He was more than ready. His resolve had shattered into pieces so small it was little more than dust. And closing the distance between them was maybe the easiest decision he'd ever made.

Their lips met—still at first—so soft and so damn warm. Felix was frozen, and Dei started to panic, but before he could pull back, Felix's hands lifted and gripped the back of his neck. He rose just before Dei's back threatened to give out, and his fingers pushed into Dei's hair, gripping him tight and holding him like he was terrified to let go.

Dei's entire body softened. His arm went around Felix's waist, hitching him close as he parted his lips, urging the kiss to deepen. The first taste of Felix's tongue was heaven. It was slick and warm and so wet. Dei shuddered with need, on the edge of collapsing from how starved he'd been for this.

Not just for any kiss but for Felix's.

"Sweet thing," Dei murmured against his lips.

Felix groaned, pushing into Dei harder, almost knocking him off his feet, but Dei held his ground, steadier than he thought himself capable of. The smell of Felix's soap and cologne was almost overwhelming, and he felt a sob in his chest because he wasn't sure he was ever going to be brave enough to take what Felix was offering, but he could see a future with him anyway.

It was right there. All he had to do was reach out.

"*On church grounds!*"

Felix broke the kiss abruptly, but instead of pulling back, he buried his face against Dei's chest and groaned. "That's my mother. If only I could forget her voice as much as her face."

Dei tried not to laugh as he eased Felix back and tipped his chin up. "Do you want me to handle it?"

"No point. I had a feeling she was going to follow me out." He took a deep breath, then let it out against Dei's shirt. "I'm gonna do this."

Dei pulled back slightly and urged Felix to look up again. "You don't need to do anything you don't want to."

Felix bit his lip, then gripped Dei tight along the hips. "Just stay right here with me?"

"You couldn't make me leave you right now if you tried, darlin'. There's not a chance in hell you're doing this alone."

Felix's eyes were bright, his jaw a little tense, and he gave a single nod before he let Dei go and turned to face the woman storming toward them. Up close, Dei could see the resemblance even more. They had the same shade of hair and eyes and the same cut of the jaw.

She was shorter than Felix, but not by much, and Dei could tell her attitude made her seem bigger.

She was lacking the warmth he had, though. Her eyes were cold and cruel, and he could see the cogs turning in her head. She was working out what would hurt him the most.

"Your grandmother would be turning over in her grave right now," she spat.

Felix laughed. "If you hadn't cremated her?"

Felix's mom snapped her jaw shut so fast Dei could hear it click. Her eyes moved over to him, widening a little when she took in his missing arm and the scars on his neck, and he wondered if she was going to be brave enough to take him on.

"The fact that you thought you could come here and parade your little...*friend* around like some rebellious teenager tells me that you haven't made any progress. Your father and I have spoken to an attorney, and—"

"So have I," Felix interrupted.

She froze. "Is that so?"

Felix laughed suddenly, making Dei jump. "Actually, yeah. See, the thing is, the shop I'm working at now? I'm making more money than I know what to do with. My buddies there told me that if I was afraid you'd start making threats, I should go ahead and get an attorney on retainer. So I did."

"I—"

"In fact, if you want to exchange information, I'm sure he'd be happy to see what evidence you have for a conservatorship."

Her eyes went narrow, and then she smiled. "How about the fact that I'm not actually your mother? That I'm not even a relative. I'm your mother's neighbor, and she asked me to do this to prove that you wouldn't recognize her if you—"

"Bullshit," Felix interrupted, calm and dry.

Dei held his breath to keep from laughing.

"You couldn't pick me out of a lineup, Felix."

He laughed again. "Yeah, that might have been true, but you opened your fat fucking mouth, and trust me, I'll never forget how you sound. My disorder didn't ruin that part of my memory. Unfortunately for me. But thank you once again for proving what a monster you are."

She swallowed heavily. "That's not…"

"You also have several social media profiles, ma'am," Dei cut in, knowing he should probably keep quiet, but it was either mouth off or get violent, and he had no desire to spend the week in jail. He had much better ideas for their free time. "I can confirm exactly who you are."

"Well, I—"

"Anyway," Felix interrupted again, now sounding tired, "this has been great and all, but my boyfriend and I need to get going."

"Boyfriend?" she sneered.

"Seriously," Felix said, "you've already been awful enough. Do you really want to add raging homophobe to the list today?"

Dei almost praised her for being smart enough to keep her mouth shut. His heart was hurting for Felix because he knew none of that had been easy. It probably wasn't even cathartic. Dei couldn't imagine what it would be like for his own mother to despise him that way.

Grabbing Felix's hand, he lifted it to his lips and pressed a soft kiss to his palm, making a big show of it when he realized people were starting to filter out of the church. They were being watched, but Felix didn't slow his pace or look back over his shoulder. Instead, he just clung to Dei and breathed slowly in and out until they reached the car.

"Kiss me again," Felix said.

"You really wanna give them a send-off, don't you?" Dei asked with a grin.

Felix looked up at him. "I really want to just kiss you. The rest is a bonus."

Dei felt like he was soaring as he leaned in, cupped Felix's cheek once more, and took the kiss he'd been longing to give for so damn long.

15

Felix was feeling too many things all at once. It reminded him a little of those people in Finland who would sit in a sauna, then roll in the snow. The shock to his system from the heavy, overwhelming grief of his grandmother's funeral, to kissing Dei, to his mother's cruelty threatened to send him over the edge.

It was only the fact that Dei had pressed him against the car and held him with their foreheads pressed together until he could breathe again that he hadn't fallen apart. Off in the distance, he could still hear his mother yelling and the voices of others trying to calm her down. He could feel people staring—people he'd once known but were now total strangers.

Not one single member of his family took his side. Not one of them stood against his mom. Not one of them attempted to ask where he'd been or how he was.

It wasn't that he'd expected them to. None of that was a surprise. But it still left an aching pit in his stomach when he thought about how—if circumstances had been different—he might still be here. If he'd made one single change in his past, Bonsai might have never happened. He'd have never met Paris and Max, and he wouldn't have been in the shop the day Zeke walked through the doors and smiled at him.

He'd be here, his brain still a mess, but completely alone and unsure if he'd ever find his way out of the maze his mother would have created for him to keep him from escaping her.

Felix felt vaguely sick to his stomach, and while some part of him wanted to put his hands all over Dei the moment they got back to the rental, he wasn't sure that he could. He hadn't even had a chance to process the reality that his grandmother was gone yet, and he wasn't sure he could now with everything going on.

What if Dei had expectations? What if he wanted more than Felix could give?

"Darlin'?"

Felix looked over and realized they were back at the house. They must have been for some time, and his face went a little hot with shame. "Sorry. I, uh…I got lost in my thoughts."

Dei sighed and reached for him, cupping his cheek with his warm, calloused palm. "Let's get you inside. You look like you're fixin' to fall over."

The soft twang of Dei's accent was an odd comfort, and Felix wrapped himself in it as he pushed the car door open and stood. Dei was at his side in seconds, and he led the way to the door, pushing Felix ahead of him the moment it was open.

Felix swallowed against the lump in the back of his throat and felt it move down to his chest, which wasn't any relief at all. He pressed the heel of his hand to his sternum and rubbed. "I, uh…"

"Bed," Dei told him.

Felix bowed his head. Fucking hell. If he rejected Dei now, there'd be no coming back from it. It would destroy what little progress Dei had made with himself, and Felix wasn't sure he could take the risk. He didn't think his dick would cooperate, but maybe if he—

"I'm putting you right under those covers, and you're gonna nap," Dei went on, giving Felix a small push toward the bedroom. "You hear me?"

Felix's gaze snapped up. "I thought you were saying you wanted to, you know…" He managed to stop himself before his lack of filter got him in any more trouble.

Dei's eyes went a little wide, and then he laughed and curled his hand around the back of Felix's neck. "Honey, I want that a whole lot with you. I'm over my hang-ups, and if you were feelin' better, I'd show you exactly how you make me feel. But I can tell you don't need that right now. So I can wait as long as you need me to. You been patient enough for me. I can do the same for you."

Felix licked his lips and felt the powerful urge to cry. "Yeah, okay," he managed to get out in a soft whisper. "Thank you."

Dei's face fell a little, and he took another step closer. "Oh, sweet thing. You want company, or do you need to be alone?"

That question was almost impossible to answer because he wanted both in equal measure. He didn't want to sleep. Hell, he didn't want to blink for too long because it meant forgetting Dei's face, and that made him want to tear his skull open and rearrange the parts of his damaged brain until they worked properly again.

But he also needed time to curl up in a ball, scream into a pillow until the tight grief in his chest let go a little, and then sleep until the weight of the day eased up off his shoulders. And he didn't want to do all of that with Dei watching.

"Maybe a nap by myself, yeah."

Dei chuckled very softly and dragged his thumb over the cut of Felix's jaw. "Come on, sweetness. I'll get you all tucked in."

Felix felt warm again, but not from embarrassment or humiliation. It was similar to the feeling he got whenever the guys took care of him, only there were far more layers with Dei. He wanted a thousand and one things with him, most of which he couldn't name, but they felt amazing. And the fact that Dei was willing to be patient with him meant more than he could ever say.

Walking into the room, Felix stared at the massive bed and felt the urge to laugh at the absurdity of the situation, though he managed to keep the sound inside. He kicked off his uncomfortable dress shoes, but before he could go for his shirt, Dei spun him around and used a curled finger to tip his chin up.

"I want you to know that more'n anything, I want to undress you, but I still haven't figured out small buttons with one hand."

"That's fine," Felix breathed out. "Do you need me to help you with yours?"

"If you wouldn't mind," Dei said.

Felix knew how hard that admission had to be for him, so he quickly went to work on Dei's button-up, moving as quickly as he could until the broad, scarred chest was exposed. Felix had done his fair share of staring over the last twenty-four hours, but not like this.

Not this close.

Now, he let his gaze linger, let his fingers graze a touch over his firm pecs and over his stomach, which was hairy and soft.

"Used to be a lot more fit," Dei murmured.

Felix snorted as he looked up into Dei's eyes, and he realized the man wasn't joking. "You're literally the hottest man I have ever laid eyes on. And please don't tell me it's because my memory is swiss cheese."

Dei swallowed heavily. "I'd never."

Felix wasn't sure he believed him, but it didn't matter. The way Dei was looking at him told him his words were important. That they meant something. He took in a deep breath and let it out, listening to the way it trembled with fatigue, grief, and all the ache of wanting this man for so long.

"Wake me up in an hour or two," Felix said.

"Sugar—"

Felix cut him off by grabbing his wrist and wrapping Dei's arm around him. He laid the man's large, firm palm against his ass cheek. "Wake me up like this."

Dei let out the softest groan, then collapsed forward and buried his face in the crook of Felix's neck. "You're gonna kill me, sweetness."

"Little deaths only, right?"

Dei laughed, his breath warm and wet. "So goddamn many when I get my way." He pulled back and searched Felix's face for a long moment. "I'd like to kiss you one more time before you get some shut-eye."

"Yes," Felix said without an ounce of hesitation. "Please." He didn't wait for Dei this time. He lifted his hands and pressed his palms to Dei's rough cheeks, enjoying the sensation of an overgrown, soft, short beard against his skin.

Dei smiled, his face transforming and becoming somehow even more beautiful than before, and Felix felt it like it was something physical. There were no words necessary between them as their gazes locked, and then Felix leaned in, and Dei met him halfway.

The kiss was as slow as the first one—a gentle touch, at first, lips grazing lips. Then Dei rumbled a soft moan, and their tongues met, warm and wet and needy. Felix swayed into Dei, who caught him and held him fast with his impossibly strong arm, and Felix lost himself in the slow dance that he knew, eventually, would lead to more.

And then it was over.

Dei broke the kiss with a series of small pecks like he wanted to pull away but couldn't bring himself to stop touching, and soon they were leaning into each other, sharing breath. "Promise me you'll get some rest," Dei told him.

"As long as you promise to wake me up soon. I feel like I could sleep for a year, but I don't want to."

Dei's face moved through complicated expressions that Felix couldn't hope to decipher, but eventually, he nodded and sealed his promise with a last, swift kiss. "Swear it."

Felix pulled back, then Dei let go, and he turned so he could undress without getting distracted by Dei's body. His slacks hit the floor, and his shirt followed soon after, but before he could climb into the bed, he felt fingers sliding alongside his spine.

"I wanna explore these later," Dei said.

Felix realized Dei was talking about his ink, and he laughed, nodding as he reached for the blanket and yanked it back. "Anything you want. When I wake up, I'm all yours."

"That's a dangerous promise, sugar."

Felix turned around as he slid his legs under the sheets and met Dei's gaze. "I'm not afraid."

Although Felix would probably never be good with expressions ever again, he recognized the surprise on Dei's face and then basked in the following grin. Neither of them said anything after that. The silence was exactly enough.

16

Warm. God, he was so warm and so comfortable. He reached for consciousness, knowing he'd never felt so safe in his entire life, and he couldn't figure out why that was so important until he felt lips on the side of his neck. He groaned, and then a massive hand cupped his ass cheek and squeezed.

Memories flooded back the way they always did these days—sort of broken shards of glass looking for where they belonged in the shattered image that was his mind. But he remembered a man he wanted with every fiber of his being standing in front of him as Felix had asked for exactly this.

"Awake?" a voice rumbled against his skin.

Felix grinned and pulled back. In all reality, he'd never appreciate his brain damage. He'd never be thankful that everyone would remain vague and strange to him at first glance. But there was something about the newness of Dei's face every time he saw it that had his heart beating against his ribs.

Dei's smile softened. "What are you thinking about?"

"Every time I see you, I can't get over how gorgeous you are."

A very faint pink flush rose along the tops of Dei's ears, then went splotchy over his cheeks. "Flatterer. I'm a damn mess."

Felix shook his head. "I don't see it that way." He dislodged one of his hands from the tangle of blankets and traced a touch over Dei's temple where his scarring was the worst. Felix knew that eye was prosthetic from the way it didn't quite move like the other one. "Does it hurt still?"

"Nah," Dei said with a lopsided grin. "Honestly, I didn't notice too much. Everything else eclipsed it."

Felix traced a touch down his neck, knotted with scar tissue. He paused over the healed ink—the mark he'd left on Dei's body that would last until he covered it up or until he died. Dei was wearing a tank top, so Felix ran his fingers over the scars and the round stump with hills and valleys that was a map of what Dei had gone through.

"And here?"

"Yeah," Dei said. "Phantom pains, mostly."

"Does it bother you if I touch it?"

Dei shook his head. "I love feelin' your hands on me."

Felix wasn't entirely sure Dei meant it. He knew below the waist was more evidence of how his body had been ravaged, and Dei hadn't explained what he could feel or what he was capable of. But it was still obvious Dei wanted him, and he'd do whatever he could to make sure Dei understood Felix wanted him back however he could have him.

"How you feelin', love?"

Felix's eyes closed against that soft word that didn't mean what he desperately wanted it to. He swallowed heavily. "Better, I think. The whole funeral feels a little like a dream."

"Mm," Dei hummed thoughtfully. "Was thinkin' about all that."

The last thing Felix wanted to do was talk about his shitty-ass family while the hottest man alive was in bed with him, half-naked, but his curiosity was getting the better of him. "Wanna share?"

Dei grinned, then leaned in and nipped at Felix's jaw like he couldn't help himself. "Let's carve out some time for you to be sad about her without the weight of your family hangin' over you."

Felix hadn't realized how much he needed that. He'd come to the funeral to shove himself in his family's face because he wanted to show them he didn't need them. He'd *never* need them. But in the midst of that, he'd forgotten that losing the one person in that family who loved him actually did hurt.

"Thank you," he whispered.

Dei nodded, then shuffled a little closer, and his stump hit the top of Felix's thigh. "Does it make me a bad person if I wanna keep touching you right now?"

Felix couldn't help a laugh, shaking his head. "Fuck no. Unless we're both bad people, which I think I'd be okay with, considering what I want to do to you."

Dei groaned, then grabbed Felix around the back of the neck and kissed him hard, and desperate, and filthy. His tongue filled Felix's mouth, pushing deep, threatening to choke him with it. Felix took it, though, going pliant because that was exactly what he wanted.

No, what he *needed*.

"More," he gasped when Dei pulled back for air.

Dei looked at him with dark, heavy-lidded eyes. "I want you, darlin'. More'n I've ever wanted anyone. But it's not gonna be like it is with everyone else."

"I know," Felix said. "You just have to tell me how I can make you feel good."

Dei bit his lower lip, his gaze cutting off to the side for a long second. "Will you touch me on my cock? No better way to get this over with than dive right in."

Felix could tell how terrified Dei was—like maybe Felix might jump up and run away when he finally saw the evidence of how different Dei's body looked. It just went to show that Dei didn't understand how profoundly and intensely Felix felt about him.

He could have been a literal Ken Doll, and Felix wouldn't have given a shit so long as it meant he got to keep him. But he wasn't going to say that. It sounded callous and unfeeling, and that was the last thing he ever wanted to be.

Taking a breath, Felix pulled back just a little, then traced a touch down the front of Dei's tank top until he reached his boxers. They were silky and slung low down around his hips, and Felix hesitated only a moment before slipping his hand past the elastic. He could feel

Dei holding his breath—feel every muscle in his body tense as he explored—and he would have given anything to be able to just prove his devotion with a single kiss.

"Lower," Dei said when Felix's fingers met thick, coarse hair.

Felix closed his eyes and moved his hand low—lower, until he came to a hard, throbbing mound.

"That's it," Dei said, slightly breathless. Felix's fingers spasmed on it, and Dei grunted. "God. It feels…no one's touched me there in a damn long time."

"This is…uh…your dick, right?"

"That's what's left of it," Dei murmured. He leaned his torso back, and then his hand joined Felix's so he could guide him lower to where his balls were hanging. "They saved the sac—gave me a prosthetic for the one I lost. I was high as a fuckin' kite when I agreed to that, but not sure I hate it now."

"Is it…does it feel…like before?" Felix asked.

Dei snorted a laugh. "The left side ain't as sensitive as the right, but with your hand there, I feel like I could go off like a goddamn rocket."

Felix swallowed heavily, then forced his eyes open as he moved his hand back up to cup Dei's dick. "Can you come?"

"Fuck. Yeah, yeah, darlin'. I can come. Want to real bad," Dei groaned.

Felix turned to face Dei better and adjusted his hand so he was cupping him, feeling the hard nub against his palm. Dei was panting, rocking his hips forward as he clutched onto Felix's hip. "Like that?"

"Harder," Dei begged. "Gonna nut all over your fingers, sweetheart. I can't hold back. I need you."

Felix was wild with desire as he rubbed the heel of his hand against Dei's hardness. It twitched and got fatter, thicker, harder, and Felix felt his own dick start to respond. "What do you need me to do? Tell me what to do," Felix all but begged.

Dei leaned back with a sharp look in his eye. "Take your boxers off, sweetness. Want you to rub your dick all over mine."

"Fuck," Felix hissed, wild with desire at being given orders. The sensation was new, and it was almost terrifying, and he never wanted the feeling to stop. He scrambled to obey, watching as Dei hooked his fingers in the waistband of his own and slid them down toward his knee. Felix couldn't look away as inch after inch of flesh became exposed.

Dei had perfectly cut hips, scarred on one side, smooth and dotted with freckles on the other. More skin emerged, and then thick, black hair. Nestled in the thatch was exactly what Felix had felt: a round, hard, thick nub he could see twitching with want. Below that hung his balls—fat and heavy, and Felix felt a sudden urge to put his mouth on them.

"I know it's—"

"You're so fucking hot. I want to use my mouth on you," Felix interrupted before Dei could give in to trying to excuse his body as though it was something that needed an apology.

Dei's jaw clicked shut, and then he swallowed heavily before nodding and putting his hand on the back of Felix's head. "Yeah. Yes."

There was hesitation in his tone, so Felix didn't dive into action the way he wanted. Instead, he used a gentle touch to ease Dei onto his back, then straddled him and pressed both hands to his pecs. "Talk to me."

Dei just stared at him.

Felix allowed himself a very small smile. "We're not strangers anymore, babe. Talk to me."

Licking his lips, Dei rolled his gaze toward the ceiling. He lifted his arm and rested it above his head, his fingers opening wide, then closing into a fist. "This is my first time."

"I know," Felix said. Not his first time ever, but his first time since he was injured.

"I don't want you to put on a performance because you're trying to spare my feelings. I know it looks weird. My whole body looks weird."

Felix frowned at him. "Different."

"Is there a difference?"

Felix couldn't help a small laugh, and he leaned in, smudging a kiss over Dei's jaw. "Yeah. There's a difference. Your body matters to me because it's yours. I'm not going to sit here and pretend like I'm gonna get railed by a big dick to stroke your ego. I'm going to put my mouth on you whatever way feels good for you because I want to make you come."

Dei dropped his arm, pushed up on his elbow, and stared Felix in the eye. "And when you find out that when I come, I squirt like I have a pussy?"

Felix's swallow got lodged in his throat. "Yeah?"

Dei's eyes went wide. "That turns you on?"

"You have a filthy fucking mouth, so yeah, it turns me on. I feel like you don't understand just how goddamn attracted to you I am, Deimos."

Dei dropped down to the pillow and groaned. "Fuck, the way you say my name."

"Deimos," Felix said, his voice going lower. He leaned in and let Dei capture him by the hair, yanking him into a messy kiss. "Deimos."

"Get your mouth on me."

Felix tore away from a second kiss, dragging parted lips and sharp teeth over Dei's left pec, then down his stomach. He paused to kiss each hip as his hand carefully cupped Dei's balls, rolling them gently along his fingers. His sac spasmed when Felix ran his thumb over Dei's nub, and it twitched at the contact. Felix looked at it and realized there was no piss hole.

"Where do you come?"

"Under my balls," Dei said, mostly breathless. "Doctors had to… *unf…*" He grunted hard as Felix thumbed him again. "M-move it. Jesus, please, darlin'. Please get your mouth on me."

Felix was done tormenting him. He shifted down, his hip resting against Dei's thigh, and he put one hand on his stump to brace himself as he leaned all the way forward and fit his mouth over the nub of his cock.

It plumped again, fat against his tongue, and he suckled against the musky, hot skin. He smelled like soap and sweat, and it was absolutely nothing like any blowjob he'd ever given before. He felt a prickle of fear, like maybe he was going to fuck up, or maybe it was too much for Dei, but the way he grabbed at Felix's hair told him different.

It told him he was good.

That he wasn't all wrong.

"Good boy," Dei murmured.

Felix moaned loudly and suckled harder.

Dei chuckled from behind a groan. "You like that, hmm? You like being my good boy?" He gripped Felix's hair tighter and pulled him off with a wet pop, though he didn't let him lift up all the way. "Lick my balls, darlin'. Get them nice and wet."

Felix's eyes rolled back in his head, and his lips parted, his tongue lolling out. He could feel Dei's gaze on him as he was directed to his heavy sac, and he dragged his tongue over them before letting them slip past his lips. He sucked gently, humming around them, and Dei dug his nails against Felix's scalp.

"Pull off, sweet thing. Come here right now." Dei let him go, and Felix sat back, swiping spit from his lips as he watched Dei push up until his back was resting against the headboard. Felix looked at him, all on display as he sat there like a Greek god, and his cock somehow managed to get harder.

He'd been ignoring himself up to that moment, but he couldn't resist palming himself and stroking a few times to take the edge off.

"You like what you see, don't you, baby?"

Felix shuddered, nodding. No one had ever talked to him like that. Ever. Everyone he'd dated in the past expected him to be some dominant asshole in bed just because he was broad and covered in ink, and he never felt entirely satisfied.

Until this moment.

Dei made him feel small in the best way—protected and cared for and wanted. He shuffled forward on his knees until he was close enough that Dei could seize him by the hip.

"Spread those legs, gorgeous. Want you to rub that dick on me."

Felix obeyed as quickly as he could, hooking his thighs over Dei's and shifting forward until his dick was resting over Dei's nub. He couldn't stop staring, so turned on he was leaking a small stream from his tip.

"God, you really fuckin' like that, don't you?" Dei said, his voice wild with wonder.

Felix met his gaze. "I really like *you*."

Dei groaned, then grabbed Felix's ass cheek and urged him closer. "Rub off on me, then, sweetheart. See if you can get yourself off that way. Wanna see you come all over me."

Felix's hips began to move, almost as though his body existed only to obey Dei's commands. He hadn't done this in so, so long that he was entirely out of practice. His thighs began to burn, and the friction was almost enough to send him right over the edge, but he hung on as long as he could. He was addicted to the soft way Dei was panting, to the way his eyes were wide and locked on where Felix was rubbing off against him.

"Come on," he urged. "Show me how much you want this. Be my good boy." His fingers pried Felix's ass cheek to the side and then pressed against his hole.

Felix's eyes slammed shut as he reached between them, using his palm to press his dick against Dei's, and two thrusts later, he was coming. It hit him all in a rush, his whole body hot like he'd caught fire. He grunted as his muscles tensed and he came in hot ropes all over Dei's stomach, and he felt the man beneath him give an almost violent shudder as his breath ripped from his lungs.

"Fuck. Fuck yeah. You're so fucking good. Look at you, losing it all over me."

Felix moaned loudly before trying to catch his breath. "Did—did you…?"

"Not yet," Dei said, his eyes still dark with want. He brought his fingers up to Felix's hair and tugged. "Get your mouth back on me."

"Yes," Felix said, breathless, as he let Dei shove him further down until his nose was buried in that thick hair, which was now damp with sweat and musky with Felix's orgasm. He pressed his hands to the mattress on either side of Dei's thighs, then parted his lips and brought them down over Dei's hard nub. He rolled his tongue over it, feeling him shudder, and Felix could tell he was close.

"Yeah. Just like that. I'm…fuck, baby. I'm gonna come." Dei began to rock his hips, so Felix sucked harder—harder, until Dei's entire body went tense. Felix heard a thud as the man's head hit the hard wood on the bed, and his fingers spasmed, pulling his hair almost painfully before he slumped back and relaxed.

Felix didn't move away immediately. Instead, he let his lips relax and then laid soft kisses over the warm, softening skin. Dei groaned lightly, his fingers stroking over his scalp.

"Darlin'?"

"Mm." Felix wasn't ready to speak yet—wasn't even sure he could. He just wanted to bask in the feeling of Dei's stomach against his cheek.

He couldn't stay that way forever, though. He felt Dei's muscles start to tense with restlessness, and then he became aware of the sticky feeling against his skin, which he hated. He pushed himself back and looked up at Dei, who was gazing down at him with an unreadable expression.

"You, um…did you…"

"Yeah, sugar. I did." Dei's hand reached down, his fingers brushing behind his balls, and they came back wet.

Felix had the sudden, wild urge to put those fingers in his mouth, but he held back. He still couldn't read Dei's face, and he was terrified suddenly that it had all gone wrong. "I'm gonna get us something to clean up with."

Dei made a sound of protest, but Felix ignored him as he hopped off the bed and rushed into the bathroom. He shut the door almost all the way, then pressed his hands to the counter, the cool marble seeping into his overheated palms, and he took several breaths.

His head was fuzzy, and he felt a little like he was drifting through the clouds. He tested himself for aura, but he was pretty sure he was just dealing with sensory overload, not an impending seizure.

All the same, the anxiety of it was crawling up his spine, and his hands began to shake by the time he got a wet cloth and wiped himself down. He grabbed a second for Dei, then found the courage to walk back through the door and found him in the exact spot Felix had left him. He was watching every step Felix took toward the bed with that same blank face, and Felix panicked for a second, thinking maybe he was losing more of his ability to read faces.

"Talk to me," Felix blurted, his voice trembling like he was about to cry.

Dei's brows dipped, and his entire expression changed into concern. Relief hit Felix as Dei reached out and snagged his wrist, tugging him close. "What happened, sugar?"

"I don't…I couldn't tell how you felt, and my head feels a little off, so I got scared."

Dei cupped his cheek, his thumb stroking over his cheekbone. "I'm so sorry. You know how some people have resting murder face?"

Felix laughed, nodding. "Yeah, sure."

"Well, I kind of have resting nothing face. I don't even know why. It was something I developed when I was in the service, and it kind of stuck. I promise you on my very soul that you are the best thing that ever happened to me. I don't…*hell*, I don't even have words for how you made me feel."

Felix understood the weight of what they'd done and what it had to mean for Dei. With a sigh, he ducked his head and gave Dei a quick cleanup before tossing the cloth on the ground and surging in for a kiss.

Dei accepted it like he was just waiting for Felix to cross that line, and he wrapped his arm around him, holding tight. "Thank you," Dei whispered when they broke apart.

Felix shook his head, then laid his head against his shoulder. "It meant everything to me too."

Dei said nothing to that and just kept holding him until Felix knew there was nowhere in the world he was ever going to want to be except curled in Dei's arm.

17

"So. Is this, like…a date?"

Dei looked up at Felix's shy tone, and he was helpless against the rush of affection in his chest. Felix had napped again, sleeping a good portion of the day, then woke up starving, so Dei searched out the nearest restaurant with enough reviews to call it edible and bustled him into the car.

He was sleep-mussed and warm all over as Dei slung his arm around his waist, holding him close while they waited for the hostess to seat them. It was a little seafood spot on the banks of a small man-made lake. It was hardly the prettiest place Dei had eaten, but there wasn't much of a late-afternoon crowd, which was something he wasn't used to, living in the Keys.

They got a table near a large window, and Felix toyed with his straw, saying nothing until that question tumbled from his lips.

Dei knew it was mostly the product of his lack of a verbal filter—something that bothered Felix to no end, so he decided not to make a big deal out of it. "If you want it to be, darlin'. I'd like to call all of this a date, but this is kind of new territory for us."

Felix smiled sweetly. "Yeah. I guess it is. And you're kind of my fake boyfriend this week anyway."

"I'd like to take the fake part out of that sentence," Dei told him plainly.

Felix blinked. "Oh. Uh…"

"There's no need for labels, darlin', but I like to think I've proven how much I like you."

Felix laughed, flushing gently as he turned his gaze out the window. "Ah. Yeah, that was, um…you definitely did."

Dei grinned widely. A small part of him wished they didn't have to go home so soon. He hadn't taken a vacation in years, and while he could hardly call this trip one, he felt worlds away from real life, and he wasn't in a hurry to go back.

After all, anything could tear them apart, and Dei wasn't ready to give him up.

"I want to call it a date," Felix said softly after a long beat.

Dei reached across and held his palm up, and when Felix's fingers grazed his, he pulled him close and smudged a kiss over his knuckles. "Then we should make it a real one. We can go for a long walk after this. I'll hold your hand, maybe kiss you at the door."

"Then meet me in the bedroom for afters?" Felix asked in a low voice.

Dei groaned, and for the first time in his life, he was grateful no one could see his boner through his pants. He stroked his thumb over Felix's hand once more, letting it go just before the server appeared to drop off their plates.

"So, did you want to—" Felix's words were cut off when Dei's phone began the shrill ring that overrode his do-not-disturb setting.

Which meant it was one of his mother's caregivers.

He felt himself go a little pale as he snatched it off the table. "Darlin', I gotta take this." He didn't wait for Felix to respond, instead answering the call as he carefully climbed to his feet and headed for the lobby.

"Yeah?"

"It's Casey," the woman on the other end said. She was one of the part-time nurses, but he liked her the most out of his mom's whole team. "I just wanted to let you know your mom spiked a fever last night, which wouldn't be a big deal, but she's also stopped eating completely."

Dei let out a trembling breath. He knew what that meant. Her team had been warning him about the spiraling symptoms that would begin when it was time for hospice care, but it was in that moment he realized he wasn't quite ready for it. Not yet. She was too young, and he still had no idea where his sister had run off to.

"Do I need to jet back?" he asked.

Casey sighed. "I'm going to say no for now. We're working on getting the infection treated and seeing if we can get something solid into her. Right now, it's definitely pneumonia. She's tested negative for everything else so far, but I wanted to give you a heads-up in case something else comes back from her labs."

"Yeah," he said, trying to shove away the dark cloud threatening to settle over him. "Thanks."

"I'll be in touch, okay? And if anything happens, you'll know with plenty of warning."

That was a promise he didn't think Casey should be making. Under normal circumstances—if there were any—there would be plenty of warning. She'd follow the textbook trajectory of her disease, and he'd have a couple more years with her.

But he also knew that even in the best medical facilities, sometimes shit just happened. Sometimes people got sick and were gone in a matter of hours. He had to trust the team, though. His mother wasn't that fragile.

He hung up and shoved his phone into his pocket before making his way back to the table. He hoped his poker face was firmly in place, and he felt bad taking advantage of the way Felix struggled to read him, but he didn't want to ruin this.

He might cut the trip short because he wouldn't be able to live with himself if he didn't get back before things went south, but he wanted to be selfish. Just for a little while.

"You okay?" Felix asked.

Dei nodded. "My momma got a little bit of a fever, and they just wanted to keep me posted."

Felix's brows dipped. "Should we—"

"No," Dei said quickly. He didn't want Felix to give him the choice. Not yet. Not when he wasn't sure he could deny the urge to go home and let everything burn down around him. "We should definitely eat this because it looks amazing, and then I believe someone promised me a long walk with holding hands and kissing. And then a little more."

Felix flushed lightly, and his shoulders hunched up near his ears, and he offered a shy smile. "Yeah. I guess I did."

"So," Felix said as they walked up to the rental, "is this how you normally end your dates?"

Dei chuckled as he moved in closer, backing Felix against the wall beside the door. He felt a little off-kilter from the stress of the phone call and then from the long walk they'd taken on the beach, which put a strain on his stump, but he couldn't bring himself to care. He braced his hand against the wall beside Felix's ear and leaned close, breathing in the scent of cologne and sea air.

"No," he murmured, letting his lips brush against Felix's earlobe. "Never."

"So I'm special?"

Dei pulled back a little, then rubbed his nose over the cut of Felix's jaw. "Very. More than I have words for."

Felix shuddered beneath him, and Dei couldn't resist his pouty lips any longer. He turned his head and captured him in a long, heated kiss. It went on and on until Dei was breathless and tingly all over.

"Need to get you inside, sweet thing," Dei said. He dragged his palm down the front of Felix's shirt until his fingers were curled in the waistband of his jeans. "But if we're movin' too fast…"

"We're not," Felix said in a rush. He clutched hard at Dei's hips. "I promise, we're not."

Dei thanked all the gods listening to them in that moment because while he would have gladly stopped without even a whisper of resentment, he didn't want to. He was slowly growing addicted to the taste of Felix, and he wanted more. Especially now that he had a small bag with supplies that would let Felix bury himself deep inside Dei.

He got the door code punched in on the first try, and the moment they were out of public view, Dei's fingers buried hard in Felix's hair, tilting his head back so he could devour his lips, so he could bite his quick-beating pulse and rub his hard nub over where Felix was starting to tent his jeans.

"Bedroom," Felix gasped out, breathless and half whining.

Dei grinned at him and released his hold, though he didn't step back far. "I think you should ask me nicely, sweet thing."

Felix swallowed heavily. "Sorry, I…yes. Please, Dei. Can we please take this to the bedroom?"

Dei groaned and rubbed his thumb over Felix's lush lips. "We sure can, my good boy."

Felix shuddered hard, his eyes slipping closed like he needed a moment—which was good because Dei did too. He didn't want to bust a nut right there in the little foyer before he got the chance to feel himself stretched around Felix's thick, needy cock.

After a beat, Dei carefully turned Felix and gave him a slight push, following along. His hip was aching to take his prosthetic off, and the rest of him ached to pull Felix apart, inch by inch, until he was a shaking, begging mess.

Dei was already tugging at his shirt the second they slipped through the bedroom door, and it fell to their feet. He quickly spun Felix around, attacking his own clothes, and with the help of his lover's clever hands, it wasn't long before they were almost entirely undressed.

Dei backed up carefully, then sat on the bed before removing his leg. His jeans came with it, and he set them off to the side as he shifted fully onto the mattress, then crooked his finger at Felix. "Come here, sweet thing. And bring that stuff we bought."

Felix's throat bobbed with a heavy swallow as he snagged the bag off the floor where Dei had dropped it. He flung it onto the bed beside

Dei's thigh, then draped himself over Dei's torso, grinning when Dei grabbed him by the hip.

"Hello, sweet thing."

Felix breathed out a sigh and knocked their foreheads together. "I never thought I'd be into being called shit like that. I have never been the sweet one."

"Oh, honey, I bet that ain't true at all. I have a feeling no one ever paid close enough attention to know the truth." Dei dragged the tips of his fingers over Felix's side, loving the way it made him squirm. He cupped his backside, then dragged a touch over his hole, loving the way it made him moan. "How would you feel about me usin' something to fuck you?"

"Like a strap-on?" Felix asked, moaning and biting down against Dei's shoulder.

Dei hadn't considered that. He'd been thinking a fat dildo, watching Felix fall apart under his hand, but goddamn if that didn't get his blood heated. "You'd like that, baby?"

Felix nodded, breathing out roughly. "I'd like it."

"Me too." Dei hooked his finger under Felix's chin and urged him up for a slow kiss. "Tonight, though, you're gonna put that pretty cock inside me, yeah? Gonna make me come like the good boy you are?"

Felix squeezed his eyes shut, a tremor running through him as he nodded almost frantically. "Want that. Want to be so good for you."

"You already are, gorgeous," Dei told him. He ran a touch down his sternum, past his stomach, over his hip, then curled his fingers around Felix's cock and gave him a hard, single stroke. Felix grunted and thrust his hips down, and Dei quickly let go. "Don't be greedy, sweet boy. I want you to save this all for me."

Felix sat up, adjusting himself so he was straddling Dei's waist, and he reached for the bag, dropping it on his chest.

Dei let out a laugh and shook his head as he grabbed the bag by the bottom and let the bottle of lube and box of condoms topple out. "Are we feeling like a brat right now?"

"I'm impatient," Felix told him. "You made me feel so fucking good, and I just want to come."

"Hmm," Dei rumbled. He liked the way Felix reacted to every noise he made, especially his patient ones. "Then I think you'd better get to work because you're not coming until I do."

Felix looked suddenly uncertain. "I…yes. But are you sure this is what you want? Do you like to bottom?"

Dei was so fucking helplessly charmed at Felix's care, and he reached for him, drawing him into a kiss. "Yeah, sweetheart. I do. Especially if it's with you."

Felix groaned as he pawed around for the lube, and he used his teeth to tear at the plastic as he shifted off to the side, then grabbed Dei's leg stump and carefully lifted it. Dei's range of motion was fairly shot from his injury, but it wasn't as painful as he was expecting. He lifted his foot and dug his heel into the bed, and he felt oddly exposed as air rushed over his naked ass.

"You okay?" Felix asked.

Dei swallowed heavily and nodded. "This is definitely a trip of firsts."

"Yeah," Felix agreed softly. He'd already poured lube onto his hand, and he was watching his fingers as he spread it around with his thumb. "It kind of scares the shit out of me, but in the best way. Is that nuts?"

"Yes, darlin'. It's fucking batshit," Dei said with a quick wink. "Just the way I like it."

Felix looked up at him with a huge grin, which turned a little feral as he glanced down at Dei's nub. It was hard as a rock and pulsing, and Dei quickly rubbed it with two fingers, sending sparks shooting up his spine. Occasionally, he felt phantom pain in his severed nerves, but right now, it was nothing but pleasure.

"I love watching you touch yourself," Felix said.

"Yeah? Maybe one day I'll make you sit on the bed with your hands tied as I get myself off."

Felix moaned from deep in his chest, shuddering as he dragged his fingers over Dei's balls, then lifted them to get to where he wanted to be touched most. He hesitated after a second, and then Dei felt a small press to the spot where the surgeons had rerouted all his internal plumbing.

"Is this…"

"Yeah. And be real careful with it, darlin'. I'm a little fragile right there."

Felix pulled his fingers away quickly, going further down until Dei felt him against his hole. The touch was hesitant at first, but as Dei shifted his hips as best he could, that seemed to spur him on because between one breath and the next, Felix had two fingers inside him.

Dei groaned, the sound coming from deep in his belly. It had been so goddamn long since he'd been this intimate with anyone. His hookups in the Marines had been quick and perfunctory. Most of the guys he'd served with had been deep in the closet, so there were rushed hand jobs and the occasional moments where Dei would drop to his knees and deep-throat them until every ounce of their self-control was tested.

And every now and again, Dei would meet a guy willing to do more. They'd steal away to some hotel on a long weekend or holiday leave and spend glorious hours tearing each other apart.

But none of those moments felt even close to this. This was passionate and just shy of fucking filthy, and it also felt like, for the first time in his life, he was making love.

He would forever lament he wouldn't be able to take Felix the way he wanted to, but this made up for it, and it would be even better once Felix was fully inside of him.

"Good?"

Dei blinked and looked up at Felix, who was staring at him with a small frown. "I could do this all night, darlin', but I need you to fill me up." He reached down and felt his way to Felix's hard cock, giving it a firm stroke, stopping to rub his thumb around his slit. Felix moaned and shuddered, his head tipped down as he fucked his cock into the circle of Dei's fist. "God, look at you. Look at you," he whispered.

Felix swallowed heavily, then pulled his fingers away and sat back. Dei's eye tracked Felix's hands as they tore at the condom box, and he saw a quick flash of white teeth as he tore one wrapper open, then rose up high on his knees to roll it on.

One day, Dei would do that with his mouth before sucking Felix's brains out through his dick, but for now, he was content to watch. He hooked his hand under his knee to pull it higher when Felix shifted closer, and Dei bit his lip when Felix carefully positioned the head of his cock against his slick, wet hole.

"Ready for me?"

"Been waiting for this all my life, sweet thing," Dei murmured.

Felix flushed with pleasure at Dei's words, and he gave a small fuck forward, his hips stuttering and his body tense with nerves. The head of his cock breached the first ring of muscles, and Dei's eyelids slammed shut as his head hit the pillow. He rocked himself against Felix as gently as he could manage as he took a few more inches, and his entire body felt overwhelmed with sensation.

His dick was throbbing hard, and he fought the urge to rub it, but he didn't want to shoot off so soon. Instead, he curled his fingers against the small of Felix's back and urged him to push in deeper.

"Come on, baby. Make me feel it," he rumbled.

Felix let out a long groan, then braced himself on Dei's shoulders before thrusting in hard and fast. He picked up a rhythm that Dei needed—the angle so perfect it railed his prostate with every pass. Dei's head tilted back as he used his hips to meet Felix thrust for thrust until his whole body felt like it was about to catch fire.

"Hold," Dei ordered.

Felix froze, almost like Dei had hit a pause button, and the only movement was his chest heaving. His eyes were wide and a little wild, and he looked like he was on the very edge.

"Good boy," he crooned, giving Felix a soft pet. "You gonna come?"

Felix swallowed heavily, then nodded, and his dick twitched, making Dei moan.

"Lost your words?"

Felix nodded again.

Dei reached up and stroked the backs of his fingers over Felix's cheek. "That's okay. All I need from you right now is to listen. Want you to push inside me as deep as you can and roll those hips. Can you do that?"

Felix squeezed his eyes shut, then gripped the tops of Dei's shoulders before shoving his hips forward. Hard. His dick reached a spot Dei didn't know it could, and white-hot sparks shot directly up his spine. His dick twitched harder, and he could feel himself getting wet under his balls.

Fuck, he was going to shoot off so hard.

"Good boy," he gasped, wrapping his hand around Felix's ass and holding him there. "Roll your hips."

Felix did. Once, then twice, as Dei's vision started to go white in the corner of his eye. His breath felt too big for his chest, and it took all his control to keep speaking.

"Reach down there, sweetness. Reach between us and rub your hand right on my dick. Can you do that?"

Felix let out a soft hum of agreement, and he managed to dislodge one hand, shoving it between them until his rough palm brushed over Dei's too-sensitive nub. It was so fucking much. His nerve endings were on fire, and for a moment, he could feel the ghost of when his dick had been long and thick and pulsing.

Then Felix began to rub, and the sensation whittled down to the round stump that was left. He never in his life thought it could be this good, but it was. Something about Felix's utter obedience while Dei was being stretched wide and pinned down was exactly what he needed.

"I'm gonna…I'm coming," he managed to get out just before his back arched and he let go.

Wetness spread out beneath him as his stomach muscles clenched, and Felix rolled his hips harder and stroked him a little faster until it was all too much. Dei shoved him back with a firm hand, but he didn't let Felix pull out.

Instead, he met his gaze and then gripped his chin. "Fuck my hole and come. Now."

Felix's eyes rolled back, and he began to mindlessly thrust, losing all rhythm until he collapsed, his whole body shuddering as the condom inside Dei went fat and hot with his release. Felix twitched hard, his breath hitching a little in his chest, and Dei held him close—a little out of fear that it was too much.

Seconds ticked into minutes, and before he could really panic, Felix finally lifted his head. His eyes were a little glassy and not entirely focused, but his mouth was curved up in the smallest, sweetest smile.

"Please tell me that was good for you because that was…I don't even have words," Felix said, slurring just a touch.

Dei laughed and gripped his chin, pulling him up for a kiss as Felix finally slipped out with a wet squelch. They both shared a groan, and then Dei laughed as he wrapped his arm around Felix and refused to let him move.

"We can shower together in a bit."

Felix moaned softly and laid a kiss on his pec. "That sounds amazing." He shifted to the side just a bit, and a few moments later, Dei felt him trace the edge of his neck tattoo.

"Admiring your work?"

Felix snorted a laugh. "I just like seeing my ink on your skin. Knowing it's there forever…" He trailed off and pressed a little harder.

Dei ran his fingers over some of the abstract shapes on Felix's ribs. "I like it too. I'd love to get more."

Felix hummed, then pushed up on one arm. "Yeah? Like what?"

Dei shrugged. "Dunno. Always wanted some kind of owl. My grandfather used to feed one when I was little, so it hung around the property. A lot of kids were scared of it. My sister hated it. But I always kind of thought it understood me. It would sit on the fence right by the porch stairs and just…be with me. It didn't want anything. It didn't need anything. It just…was."

Felix blinked slowly, then opened his eyes like he was struggling to stay awake. Dei knew they'd regret it if they slipped off before cleaning up, but falling asleep surrounded by the musky scent of their lovemaking wasn't the worst thing in the world either.

Felix's head dropped back down to his chest, and Dei sighed, holding him a little closer. He was dangerously happy—dangerously content. It felt like everything he'd ever wanted was being handed to him, and he was terrified that at some point, the universe would come asking for him to pay.

18

Felix felt a huge rush of nerves as he headed for the door of his old shop. It wasn't so much the look of it that triggered his memory, but the smells of the taco truck a few feet away in the laundromat parking lot, and the ocean breeze coming up the street, and the sounds of rumbling cars from the locals since tourists rarely flocked to their neighborhood.

Bonsai was away from the hustle and bustle of shopping and fancy hotels and the Santa Monica Beach. This place was home in ways he knew that the Keys would never be—even if he didn't feel compelled to go back there. But sharing a piece of him with Dei felt important, and that made his nerves even worse.

"You don't need to do this, baby," Dei murmured, leaning in close to the back of his ear. "You don't owe anyone anything."

Felix ducked his head and laughed. "I actually want to. I just didn't think it would feel this strange to be back."

Before he could open the door, it was wrenched away from him, and he was tugged into the arms of a man he only recognized from his absurd height and the way that his skin was blacked out from his wrists to his elbows.

"Holy shit, you look amazing," Leif told him. He was the acting manager of Bonsai since the owner, Garrett, only showed up for his occasional appointments, then fucked off to do whatever rich business owners liked to do in LA. But Leif had been the one to hold the fort down whenever shit got ugly. He'd been the first person at Felix's side when his seizure turned his life upside down.

And he'd been the first person to take Felix by the shoulders and tell him that he needed to go when Zeke showed up and asked Felix to uproot his life and get out.

Felix looked up at him and wished to god he could remember his face better. It felt like staring at a stranger with his light hair and temple tattoos and dark eyes. But his smile stirred nostalgia in Felix's gut, and it put him at ease.

"You know who I am, right?"

Felix rolled his eyes. "Yeah, fucker. I couldn't forget this ugly mess." He flicked Leif on his arm right over his wrist, and Leif quickly flipped him the bird.

"Someday, you'll have the balls, young Padawan. But I guess today's not that day."

Felix's grin was so wide it was starting to make his cheeks hurt as he stepped back and beckoned Dei a little closer. "Uh. This is my…um. Boyf—er. My…"

"Boyfriend," Dei said smoothly, extending his hand.

Leif did what everyone did when they first met Dei. He hesitated, staring at his stump, then down at his prosthetic, which was obvious beneath the hem of his shorts. Then his gaze lingered on the exposed scars along his neck and then at his eye, which was at a slightly off angle.

It was only a second, really, but it felt like forever, and Felix wondered if Dei even noticed anymore.

"Boyfriend," Leif said slowly, adjusting his stance so he could take Dei's hand. "So are you saying I lost my chance?"

Felix flushed lightly. Leif had always flirted with him, but he never took him seriously. "Weren't you dating some model last time we talked?"

Leif waved him off. "Hon, that mess ended like a year ago. And if you'd keep up with your friends on Instagram, you would have seen my emo poem posts about it."

Felix laughed and dragged his hand down his face. "That is so embarrassing. I changed my mind. I didn't actually work here—I lied. Come on, babe. Let's go."

Leif cackled and grabbed Felix again, tugging him into another hug. "You seriously look so good. You look happy." He pulled back and shook him by the shoulders. "Forgetting us was the best thing that ever happened to you."

Felix swallowed heavily. "I didn't forget you. I swear."

Leif gave him a look of slight disbelief. "Heard those Irons and Works fuckers have all been out to visit you, and we don't even get a phone call. I mean, I don't blame you, but…" The door chimed, and Leif's words died as he looked over Felix's shoulder and frowned. "You hooking up with any of your old clients?"

Felix shook his head. "I didn't tell anyone I was stopping by. I'm gonna give Dei something small while we catch up."

"Fuck. Okay. Give me two minutes. We got no one on walk-ins today."

As he stepped away, Dei moved in close and lashed his arm around Felix's waist. "Tell me I don't need to be jealous."

Felix couldn't stop a small chuckle. "You don't need to be jealous. He's like that with everyone."

"Mm. I don't think so, sweet thing. The way he was looking at you was a little too familiar because that's the expression on my face all the damn time."

Felix looked up at Dei and smiled softly. "Luckily for you, there's only one man who has my attention."

"It better be me," Dei growled.

Felix reached up and curled his fingers around the back of Dei's neck, tugging him into a kiss. It felt like an odd thrill. The shop had seen a few questionable artists over the years, and the guys had never really been big on PDA, no matter who they were dating, but the queer ones had kept it even more quiet.

Max had been the only one who ever really embraced loud and

proud, so it felt almost like a rebellion to kiss his boyfriend right there.

And he only stopped when Leif wolf whistled. "Get a room, fuckers."

Felix laughed and flipped him off again before he took Dei's wrist and tugged him toward the back. The shop was different from Irons and Works. There were no perfectly sculpted stalls with short partitions that kept them private but together. There were just tables and chairs haphazardly flung into corners with every inch of shelf space occupied.

He chose the space that had the least amount of hand-drawn art on the walls, assuming that it was for a part-time artist and he wouldn't be kicked out midway through Dei's piece. "Sit. Then show me where you want me to mark you," Felix told him.

Dei bit his lip and grinned before dropping onto the chair and then hiking up the hem of his shorts. Felix watched as he pushed a button on the side of his prosthetic, and then it released with a small noise, and Dei groaned with relief as he rolled his shorts up to expose his stump, setting his leg to the side.

"Can you ink here?"

Felix raised a brow. "Do you want me to? I know your nerve endings are frayed."

Dei nodded. "Yeah, sweetness. It's what I want. This spot is for you and you alone."

Felix felt a hot flush spreading from his chest all the way up his neck, and he had to turn around and start fiddling with his case before he said something that sent Dei running. He could hear Dei shifting behind him as he began to unpack his machine, ink, and needles, and it was only when he had his heart under control that he looked back at his lover.

"You okay?" Dei asked.

Felix set his things down on a rolling tray, then walked over and set his hand on Dei's stump. "This is big."

Dei nodded. "Yes."

"And if we get back and you realize that you don't actually want to be with me—"

"Felix," Dei said, interrupting him before he could get the most painful part of his sentence out. He laid his hand over Felix's and pressed down. "I can't predict the future. I have no idea how we're going to feel about each other when real life kicks back in. But I know for a goddamn fact that even if the worst happens and we decide to go our separate ways, I won't regret this."

Felix laughed softly—a little bitterly. "You have no idea how many times I've heard people in my chair say that."

Dei moved his hand and hooked a knuckle under Felix's chin, drawing in his gaze. "Am I people in your chair?"

"No," Felix breathed out.

"Am I just *people* to you?"

"No," he said again.

Dei cupped his cheek. "I mean it. This isn't just because you make me feel amazing, okay? Or that we're in some honeymoon phase that's gonna fade in six months. I want this from you because I trust you with every inch of me—including all my soft spots that could take me down to my knees."

Felix swallowed past a lump in his throat as he looked at Dei. "Okay. I trust you too."

He could easily say Dei believed every word that was coming out of his mouth now. Felix had heard the most impassioned reasons for people getting ink, and in that moment, the words were utterly and completely honest.

But he'd lost count of how many return clients he'd had over the years who came in—sheepish and embarrassed—with a cover-up request. Felix always did his absolute best to never, ever say I told you so and never, ever make them feel humiliated for being wrong. But there was a small part of him that wished people would listen to him the first time.

Still, as he stared down at the knotted, scarred skin on Dei's leg, he didn't have that same feeling of warning in his gut. He had nerves, because he couldn't fuck this up. But there was something else behind that. It was warm and careful, and he never wanted to stop feeling this way.

"Do you have something in mind?" Felix asked.

Dei shook his head and grinned as he leaned back against the chair. "This time, I want it to be something from here." He pressed the tip of his finger against Felix's sternum.

Now, *that* was a lot. It was more than he really wanted to deal with, but it didn't matter. He didn't even need to think. The design came unbidden and willing into the pads of his fingers. He wouldn't even need to draw it.

"You know, don't you?" Dei asked.

Felix looked up and took a fortifying breath before nodding. "Yeah. I know."

FELIX HADN'T ANTICIPATED TAKING MORE than an hour, but he also hadn't anticipated going freehand on a piece that took up most of the top of Dei's thigh. Over the valleys of his scars, he inked wings that stretched up toward his hips.

He could tell Dei was in pain through it, but he didn't complain. Not once. Not even when Leif came and sat beside him and asked him a thousand questions about how he was injured and how he'd survived.

When he was finished, Felix cleaned him up, then spread the plastic shield over his skin, laying a kiss to where it was feverishly warm. He knew Leif was watching, but he couldn't bring himself to care. He looked up into Dei's face, but Dei was staring down at the image on his skin.

"Is it okay?" Felix had to ask.

"It's my owl. You remembered," Dei said quietly. He traced the outline of the bird, then looked at Felix. "I said that minutes before you were asleep."

"I still listen. I always listen," Felix told him.

Dei groaned and dragged him into a kiss. "We need to get the fuck out of here."

Felix couldn't agree more. He'd said all of his hellos to everyone, and while Max had gently suggested that Felix make the day a little tour of his past, he realized this was enough. There was only one stop he wanted to make, and now that it was days past the funeral, he felt safe to do it.

"One more stop?" he asked.

Dei nodded without looking even a little disappointed that they couldn't rush back to the rental and fuck like rabbits.

It didn't take long for them to clean up, and as Dei was getting his leg back on, Leif dragged him into another hug. "Do me a favor and don't ice me out anymore," he said when he pulled back. "I know this place wasn't the best for you to recover after all that shit happened, but you were my friend. You *are* my friend."

Felix bowed his head and nodded. "Yeah. I don't know what else to say except I'm sorry."

Leif shook him by the shoulder. "I know you won't remember my face, but you got my number. Use it."

"I promise," Felix said, and he meant it. Mostly because he saw something in Leif that told him maybe there were more he'd left behind who were looking for a way out, and maybe it was time to let Zeke know that they needed to make room for at least one other poor bastard who needed something else.

Felix stepped aside as Dei shook Leif's hand, then pulled him into a hug. Leif let out a small laugh as Dei picked him up with his one arm and gently shook him.

"Take care of each other," Leif said when he was back on his feet. "You two don't know how lucky you are."

Dei captured Felix's gaze. "You know, I think we might."

They were both quiet on the way home, and Felix excused himself to shower while Dei headed into the kitchen to fix them something for dinner. He wasn't feeling particularly hungry—at least, not for food, and not even for sex, really.

He wasn't sated by any means. He most definitely wasn't tired of the way Dei made him feel, but he wanted something else. Something that was almost deeper than fucking. It was the place he went in his head when Dei commanded him. And not necessarily with words, but with his presence. With the way he held Felix and made him feel safe, and content, and *good*.

The ache followed him as he washed stray bits of ink from his skin and then the salt from his hair. It nipped at his heels as he got dressed in soft sleep pants and a T-shirt and as he finger-combed his wet locks, then made his way to the living room, where Dei was setting out a second plate of what looked like freshly made pasta.

"How long was I in the shower for?" Felix asked with a frown.

Dei glanced up and smiled. "It's a quick recipe, but they're pretty good. Jeremiah wants to put them on the menu."

Felix grinned as he slid down onto a cushion in front of the sofa, his legs stretched under the coffee table. "What are you going to call them?"

Dei sighed as he flopped onto the couch and began to pull his leg off. It came off with a slight pop, and he set it to the side as he positioned himself so close to Felix their hips pressed together. "Send Me Noods."

"Send me—" Felix repeated, and then it clicked, and he rolled his eyes with a laugh. "Cute."

Dei touched his chin, turning his face for a quick kiss. "I thought it was." He stared at Felix for a long second. "Can I ask you somethin' about your head?"

"Go for it," Felix said, entirely unbothered.

"Do you remember stuff in photos?"

Felix bit his lip and shrugged as he pulled one of the plates close to him. It smelled rich and cheesy, and though he wasn't really hungry, he knew he was going to devour it. "Not really. It's…hard to explain. Everything feels a bit fuzzy to me, and I get this weird sense of like… déjà vu, I guess? Some things come back quicker than others, but it's all kind of a struggle."

"And it'll never get better?"

"Fuck knows," Felix told him, feeling a small pulse of irritation.

The one thing he'd been worried about was meeting someone and letting them hope that he'd go back to the man he was before the Incident. He didn't have the strength left to hope for that anymore. He just wanted to live and be happy.

"Hey," Dei said softly.

Felix looked up again.

"I'm sorry. I didn't mean it like that. I don't want you any other way."

Felix was still annoyed, but somewhere, a small voice in his head reminded him that if anyone understood what it was like, it was Dei. Only where Felix might actually find his miracle, Dei never would. He settled, then leaned his cheek against Dei's stump, turning his face to kiss his warm skin.

"Sometimes my scrambled-egg brains make me kind of a dick," Felix murmured.

Dei chuckled and kissed him back on the crown of his head. "Nah, sweet thing. I said it all wrong, and it was my fault."

Felix wanted to argue, but he figured his time was better occupied with eating what Dei had cooked for him and showing him appreciation that way.

19

Dei had trained himself to stop jumping up at the slightest disturbance in the middle of the night, but the one thing he couldn't ignore was the sound of his mom's caregiver ringer. It was muffled, coming from under the pillow where he'd lost his phone while doom-scrolling after Felix had dropped off, and he scrambled to get it before Felix could wake up.

Luckily, his lover seemed dead to the world, so Dei managed to answer before balancing on his leg and hopping out of the room. It was late in California, which meant it was too early in Florida for just a quick hello.

His heart was in his throat.

"What happened?"

"I hope I'm not disturbing you." The voice was a man's, one Dei recognized as his mom's primary doctor—Ethan Fuller, who was very kind but also very blunt.

Dei rubbed at his eye tiredly. "It is what it is. Did something happen?"

"Her blood pressure dropped significantly tonight. We managed to stabilize it, but she's stopped eating, and nothing we've done is working consistently. Carol's her nurse on duty tonight, and she said you were away, and I hate to interrupt your vacation, but this isn't something we can ignore. We need to sit down and have a frank talk as soon as you can."

Dei managed to get to the back door, and he slid it open, collapsing on the deck with his back pressed to the rough stucco. He stretched his leg out and pinned the phone between his stump and his ear, using his fingers to pinch the bridge of his nose. "Ah. Yeah, I'm in California. Is this like, get on a flight right now and you'll be lucky if you don't miss her, or…"

"This is a 'I'd like to sit down with you within the next week or two' sort of thing," Ethan said. "Not because she's in danger of passing away, but because she's severely malnourished, and it's time for us to make some decisions regarding hospice."

Dei swallowed heavily. "Yeah, I…okay." He felt defeat rush through him so profound he felt like he was going to choke on it.

"I'm sorry. Sometimes things spiral faster than any of us could have predicted. It's not a fun conversation, and it's definitely not one we want to have on the phone if we can help it."

They were kind words, and honest ones, but in truth, Dei had seen this coming. His mom's condition had never been a slow decline. It had been long plateaus with massive valleys that she never recovered from.

Maybe, for her, it was lucky. He couldn't imagine what it would be like to be locked in her own brain like that for years and years.

"I need to try and get ahold of my sister," he said. "Then I'll book my flight. Will you please have someone call me immediately if things get worse?"

"Of course," Ethan said, "but I've been doing this for many years, Deimos. I promise you'll have time to say a long, long goodbye."

He wanted to believe him, but maybe this was the price he was paying for happiness. It was cruel, and it was unfair, and he wasn't really sure that was even possible. After all, why would god care about someone so small and insignificant as him?

And why would He rest the weight of that on the way Dei had fallen in love with one of the kindest men in the world? He picked at the edge of his Saniderm. The tattoo was aching and itching a little, and the plasma beneath it had mixed with the ink, so he couldn't make out the owl anymore, but he could picture it in his mind.

And he could picture the way Felix had looked up at him over and over with that sly little grin, knowing what he'd done.

Fuck.

Dei didn't want to complicate what progress he'd made by all of this.

After hanging up, Dei took a trembling breath, then scrolled through his contacts for Sofia. He hadn't tried calling her since well before he left, and he was pretty sure there was no chance in hell she was going to pick up, but he had to do everything he could to find her.

It rang four times, and then he was met with silence before, "Is Mom dead?"

The sound of her voice startled him so badly it took him a second to find his voice. "Uh. Hey. And no. Not yet."

"But she's getting close." It wasn't a question, and she sounded more resigned than sad, which made sense.

Dei swallowed down his anger and frustration with her because now wasn't the time to berate her for disappearing on him. "The doctor said it's time to talk hospice."

Sofia was quiet for a moment. "Are you with her? Can you put the phone to her ear?"

"I'm in California," Dei said.

Sofia made a noise of outrage. "Are you fucking serious? You're in California right now? And you just what, left her there to—"

Before Dei could defend himself and point out her absolute hypocrisy, he heard someone on the other end of the phone speaking very softly. Sofia had obviously covered the phone, but she came back a second later. "Sorry."

He took a breath. "You have some fucking nerve, Sof. Like, the size of your goddamn balls—"

"I know," she said in a rush. "I know. I'm not…I'm not well, okay?"

He pressed his finger and thumb against his eye, letting himself push extra hard on his prosthetic since he could barely feel it. "How bad is it?"

"I'm in rehab."

Well. That was…something, he supposed. "Voluntary?"

"Kind of. I got arrested, and I was ordered thirty days outpatient as part of my probation, but I'm going to stay in it longer," she admitted.

"Are you allowed to come see her?" he asked.

She took several breaths before she answered him. "Probably, yeah, but I don't think I'm going to."

That was the answer he was expecting. Sofia's first major spiral had come on the heels of their mom forgetting her name for the first time, and it had only gotten worse after that. All he could really do was hope she wouldn't live to regret her choice.

"If you promise to pick up, I'll call you when I get home."

"When?"

"Probably tomorrow," Dei told her.

"Why are you in California?" she asked him.

Dei laughed. "That's not your business, and I don't really feel like telling you."

"You know what?" she started, then stopped again and let out a calming breath. "Dei, I need to hang up now. I love you. So much. But I'm not really in a place right now where I can talk to you without falling apart. I'm sorry." And then the line was dead.

Shock stole over him—some because of his mom, but mostly because of Sofia, and anger was quick on its heels. Behind that was a powerful, endless feeling of grief because he wasn't even allowed to be angry at her for trying to get better.

It's what their mom would have wanted.

Dei knew enough about addiction to know that the only way Sofia was going to get to a place where she could be healthy was if she was entirely focused on herself. But a part of him wanted to scream that she'd been putting herself first for longer than he could remember, and it felt so fucking unfair she'd chosen this moment—the moment when his mother was reaching the end of her life—to decide it was time for all this.

He eventually let the phone go, and it clattered to the deck beside him. His head thudded back hard against the stucco, and he didn't move, even when he heard the sliding door open again and Felix's soft, bare steps padding over to him. Dei didn't do much besides move slightly to the right to give Felix room to cuddle up under his stump, and Dei laid his cheek against his lover's head.

A warm, stubbled cheek rubbed against the sensitive end of his arm, and Felix pressed a kiss to that tender spot before wrapping an arm around Dei's middle.

"How much of that did you hear?"

"Enough to know I shouldn't ask questions right now," Felix told him.

Dei laughed, the sound a little pained, but he still felt a small pulse of joy, which was odd considering how much it all hurt.

"We need to leave, don't we?"

"I'm so sorry, darlin'. I know you weren't done showing me around," Dei said, but Felix interrupted him with a laugh.

"My sweet, amazing, wonderful man. This is all I really wanted with you. The rest was details."

Dei tucked those words behind his ribs and held them close to his heart. "How about we stop by the cemetery on the way to the airport. Likely enough we're not gettin' a flight out of here until late, so we might as well let you say your goodbyes."

Felix let out a slow breath. "I think…I think I already said them. I mean, it's just a piece of granite with her name on it. She's not even interned there. My mom took her ashes home."

Dei bowed his head. "Ah, my sugar…"

Felix grinned and kissed his stump again. "My baby."

Dei felt a profound, intense warmth in his chest at those words. He lifted his gaze, then used his finger to tilt Felix's head up. "The doctor said she was hanging in there, so we can wait a few days if you want to. I promise it's okay."

"No," Felix said. "I don't need that. I need to know you're home with her."

Dei turned slightly and cupped Felix's chin. It felt like his heart was bleeding out in his chest. "Oh, sweet thing. What if you regret it?"

"Then I can fly back," Felix said. "The funeral's over. I saw my family, and anything that needed to be said already was. There were other things I wanted to show you, but they're not important enough."

"Felix…"

"Deimos," Felix shot back, his voice small and so tender it almost physically hurt. He surged in and pressed his lips to the corner of Dei's mouth. "Let's go home, okay?"

Dei curled his fingers into the back of Felix's hair and held him there. "Just do me one favor."

"Anything," Felix promised.

"Don't let me push you away. I have no idea how bad this is going to get for me. This is something I've known was comin' for a long damn time, but in the end, I don't know if I'm gonna lose it a little."

"Okay," Felix whispered.

Dei moved his hand down to the back of Felix's neck and stroked absent lines over his warm skin. "The last thing in the world I want is for my earth to be scorched when this fire passes. So please, just… please don't run."

"I'm not going anywhere," Felix vowed fiercely, and while Dei was petrified that Felix didn't know what he was getting into, he wasn't willing to let him take it back.

THERE WAS a particular kindness about the men from the tattoo shop that surprised Dei, even after knowing them for as long as he had now. Paris picked them up from the airport and was quiet the entire drive back to their street, doing little more than offering a fist bump when Dei climbed out of the truck and grabbed his bags from the back.

He waited on the sidewalk as Paris and Felix talked for a few, and then Felix got out and walked Dei to the door.

For a brief moment, Dei was petrified Felix was going to invite himself in. The last thing in the world Dei wanted was to sleep alone, but he needed some space to let himself fall apart. There would come a time that Felix would see him at his worst and at his most vulnerable, but he wasn't ready for that yet.

But instead, Felix just leaned against the side of the truck and tugged Dei in for the softest, sweetest kiss that made Dei regret his need to be by himself. "You know where I'll be if you need me," Felix murmured against his lips. "Promise you'll call if you do."

"Sweetness, I just don't know if I'm gonna be in the right headspace for—"

"No," Felix interrupted. He leaned back and held Dei by the chin in the same way Dei often did to him. "If you need me. That's all I'm asking."

Oh. *Oh*. He understood. He let his eyelids fall shut as he surged in for a second kiss and breathed in the scent of Felix until it felt imprinted on his soul. "It won't be forever, darlin'."

"I know. Because you made me promise not to let you go," Felix said with a tiny smile.

It took every ounce of his control to pull his hand back, but eventually, Dei stepped far enough away that Felix could move around him, and he got back into the truck. Paris gave him a quick salute, then took off down the driveway, and it was clear they weren't going to the house. Felix disappeared out onto the main road, and then Dei was alone.

The feeling was a heavy weight in the center of his chest, and the inside of his place felt cavernous in the strangest way. It was clean, so there was nothing to do, and after five minutes of just standing in the middle of his living room, he grabbed his cane and walked back outside, got into his truck, and took off.

It was absolutely no surprise when he found himself parked out front of his mom's care facility, and it was also no surprise when it took him twenty minutes to find the strength to turn off the engine and get out of the truck. He leaned heavily on his cane, his knee weak and both hips plagued with a sort of trembling sensation like they might give out at any time.

He was pretty sure the staff there were used to people falling apart for one reason or another. He just never expected to be one of them. His heart was beating in his throat when he walked through the front doors, and there was a look of pity on the receptionist's face when she saw him.

"She's in her room. You can head in," she said softly.

Dei tried to breathe through the bizarre fog that had settled in his lungs, and he forced himself to cough a few times to loosen it all up. The door was mostly shut, so he peered around the corner and turned his head so he could see where her bed was. They'd moved it further away from the window, and while she wasn't on any monitors, it felt far more like a hospital room now than it did before.

Dei shut the door behind him, then walked in and saw her dark, grey-streaked hair fanned out over her pillow. She looked thinner, which was ridiculous since he'd only been gone a couple of days, but it was also the first time he hadn't seen her for any stretch of time.

It felt like no time at all had passed, and it also felt like he'd lost a hundred years.

Dei grabbed one of the chairs that was pushed up against the wall and dragged it to her bedside. She hadn't moved since he'd gotten in, and he wasn't sure she was going to wake up for him. Not that it mattered. Her body was limp except for her hands, which were curled into tight fists, and her breathing was a little shallow, probably from the pneumonia.

"Hi, Momma," he murmured. He set his cane to the side as he sat, then curled his big hand around her tiny fist. Her skin felt papery and her knuckles too bony—nothing like the strong woman who had been able to pick him up with one arm and haul her around on her hip. "I'm back."

He watched her nose twitch, but he didn't think that meant much.

"I was in California, and I can't even tell you how beautiful it was there. The water there was real cold, and the smell of the sea stuck to everything. You'd'a loved it." He stroked his thumb over her wrist. "I'm hoping I can bring Felix in to meet you too. I, uh…I really like him, Momma. I was fixin' to spend the rest of my life alone with some good friends and maybe a cat later on down the road, but he came in like a damn tornado and turned everything upside down. You'd like him too. He's real sweet and real funny."

She was too still, and he checked her breathing before going on.

"I haven't thought much about a future since I lost a bunch of my body, but now I'm hearin' wedding bells, and that's…strange. Last thing I wanna do is get married without you here, but you're not givin' me much choice, are you?" His throat went thick and hot, and he had to stop because he wasn't going to lose it here.

It was easier to just let himself think—to get lost in the feeling of his grief instead of trying to say it aloud. He bowed his head and felt the air flow in and out of his lungs as her hand warmed beneath his.

And nothing happened.

The sound of the door startled Dei upright, and he let out a small sigh when Ethan appeared in some scrub pants, white shoes, and a very tight T-shirt that might have had Dei looking twice under entirely different circumstances. It was the first time Dei had seen his bare arms, and he noticed a flowers-and-vine tattoo going up from his inner forearm to his shoulder.

"When did you get in?" Ethan asked.

Dei let his mom's hand go and rubbed his sternum. "Ten minutes ago? Twenty? I think I dropped off a bit. Jet lag's a bitch."

Ethan nodded and stepped closer. In the light, Dei could make out a few streaks of grey in his dark hair and just the barest start of crow's feet in the corner of each eye. He wanted to believe that it was from smiling because Ethan was a good guy—one of the few doctors there that Dei believed actually gave a shit about his patients as people.

"Did she wake up for you?"

Dei shook his head and wrapped his arm around his middle, leaning forward a bit. "Nah. Should she?"

"She's been up and down a few times today, but she's pretty medicated right now. We got a little liquid in her, but we do need to talk about the next steps regarding hospice treatment."

"Because she's dyin'?"

Ethan sighed. "This is the trajectory of her disease, and it's always a thousand times more heartbreaking when it's someone so young."

Dei wasn't quite sure that was true. He was pretty goddamn sure it would hurt this bad no matter what age his mom was, but he knew what Ethan was trying to say. He rubbed the back of his neck. "She gotta transfer out of this place?"

"Not at all. But she's going to need different care. She's at risk for infections and becoming severely malnourished from not eating. We can keep her on an IV, of course, and we will. Our main goal is her comfort as things start to shift."

"Shift how?" Dei said. He was pretty sure he'd been given all this info when she was admitted, but his brain felt like white noise.

"Decrease in mobility and bodily functions," Ethan said plainly. He clasped his hands in front of him. "She's already lost most of her speech and the ability to eat. As time goes on, some patients can forget how to breathe. Most of them sleep all day, and some of them will go days without any sort of rest."

"She's already a risk for wandering. And that sundowning thing you told me about at the beginning," Dei said. It had been a while since he'd gotten a call that his mom wasn't where she was supposed to be, but if she got a wild hair now?

"Which is why we want to adjust her care," Ethan said. He walked over and dropped a hand to Dei's left shoulder. The pressure always felt strange when someone squeezed all his scarring, and it wasn't nearly as nice as when Felix did it, but he didn't mind right then.

He looked down at Ethan's ink, and he realized it looked fresh. "You get that done here?"

Ethan blinked, then laughed. "Yeah. My…fuck, I don't know what you'd call him. My sister's husband's brother?"

Dei snorted. "Right?"

Ethan's eyes crinkled in the corners with his grin. "He met some guys here that opened a tattoo shop a year ago."

"Irons and Works," Dei said.

Ethan's smile widened. "You know them?"

"I'm the chef at Midnight Snack. We share a parking lot."

Ethan's brows shot up. "I know that place. I eat there!"

Dei laughed. "Good to know my momma's doctor has tried my hot, sweaty balls."

Ethan burst into a fit of giggles, covering his mouth with his free hand. "Oh my god, okay. We cannot have this conversation here."

Dei chuckled but agreed, though it felt good to laugh in spite of the situation. After a beat, the mood sobered again, especially when he realized his mom hadn't moved at all. "Look, just…tell me what we need to do here, okay? Money and time don't matter. I'll figure it out."

Ethan gave him a careful look. "Let me put together a treatment plan for her. Can you come by tomorrow around two? I'll be done with my rounds then, and we can sit and go over everything."

Dei nodded, hating that he had to agree. A part of him wanted to just let Ethan and the rest of his team do whatever they wanted to do so he could bury his head in the sand. But his mom deserved better than that.

"I'll be in touch," Ethan said after a long silence. He gave Dei's shoulder a last squeeze, then left the room.

The door shut with a firm click, and Dei let out a heavy breath before bracing himself on the arm of the chair and pushing up to stand. He shuffled closer, ignoring all the pain zinging through all the wrecked parts of his body, and he leaned down to press a kiss to her forehead.

"I'll be back soon," he murmured.

Once again, she didn't move, so he backed away, grabbed his cane, and got out of there as quickly as he could manage.

20

"Just use the goddamn gun. I've seen it done on TikTok, okay? Stop acting like I'm being unreasonable!" The voice was loud and piercing, the tone of someone being *entirely* unreasonable.

Felix pushed his way through the swinging doors and came to a stop near the back stall. He blinked and tried to let his brain calibrate since he'd been in the drawing room for the last two hours, and it took a second for him to recognize Rafe and Jamie, who were hovering near him, watching the scene play out at the front of the shop.

"Wanna get in on the bet?" Jamie asked.

Felix raised a brow as he looked from the woman to Linc, then to Zeke, who was standing a few feet away with his arms crossed over his massive chest. "Are you betting that Zeke's gonna grab her by her ponytail and drag her into the street?"

Jamie choked on a laugh, slapping his palm over his mouth as Rafe grinned and said, "That's *my* bet. Jamie thinks Zeke's going to cave."

"What's happening?" Felix asked.

"This lady wants her nose pierced with a piercing gun. I don't think Linc even owns one, and she threatened to report him to the FDA," Jamie said from behind his fingers.

It took all of Felix's control not to laugh. "Seriously?"

Jamie shrugged. "I think Zeke should make Linc do it. She'll be the one to pay the price."

"Linc values himself and his job way too much for that," Felix said, then turned his attention back to the trio. The woman's voice was rising, and he could see Zeke's face going a little redder, which meant he was reaching the end of his patience.

"And it's time for you to leave now, thank you," Zeke said. He took a step closer to her, and the woman whipped out her phone with shaking hands and pointed it at him.

"You're seriously kicking me out of here because you don't want your employee to do his job?" she screeched.

Zeke pinched the bridge of his nose and glanced over at Linc, who hadn't moved a muscle the whole time Felix had been watching. "I'm asking you politely to leave my shop since you don't want to comply with our policy." He took another step closer to her.

"Oh my god! Don't touch me! Don't hit me! I'm being attacked!" She started to scream at the top of her lungs, and before Felix could react, Eve jumped over the counter, grabbed her by the arm, and shoved her through the door before locking it.

The woman started throwing herself against the glass as Eve backed up a few paces. And then, in the stunned silence of the shop, there was the sound of a small child crying.

Felix's eyes went wide when he realized there were customers, and one of them was a kid. "What the fuck?" he whispered.

Rafe pointed to the front stall where Paris worked, and Felix brushed past them both and came to a halt when he saw a dad in the tattoo chair with his leg half-done and a boy of about five sitting in another chair next to Max, who had his machine hooked up to a ball-point pen.

"Hey, kiddo," Felix said. "Are you getting some ink like your dad?"

The kid sniffed and looked over his shoulder at the sound of the woman still hitting the glass. "Um."

Felix looked up at Linc, who had his phone to his ear, then back at the kid. "Do you like painting?"

The kid nodded.

Felix looked at the dad. "I've got some really amazing fingerpaints in the drawing room. Think that sounds like fun?"

The dad's face fell in a look of relief. "What do you think, Connor?"

"I've only got maybe ten minutes left," Paris said. "It could be fun. Maybe Max will go?"

Max set his machine down and used a dry paper towel to wipe the kid's arm in a mimic of what Paris was doing to his dad. "You're all done anyway, champ. We can get a snack too, okay?"

The kid—Connor, apparently—hopped up and situated himself between Max and Felix. "'Kay."

Max offered his hand, so Felix did the same, and they quickly led him through the doors and into the back room, where he saw the sprawling art table covered in paper and pencils. They kept a small stock of the cheap-ass Crayola fingerpaints for moments like this—or moments when kids were having a meltdown. It wasn't his favorite thing in the world, but he was grateful they had it in that moment.

"Here you go," Max said, shoving a bunch of paper toward Connor and then opening up the jars of paint. "Go nuts."

Connor's eyes lit up as he dug his hands into each jar and began to smear everything around. Felix couldn't help a small grin as he shuffled closer to his friend and tipped his head down low toward Max's ear.

"Uh. What the fuck, dude?"

"I don't know," Max murmured back. "I think she was drunk. She stumbled in like ten minutes ago, demanding that Eve pierce her, but she was with a client. Then, when Linc stepped up, she had a fuckin' toddler tantrum about his hands. *Then* she said she'd only do it if he used a gun, which…obviously, he doesn't have that shit."

Felix rubbed a hand down his face. He'd been hoping for a quiet week back since he hadn't heard from Dei in a while, and he was doing everything in his power not to act like a clingy, worried asshole. But he'd had two fainters that week, one woman who'd tried to change her mind an hour into the tattoo, and a man who'd started screaming at him because he was told tattoos didn't hurt, and his did, so it was obviously Felix's problem.

And while this had nothing to do with him, it felt a bit like the cherry on a shit sundae.

"You okay?" Max asked after a second.

Felix laughed, shaking his head. "Not really, no."

"Head stuff or other stuff?"

"Other stuff. My head's the only thing that decided to be nice to me since I got back." He tried to smile, but it felt plastered on and completely fake.

Max reached for him, tangling their fingers together in a comforting hold. "Talk to me."

Felix glanced over at the kid, who was definitely lost in his own world. "I think I'm in love with Dei."

Max laughed softly. "Water's wet. The sky's blue…"

Felix smacked him on the arm. "It might have been easy for you to figure shit out with Jeremiah, but—"

Max's smile fell, and his brows shot up. "Seriously? You think any of that was easy?"

Felix shrugged. "I mean, at least you could remember his face in the mornings. And at least you knew he wanted to kiss you."

"Have you two not—"

"We, uh," Felix said, then flushed and glanced away. "We did. A lot. And it was maybe the most amazing thing I've ever felt."

Max leaned against the wall and reached for Felix's hand again, squeezing him tight. "How did you leave things?"

"With a kiss and a promise that it wasn't over, but he asked me for space," Felix told him. "I'm trying my best to respect what he needs, but I feel like I'm losing my goddamn mind. It feels like there's no chance in hell he doesn't realize that I'm way too much work. Especially with his mom and sister already taking up so much of his time."

"Dude, you really think he's that kind of guy?"

"It wouldn't make him a bad person," Felix insisted, his stomach hurting at the thought of it being over before it started. "That would make him human."

"You have your own struggles," Max pointed out. "Do you feel like he's too much, even with all his complications? I mean, you almost got your ass kicked by his sister's boyfriend."

Felix couldn't imagine not loving Dei, no matter what was going on, but he was also clingy and needy and lonely. He was the kind of guy people fucked, not loved, and he always had been. So why would that change with Dei?

"I don't—" he started, but his phone buzzed, and he went quiet as he pulled it out of his pocket. He saw Dei's name on the screen, and his heart did a funny pitter-patter in his chest.

> Dei: Gonna start prepping for dinner rush, but can I pick you up after? We need to talk.

And then his heart shattered into a million pieces.

We need to talk.

He knew what those four words meant. Not a damn soul on the planet didn't, and he wasn't ready. He wasn't ready to let this go, and even if he had promised not to let Dei push him away, Felix wasn't sure he knew how to fight for them. He needed time. He couldn't roll over and let this end, but if Dei decided it was over tonight, Felix would fold.

> Felix: Busy. Maybe tomorrow. Text you later.

It was all he could say. He looked at Max and felt his eyes get hot. "I think he's telling me it's over," he managed in a whisper.

Max took the phone from him, and the expression on his face said everything. "You should get out of here."

"I have clients," Felix said, then cleared his throat and squared his shoulders. "Just because one thing's going to end doesn't mean the rest of my life needs to fall apart."

It was telling that Max didn't stop him as he pushed his way out of the drawing room and headed for his stall.

"Do you like dolphins?"

Felix glanced up from where he was wiping down his station and saw Jamie smiling at him over the partition. "What kind of monster doesn't like dolphins?"

Jamie laughed. "I mean, to be fair, they're kind of dicks. But there's this one guy over at the sanctuary who just got a new prosthetic tail, so I thought you might want to come with me and meet him after I drop off some paperwork."

Felix knew what Jamie was doing. Max was quiet about it, but gossip spread like wildfire in the shop, and by that evening, even the guys who had the day off knew that Felix's heart had been shredded into a million pieces.

A small part of him wanted to tell Jamie to fuck off—that he could handle his own pain—but the idea of not being alone had way more appeal. "I need to get something to eat, but…"

"Got you covered. Zeke just got back with sushi. He ordered inari for you."

Felix wanted to cry just from that little kindness alone. "Sweet. Uh, give me ten minutes to put everything away and text a couple appointment reminders."

Jamie shot him a thumbs-up before turning back around, and Felix quickly put his machine and ink bottles back in his toolbox before heading to the bathroom. His last client of the night had been a woman, which meant fewer breaks, so he stood there having a full-on Austin Powers piss, which might have even been funny if he wasn't feeling so wrecked.

He'd checked his phone twice, but his message to Dei hadn't been read, just delivered, and he didn't know what that even meant. A small part of him had hoped Dei was going to walk his words back, but he supposed it was just his shitty luck.

Washing his hands, Felix splashed some water onto his face in hopes that it would make him look less like he was fighting back tears, and then he slipped out and headed into the back room to grab his things. He checked his phone one last time—and there was still nothing—so he headed back into the main shop and glanced around.

Jamie was one of the people he was still struggling to recognize on sight, so Felix went by process of elimination. He wasn't the man sitting up front—that was Paris. And Rafe with his temple tattoo was sitting behind the computer. That only left the one man, who was staring at him with a grin, and Felix tried to smile back.

"All set?"

Felix nodded as Jamie hopped up, and he laughed just a little when Jamie grabbed his arm and all but pulled him through the shop and out the back door. "You know Eli?"

Felix's brow furrowed. "Uh…is he a client?"

"Nah. He owns that big-ass resort up the street. The one with all the white columns," Jamie said as he unlocked his car and waited for Felix to get in.

Felix offered him something between a grimace and a smile. "I don't think I've met him, and if I did…" He trailed off, tapping his temple.

Jamie flushed in the low light of the car before slamming his door. "Fuck. Sorry. I don't mean to be insensitive."

Felix waved him off. "Please don't apologize. I'd rather people forget than treat me like I'm a freak all day long."

Jamie stared at him, then shook his head and smiled down at the steering wheel. "Well, anyway, he's like rich as fuck, right? And I will die on the hill that there are no good billionaires in the world, but he literally just gave the sanctuary a year's worth of funding."

"That's amazing."

Jamie nodded as he pulled out onto the main road. "I also don't think he has billions, but probably close enough to be able to just throw cash around like that. Anyway, he's going to be there tonight."

"How, uh…how should I know this guy?" Felix asked.

"Oh. He's, like, really good friends with Paris. He's the one who paid for the ramp Paris put up in his house."

Felix's eyes widened. Everything in his head was foggy, but he had a very vague recollection of a guy in a wheelchair who wasn't from Colorado. Someone else—someone new. "Well, hopefully, I haven't met him. Those conversations are awkward as hell."

"I don't think he'd judge you," Jamie said, his voice softening. "He's really cool."

Felix stared, and then his eyes widened. "You're into him."

Jamie flushed harder. "Uh. Not…I mean. I *was*. But we're just friends. We had a little thing a few months back. No strings," he said very quickly, which told Felix that maybe he wasn't being entirely truthful. "His ex came back into town, though, and they wanted to work things out."

"Kids?" Felix asked. He wasn't sure what the hell he'd do if Dei had kids. Not that it mattered now.

God, that made his chest hurt.

"Nah. That was one of the reasons they split. We haven't talked about if they're actually trying to work things out. But all that shit's a little too complicated for me, you know? Like, it's hard enough being gay and having these cis dudes freak the fuck out when they realize my dick doesn't look like theirs." Jamie stopped abruptly and slapped his hand over his mouth. "Sorry. TMI, and my Adderall wore off three hours ago."

Felix chuckled very softly. "You're good, man. This actually means a lot. I was kind of terrified about going home and being alone with my thoughts. You're definitely doing me a favor, so please keep talking."

Jamie winced, but he kept rambling on about the sanctuary for the next ten minutes as they made their way over the bridge toward the seaside building. Most of the guys hung out there with Jamie a lot, but he'd only been twice. Felix wasn't big into social situations where he'd be expected to remember people.

His clients and the shop were bad enough.

He felt a little less nervous, though, seeing as the place was closed to the public and the parking lot was almost entirely empty. "Am I allowed to be here right now?"

"I mean, I can't let you swim with the dolphins or anything, but yeah," Jamie said with a smile. "Callisto brings Ben and Paris here all the time after the gates close."

Felix was only familiar with Callisto since he'd moved onto Ben and Paris's property. The guy had an adorable kid and was so painfully shy he'd only spoken about six words to Felix in the year they'd been in each other's social circle.

But Felix liked him. He liked almost everyone they hung around with. The last time he'd been uncomfortable was back home, and even then, he'd been with Dei—safe, protected, wanted. His throat got hot again, and he cleared it. "So, uh…should we go in?"

"In a minute." Jamie frowned at him for several seconds. "Look, I know you know Max opened his fat mouth and told everyone you had your heart stomped on, but are you okay? Seriously?"

Felix let out a watery laugh and sniffed. "No. Isn't that what we're doing here?"

"A pity trip to see dolphins?" Jamie asked with wide eyes.

Felix shrugged. "Well. Yeah."

"Dude. I just wanted to spend time with you. Our schedules suck, so we never hang out, then you came back in a relationship thing, so I knew if this worked out with Dei, I'd definitely never see you."

Felix sat back, stunned. Jamie wanted to hang out with *him*?

"Why are you staring at me like that?" Jamie asked, folding his arms around his middle.

Felix bit his lip, then said, "I didn't know you wanted to."

"Oh my god. Dude. I've had a friend crush on you since the shop opened, but you're always so quiet, and you get even more quiet when I come around."

Felix covered his face with both hands, feeling the need to laugh and cry at the same time. "I don't know what to say." He looked up when he felt a light touch on his elbow, and he glanced at Jamie's contrite face. "I'm such an awkward nerd, but you're the best, Jamie. I fucking love spending time with you. I just kind of assumed I was too much for most people."

"Never," Jamie said, his voice low and fierce. "Jesus, dude. You're never too much."

Felix let out a weak, watery laugh. "So we're best friends now?"

"Yep. As long as we can pretend like neither one of us are socially inept, awkward nerds."

Felix did laugh this time, and somehow, he felt just a little bit better. "You got yourself a fucking deal."

"Hell yeah," Jamie said, his light eyes crinkling in the corners. He reached up and scratched at his short curls before slapping both hands down on his thighs. "Come on. Let's get inside so we can forget all about real-life problems and play with dolphins."

21

Dei was rushing toward Jeremiah's office when he heard a raised voice and came to a skidding halt. He'd had the misfortune of walking in on Jeremiah and Max arguing once or twice, and the last thing he needed right then was to get involved in more of their drama.

He almost turned away, but then he heard Max all but shout, "…going to murder him. He fucking broke my best friend's heart. You have to fire him. I don't care if you don't have a chef. I'll learn to cook and take his place."

"Babe…"

"Don't babe me. You don't hurt my friends, Jer. You just *don't*."

Dei sagged forward, his forehead thudding against the wall as his worst nightmare came true. He'd been balls to the wall busy when he'd sent Felix the text that morning, and it had taken him all day to be able to look at his reply. The response had been short and terse—exactly what Dei hadn't expected, and it took him another ten minutes before he realized what he'd done wrong.

He had meant they needed to talk—but not because he wanted to end things. He needed Felix to know that space was the last thing he wanted. He needed to be with him. When he came home from a long day at work or a painful day with his mother, he didn't want to be alone anymore.

He had no goddamn desire to be an island.

But he'd fucked up. He tried texting Felix, but the messages remained undelivered, so either his phone was off, or he'd been blocked. And right now, a very pissed-off Max was his only hope in fixing it. He just had to be able to explain himself before Max murdered him.

His hand trembled as he reached for the door and slowly pushed inside.

"Hey…"

"*You*," Max said in a low growl, shooting up to his feet from where he'd been perched on Jeremiah's desk.

Jeremiah had his eyes closed, his hand pinching the bridge of his nose. "Please don't make me sit here for this."

"I'm gonna need a witness. An alibi," Max said.

"They won't take my word for shit, babe. I'm blind," Jeremiah reminded him.

"That's ableist and bullshit," Max said. "And I know you wouldn't tolerate that crap, so try again."

Dei put up his hand in surrender. "Hey, listen. For what it's worth, I know I fucked up, but I didn't mean to. We got hit with a reservation for three tour busses who asked us to cater, and your boyfriend there said yes."

Jeremiah opened his eyes and crossed his arms over his chest. "I gotta pay y'all, don't I?"

Dei sighed and ignored him, turning his attention back to Max. "I wasn't thinking. I wanted to pick him up and tell him that I'm in love with him and that space is stupid. I just said it all wrong, and now he's not answering my texts."

Max stared at him for a long, long while before sagging against the desk. "God. Why are men such emotional morons?"

Dei shrugged and offered him a hopeful smile. "Wish I could tell you, but the only answer I want right now is to know that I can fix this."

"You can fix this," Max said, rolling his eyes. "That fucker is so in love with you, you could probably run over his feet with your car, and he'd make sure you weren't feeling bad about it."

Dei wanted to argue, but he knew it was true. Mostly because he felt the same way. "Did he block me?"

"He probably turned his phone off. He didn't want to meet with you tonight because he wanted one more day to say you were his."

"Fuck," Dei whispered, clutching at his sternum. He loved Felix so goddamn much, and the idea that he was hurting was threatening to send him over the edge. "Is he home? Do you know if—"

"He went out with Jamie," Max cut in.

Dei's face pinked. "Like a date?"

Max blinked, then burst into laughter. "No, you absolute fucking *nightmare*. Jamie took him to the Sea Sanctuary to feed the dolphins or whatever and distract him from how shitty he feels."

Dei rubbed his face, then dropped his hand to his side. "Should I go over there?"

"It's closed, bud," Jeremiah cut in.

"Then I'll wait," Dei said firmly. "I'll sleep in the goddamn parking lot if I have to, but I can't let him think… God, I fucked up so badly, and I can't let him think I wouldn't offer him the universe if I had the means to do it. I just need to finish cleaning up the mess after that service, and—"

"Go," Max barked at him. "Jer and I will handle it."

"Thanks," Jeremiah said dryly, then grinned. "Seriously, Dei. Fucking go."

As Dei turned on his heel and rushed out of the office, he heard Max's quiet voice say, "Were we this bad?"

And Jeremiah answered, "Baby, we were worse."

DEI DID his best not to commit felony speeding as he followed his GPS to the Sea Sanctuary. He'd seen the entrance a few times as he drove by it, but he'd never bothered to give it a second thought. Now, it was a place that stood between him and the love of his life, and he felt like he was going to lose his mind if he had to spend all night staring at the brick walls.

Luckily, the parking lot gate was open, and while he felt like he was committing some crime driving past the entrance booth, he rolled around to the employee section. The lights were dim, and there was a vaguely familiar car parked at the curb near a heavy metal door marked Staff Only.

Dei pulled up alongside the curb and let his engine idle, staring at the door, then pulling out his phone. He brought up Felix's text thread, and his heart leapt a little when he saw a single word under the last message he'd sent: *Read*.

Dei's fingers started to shake as he opened up the keyboard and stared at the letters. What the fuck did he say now? He'd already sent a barrage of "I'm sorry, I realize how that sounds and it's not what I meant, please call me baby, I'm a complete moron and I don't deserve you."

He supposed an "I love you" could work, because god, he did. With his whole heart. But that was better left coming from his own lips where Felix could hear just how much he meant it. He sighed and dropped his forehead to the steering wheel, preparing to literally wait all night if that's what it took.

Everything in his life was upside down, and he wasn't going to let go without a fight. Not over one of the few good things he still had to hold on to. He hadn't ever thought he'd fall in love. At least, not like this. He'd known one day he'd get over the fear of showing his body to other people. He'd known one day he'd let someone touch him again.

But he hadn't expected Felix.

A tapping sound damn near shook him out of his skin, and Dei sat up, ready to throw fists, when he blinked through the window and saw the only person he wanted to see standing there. Felix was a few feet away from the door, his hands stuffed into his pockets, his brow furrowed.

Dei wondered for a second if Felix recognized him, but then he caught the look in his eyes, and he knew. Felix was scared.

And he was pissed.

"Oh, sweetness, I'm so sorry. I'm such a moron, I didn't—" He stopped abruptly when he realized Felix couldn't hear him, and he twisted his body, missed the door handle twice, then finally flung it open and almost fell on his face. "Baby," he gasped.

Felix, in spite of his obvious complicated feelings, darted forward to steady Dei so he didn't eat shit on the asphalt. "Max called," Felix said in an even tone.

Dei braced himself on the truck, bowing his head as he collected himself. "I was hopin' he would. I was fixin' to stay out here all night if I had to, but I really wanted to talk to you before the sun came up."

Felix rolled his eyes as he stepped back, giving Dei a bit more space. "I read your texts. I was going to call you in the morning."

Dei nodded, meeting Felix's gaze and holding it. "I'm not ending things. I mean, you're free to since apparently I'm no good at this, and I know you were hurtin' all damn day."

Felix took in a tight breath, then shrugged. "Yeah, I figured that out from all the 'I'm sorries.' And Max told me what happened at the restaurant. I get why you didn't see my message until later."

"That's no excuse," Dei told him. "I'm madly in love with you, Felix. I have been for a while now, and the last thing I want is to cause you any more pain."

It almost felt like someone had muted the world. Dei would have heard a pin drop a mile away if there was a sewing circle nearby. He couldn't take his eyes off Felix's face, but his expression was completely unreadable.

"I'm not askin' you to love me back," Dei said into the tense silence. "I don't want anything more than you're willing to give. But I asked you to come with me to talk cuz I was fixin' to tell you over dinner."

"You're...I don't," Felix stammered, then rubbed both hands down his face. "You don't preface the first I love you with 'we need to talk,' you *asshole!*"

Dei's face went white-hot with shame. "I know. I should'a known when I sent the damn text, but I wasn't thinking. I am so sorry, darlin'. So goddamn..."

He didn't get the chance to finish the rest of his sentence. Felix was suddenly in his space, cradling his cheeks between two warm hands. He smelled a little like old fish and seawater, and it was the strangest, grossest, most amazing thing in the world because his lips came after that—and his warm tongue.

Felix kissed him for so much more than he was worth, knocking Dei against the side of his truck as their bodies pressed together like they were drawn by magnets. Dei felt like he was going to lose his mind with how much he loved this man. He felt like the force of it would literally break him.

And he never wanted it to stop.

"Sweetheart," he murmured against Felix's mouth.

Felix slowed down, taking a deep breath as he pressed their foreheads together. "Sorry. I was so fucking scared earlier, and I'm…I don't even know. I don't know how I feel."

"That's alright," Dei told him. "But is there any chance you wanna come home with me? My leg's killin' me, and I just want to lay in bed and hold you."

Felix pulled back just slightly, his eyes narrow and dark with purpose. "Is that all?"

Dei felt a quiet rumble of need rush through him, and he cupped Felix's cheek, running his thumb over his lush lower lip. "I suppose I could be convinced otherwise. So long as you're there."

"I need you," Felix said. "I feel really insecure right now."

Dei squeezed his eyelids shut and wrapped his arm around Felix, holding him a bit tighter. "I'm so sorry."

"I know. And it's ridiculous that I'm all worked up over a few words and a misunderstanding, but…"

"No," Dei told him. "It's not ridiculous. I've been pushin' you away all week with all the shit I have happening, and then I came at this all wrong. I should'a talked to you first before all this. Told you that I didn't want space and that I needed as much of you as you could give me. And I'm gonna work on bein' better for you."

Felix met his gaze, then started to lean in for another kiss when the sound of the metal door slamming shattered the moment. Dei turned his head just in time to see Jamie and another guy behind him following in a wheelchair. Felix let out a soft groan and shook his head.

"Unless you want to have a whole conversation about what happened," he murmured against Dei's shoulder, "we should get the hell out of here. Like, now."

Dei cupped Felix's chin, lifting his face, and he kissed him fierce and firm. "Get in the truck, gorgeous. We have somewhere to be."

22

Felix couldn't stop his knee from bouncing as he rode beside Dei. He wished he could hold his hand, but it was worth it just to be near him as he processed Dei's earlier words. Felix had envisioned those three little words about a hundred times since coming back from California. He'd come up with a hundred and one scenarios about how he'd react.

None of those had been by the side of Dei's truck after a long day of Felix believing his heart was about to be shattered. He should have said them back in that moment. He was absolutely in love with Dei in ways he didn't think he could be, but when he tried, the words refused to come out.

Maybe it was leftover fear that everything was about to fall apart. Or maybe he just wanted to be somewhere he felt safer. Dei didn't seem to mind either. He just laughed as they escaped Jamie and Eli.

"The whole shop hates me, don't they?" Dei asked after a long beat.

Felix winced. "Hate is a strong word. And Max is the world's biggest fucking gossip queen, so I promise you everyone's going to know part two by morning."

He stared down at the last text on his phone, his chest warm and happy.

> Jamie: As your newly appointed best friend I just need you to know that if he hurts you, I'm coming for him. Eli says same. He'll run over his toes, and believe me that shit hurts.

"Sugar?"

Felix looked over at Dei, and it was only then he noticed how dark the bags were under his eyes and how exhausted he was. He felt a surge of guilt because Dei was now doing everything to apologize when Felix had been the one to panic and shut down. If he'd taken the time to wait for Dei—to be patient and trust him—he wouldn't have worked himself up.

"Yeah?"

"You okay there?"

Felix rubbed at his eye. "Uh…no. Not really."

"Honey, I am so sorry I—"

"No," Felix said in a rush. He let out a small growl of frustration. "It's not you. I promised to trust you and not let you push me away, and the second I felt like I was losing you, I just…lost it. I broke my promise, and I feel like shit about it."

"Oh, darlin'," Dei said from behind a sigh. "This is all a big mess."

Felix laughed, the sound broken and watery. "Yeah. A bit."

Dei made a quiet hum in the back of his throat. "Part of me wants to offer to drop you off at your place and talk about this in the morning, but I think I need you tonight if you're up for it."

"I don't want to be alone," Felix said very softly. The very thought made his stomach hurt. He wrapped his arms around his middle and said nothing else until they pulled up in front of Dei's, and he couldn't bring himself to move.

"Want me to carry you inside?"

Felix snorted and rolled his eyes. "No. But another kiss would be nice."

"I can do that." Dei turned and cupped Felix's cheek, drawing him in for a soft press of lips. It held none of the desperation of before. It was just quiet comfort that Felix hadn't realized he needed until right then. "I love you. I hope it's okay for me to say that now."

Felix nodded, kissing Dei again. "Please don't stop telling me."

"I love you," Dei whispered again.

For a moment, Felix felt like he was walking through a dream, and he took a moment to collect himself before pulling away. They locked gazes for a moment, and then he got out of the truck and heard Dei follow as he walked around the back to meet him at the door.

His place felt oddly strange since he'd been away for so long, but the smell inside was a warm blanket of familiarity, just like the hand that pressed to the small of his back. Dei crowded up against him and kissed the side of his neck. "Meet me in the bedroom, darlin'. I just need to put a few things away."

Felix nodded, basking in the touch until Dei let him go, and then he headed to the bedroom and flicked on the light. It looked barely touched, and the bed was made, which had Felix wondering if Dei had slept in there at all since he'd been back. He hadn't looked at the couch, but he had a feeling he'd find blankets and pillows there.

Dei had wanted his own space, but it still broke Felix's heart to know he'd been going through his mom's declining health all on his own. He didn't think Sofia had changed her mind about coming back to the Keys, which meant every decision had been resting on Dei's shoulders.

Felix sighed, kicking off his shoes and peeling away his clothes until he was left in his boxers and T-shirt. He pulled the covers back, and just as he was climbing onto the bed, he heard Dei's soft groan behind him.

Glancing over his shoulder, he grinned. "See something you like?"

"Oh, sweet thing, don't even get me started tonight."

That wasn't the deterrent Dei wanted it to be, but Felix knew they needed a moment to talk before they went any further. He pressed his lips together and shuffled toward the wall, turning to watch Dei undress.

He moved like an interpretive dance, the way he peeled himself out of each layer. Felix knew that no matter how much he wanted Dei —how wild he was about every inch of him—he was still insecure. And Felix understood that feeling more than he wished he had to.

"Gotta stop hittin' me with them bedroom eyes, baby," Dei rumbled as he walked toward the bed and sat.

Felix shifted over and wrapped around him, pressing his chest against Dei's back as he took off his leg and set it to the side. He felt Dei's sigh of relief more than he heard it, his broad shoulders rising and falling and moving Felix with him.

Unable to help himself, Felix pressed a line of kisses along the back of Dei's shoulders. "I thought I lost you," he admitted. It was easier to speak when he wasn't looking at Dei's face.

"I know. I'm so damn sorry."

Felix shook his head and finally forced himself to let go so Dei could slide up on the bed and stretch his leg out. Felix could see the tension in his muscles. His arm stump hung there the way it always did since it had little motion, but the corded ropes along his thigh were in knots, like a dozen charley horses.

Felix shifted around until he could pull Dei's stump into his lap, and he began to carefully knead along his skin.

"Oh, darlin'," Dei groaned, head tipped back against the headboard, eyes shut. "You don't need to do this."

"Can I, though? I'll stop if you want, but it's obvious you're in pain."

Dei opened his sighted eye. "Only if you want."

"I do. I feel like I need to have my hands on you right now," Felix confessed. He wanted tangible proof that this was real. That it hadn't all ended at the sight of a single text. He hated how weak his emotions were now—how out of control he felt. And he hated that he didn't know if it would ever get better.

"My body's yours," Dei said very quietly.

They fell into silence, punctuated only by an occasional grunt as Felix found a tender spot, but soon enough, Dei was relaxed, and Felix's hands were tired. He shook them out, then curled into Dei's side, grinning when his lover picked his arm up by the wrist and pressed a kiss to each fingertip.

"How'd I get so lucky?" Dei asked.

Felix wanted to argue about luck, but that felt unfair. "So," he said instead, "you wanted to talk to me about something?"

Dei let out a long, deep sigh and shrugged. He continued to play with Felix's fingers as his brow furrowed in thought. "I know I said I love you quicker than you were ready for…"

"No," Felix interrupted. He didn't want Dei to go a single moment more without knowing. He sat up and waited for their gazes to connect. "I'm having a hard time with those words. I don't know why. I might just be afraid, but I'm…it's." He stopped and licked his lips. "It's the same for me."

Dei cupped his cheek. "You don't need to convince me how you feel. I already know."

Felix bowed his head and took a slow breath. "I just don't want you to think I'm in this any less than you are."

"I don't," Dei murmured. "Things are gettin' real complicated in my life right now, and I thought it would best for us if I did it alone. But it didn't take me long to realize that's not what I want. I need you, baby."

Felix felt suddenly restless, like being side by side with Dei was far too much space. He shifted his body around and slid a hand over Dei's thigh. "Can I?"

"What, sweet thing? What do you want?"

Felix didn't answer him with words. He shifted up onto his knees, and at the sight of Dei's damn near feral grin, he straddled him and shifted as close as he could. Dei's hand immediately moved to his hip, where he squeezed and tugged Felix forward.

"God, sweetheart," Dei murmured. "You are somethin' else."

Felix went hot all over, then felt a rush of emotion because for a short while, he thought maybe he'd never hear Dei call him that again. He bowed his head until their foreheads were resting together. "I'm sorry I lost faith."

"I'm sorry I didn't give you reason to believe," Dei shot back. His arm moved around Felix's waist, and he tipped his head up, kissing him softly, deeply, slowly.

Felix immediately lost himself in the slow, push-pull dance of Dei's mouth, his tongue heavy and wet and dominating as it licked against Felix's. His entire body was hot with need, and as he began to harden, he rocked against Dei.

"Yeah. Fuck," Dei groaned. "I'm okay if you're not ready, but darlin'..."

"I'm ready. I need it. I need you," Felix all but begged as he rocked his hips. Dei held him tighter, catching his moan with another kiss.

Felix let Dei take the lead because he needed him to. He needed to let someone else take control. He wanted to be beneath Dei—to be taken apart with careful fingers and biting kisses and a massive, warm body pinning him to the sheets, dragging his orgasm out of him like Felix owed Dei every ounce of pleasure.

"How do you want me?" Dei asked.

Felix took in a shuddering breath before letting one hand drift between them. The heel of his palm felt for the hard nub, and he rubbed it the second Dei's breath caught in his chest. "Anything," Felix told him. "Just need to feel you. I want to be good for you."

Dei's eyes were dark, his pupil swallowing up his iris. "Undress," he ordered. "Then lay on your stomach."

Felix's limbs felt loose and lazy as he rolled away, his feet hitting the floor. Dei's gaze on him was almost like a physical touch as he stripped away his clothes, letting each piece fall beside the nightstand. He was on display, and it made him feel strange and a little too seen, but he also never wanted it to stop.

"Come here," Dei ordered.

Felix shuffled closer, stopping right at the end of the mattress. Dei's fingers pressed to his sternum, drawing a line down to his hard cock jutting out from his nest of dark hair. Dei stared at it, then grabbed him and squeezed, rubbing his thumb over his hole.

"This for me, baby?"

A single tremble moved through Felix, and he nodded. "Yeah."

"Mm. So fucking good for me. You have no idea what it does to me watching you respond like this." Dei let him go, then reached between Felix's legs and gave his balls a gentle pat. Felix twitched. Hard. Fuck, he hadn't realized having his balls lightly smacked would feel good. Dei's expression darkened. "Like that?"

Felix whimpered, unable to form words, but his legs spread just a little, and Dei's hand pulled back, slapping him again—a little harder this time. Felix grunted and moved, almost like he was trying to chase the light sting.

Dei let out a shaking breath, then dropped his leg off the side of the bed and pointed to the space beside him. "Face down."

Felix crawled, his entire body lit up like every nerve ending was being electrocuted. The bed felt too hard, the comforter too soft. The fabric was oddly rough against his skin, and he wasn't sure he'd be able to handle lying there, but Dei was relentless.

He pressed his hand to the small of Felix's back, forcing his hard dick to rub against the cotton. Felix shifted his hips, and Dei groaned.

"Look at you," he murmured. "Horny and needy for me. Can't even keep still, can you?"

Felix knew he probably looked like a fucking cat in heat, the way he was humping the mattress, but he couldn't help himself. He needed to take the edge off whatever the feeling was crawling through his limbs. "Not enough," he managed to say.

Dei hummed in thought, and then his nails dug into Felix's hip, and suddenly, the world was right again. "Thought so," Dei whispered as he leaned in. His teeth grazed the top of Felix's shoulder. "I ain't gonna hurt you tonight, but at some point, we're gonna talk about this because I wouldn't hate it if you let me paint your ass red with my hand."

Felix's breath left him in a rush at the thought, and his hips began to move faster until Dei's firm grip stopped him.

"Don't you fuckin' dare, sweet thing. You're savin' that come for me. Got it?"

"Yeah. Yes," Felix said. Forcing himself to sit still was torture, but the idea that Dei was happy with him was enough to keep him obedient.

"Fuck, you are such a good boy. You're so fucking perfect, Felix. I can't believe you're here. I can't believe I've done anything to deserve you."

Felix squeezed his eyes shut harder as Dei's hand traced a pattern around the ink on his back, finally pulling aside his ass cheek. Felix felt exposed, and the feeling only got worse when he felt the rough scratch of Dei's beard seconds before warm lips kissed his hole.

"Oh. Oh...*fuck*," Felix sobbed.

"My sweet, sweet, precious baby," Dei told him. He licked a stripe over him, then deepened the kiss, the tip of his tongue just barely breaching his muscle before pulling away.

Felix sobbed a little louder. He didn't want more than that—it was too much—but before he had to beg for it, Dei pulled back, trailing kisses up his spine until he was gently biting the back of his neck.

"I know," Dei murmured. "I know. I've got you."

Felix realized that Dei was telling the absolute truth. There would be some days he would have to spell things out, but Dei paid attention to him like no one ever had. He knew the most subtle shifts of his body, like reading Felix was no harder than reading a book, and that thought was almost terrifying.

Would he ever be able to keep secrets?

Would he want to?

Dei kissed along his shoulders, then gently rolled Felix onto his back, where he bit at his Adam's apple, sucked a mark into the crook of his neck, then went right for his nipples. Felix groaned, the feeling shooting right into his balls as his hips bucked, and Dei just laughed, pinning him with his hand as he continued to torture the sensitive nubs.

Before begging words left Felix's lips, Dei moved onto his stomach, to his tender ribs, and the cut of his hip. Felix was wound up and ready to ascend to the fucking heavens by the time Dei licked a stripe along his cock, and he knew he didn't have the control to hold back.

"I c-can't," Felix gasped.

Dei curled his fingers around Felix's cock and squeezed tight enough to hold back his orgasm. "I want you to come in my mouth, sweetness."

Felix pressed his hand over his mouth to hold back a moan, but Dei wasn't having it. He dropped Felix's cock and ripped his fingers away from his lips. "I don't think so. You want to be good for me, don't you?"

Felix swallowed heavily, panting as he nodded.

"Then give me all your sounds, baby. Those moans are mine. You hear me?"

"Mm-mhm," Felix managed.

That seemed to be enough for Dei, who quickly went back to work on Felix, holding the head of his cock between his lips while his fingers played with Felix's heavy balls. The touch was gentle at first, but as Dei sank lower, the grip on his sensitive sac became firmer. And just as it started to crest into pain, Dei let go.

Felix gasped, thrusting upward into his mouth without the ability to stop himself, but instead of Dei pulling away, he sank further. His fingers pressed hard into Felix's hip, urging him to fuck forward, and Felix lost himself to the pleasure racing through his body.

He wasn't even aware he was coming until Dei was swallowing it all down, and his whole body trembled with aftershocks. He felt ecstasy like little bubbles popping under his skin as Dei let his spent cock slip from his lips, kissing the head, then kissing down his softening shaft.

He moved lower, licking along his balls before kissing up his hip. His body moved as fluid as water, sliding up Felix's prone form until they were nose to nose, and then he kissed his mouth. Felix tasted himself on the edge of Dei's tongue, and he sucked on it until Dei was rocking against him, moaning softly with each panting breath.

"Baby," Dei murmured.

"Tell me how to get you off like this," Felix begged. "What can I do?"

"Just lie there. Fuck, just—just lie there," Dei said. His voice was trembling, tone shattered as he pressed his hard nub into the cut of Felix's hip, bore down, and began to thrust against him. Felix matched his rhythm, going pliant when Dei grabbed him by the shoulder to brace himself.

After a short forever, Felix felt his lover stiffen, then shudder with his release. Dei let out a long groan, burying the sound against the crook of Felix's neck as his hips finally stilled and the heavy weight eased.

"Tell me I didn't hurt you," Dei whispered.

Felix shook his head. "Not in any way I didn't want."

There was a moment's pause, and then Dei gently rolled to the side, resting his stump against the pillow and taking Felix by the cheek. His palm was warm and smelled like sweat and come, and Felix was pretty sure there was nothing better in the world.

"We're gonna talk about some of that later," Dei said. "But I need to know if you've done any of that before?"

Felix shook his head. "I don't think so. I've had a few people get a little rough, and I liked it in the moment, but it was always over really fast, and they never stuck around."

Dei's expression cracked. "Oh, darlin'…"

"I'm glad they didn't," Felix said quickly. "I was so starved for affection I might have stuck around with some mediocre asshole and missed out on this."

Dei blinked, then burst into laughter, shaking his head as he fell back against Felix and let his cheek rest against his shoulder. "I'm so in love with you. And if you want me to give you a pretty, cherry-red ass one of these days, I will."

"I think I…yeah," Felix said.

He didn't know how to describe the way it made him feel, but it wasn't just the pain. It was also the fact that it was Dei. It was that he was with a man he trusted beyond all reason. A man he knew loved him and would die before going too far. It was being with someone who wanted to give Felix everything—who didn't judge him for the things he needed…or the things he wanted.

"Talk to me," Dei said softly.

Felix closed his eyes and shifted his arm so he could tangle his fingers in Dei's soft hair. "I'm shit-scared of losing you. I'm…Jesus Christ, I am so in love with you, Dei, I feel like I'm losing my mind. This is the kind of love that could ruin a person if they lost it."

"You're not gonna lose me," Dei whispered, holding him just a little tighter. "Not if I have anything to say about it."

Normally, Felix wouldn't let someone make that kind of promise to him. He knew better than anyone that things could change on a whim, and not even Dei could control the universe. And yet, he couldn't bring himself to refuse Dei's vow because somewhere deep down, he felt the same way.

He couldn't imagine a world where he wasn't this in love—and maybe it was dangerous and reckless, but he was ready for that in his life.

He'd been cautious for so long, and he was ready to just let himself be loved.

"Can I stay?"

"Darlin'," Dei murmured, kissing the side of his jaw, "if you tried to leave, I'd chase you down."

Felix laughed. "Okay, creeper."

"Not sorry," Dei murmured. He pulled away abruptly, lifting himself off the bed a few inches, and he stared at Felix. "Say it again, sweetness. I need to hear it."

Felix didn't need to ask what Dei meant. He owed him a few more of those words—from now until the day he died. "I love you," he said.

Dei's smile was like the sun, and the kiss he gave after was somehow even brighter.

23

"You got a light touch, bud. How the fuck are you not booked for the next three years?"

Rafe looked up at Felix and laughed. "Stop kissing my ass. It's a bad look."

Felix grinned unrepentantly. He'd been out of work for the last week after a grand mal seizure had taken him down, but it had been expected. He would always have ups and downs, and medication wouldn't always be the most effective, but it was starting to matter less and less because he was happy.

Dei was a huge part of it, but Felix was starting to feel like this was his family—like everyone at the shop were all the missing pieces of the puzzle he'd been putting together for years. He wanted to believe that he would have eventually gotten there if he and the other guys had stayed with Bonsai, but he knew that coming to Key Largo—that signing with Irons and Works—had healed parts of them they hadn't even realized were wounded.

He stared down at the band around his ankle and grinned. Rafe's style was unique, and Felix had been craving a piece by him for months now, and with his time off, he was finally able to get it. It was also distracting him because Felix was supposed to be heading over to meet Dei's mom for the first time that evening.

She hadn't gone downhill as fast as Dei had been worried about, but he knew she was slipping. She didn't remember him anymore, and it was a good day when she ate a few bites of a meal. Felix knew Dei was struggling with the slow loss, and Felix was struggling with the fact that there was nothing he could do except be there.

He couldn't stop the inevitable. He couldn't take Dei's pain away.

All he could do was exist and trust Dei when he said that was enough.

"Hello, my children," came a voice from the front of the shop, and Felix looked at Rafe, who mouthed, 'Tony.'

He'd been coming around a lot more lately, and Zeke had finally fessed up that Tony was preparing a couple of the other guys to take over the shop in Colorado because he was looking at a partial retirement, and the Keys were definitely on his list.

A face appeared over the partition a second later, and by process of elimination—and the shit-eating grin on the man's face—Felix knew who it was.

"That looks badass, man," Tony said.

Rafe flushed and shrugged. "It's nothing."

"Fuck you. Don't insult my ink like that," Felix said, kicking at Rafe's arm.

Rafe laughed and shook his head. "Fine, fine. It looks amazing on your leg, princess."

Felix flipped him off as he smiled at Tony. "Good to see you again."

"You recognize me?" Tony asked. There was no mockery or malice or even that gross, invasive curiosity people tended to have with Felix when they knew about his face blindness.

"No, but I Sherlocked it," Felix said.

"By that, he means I told him," Rafe cut in.

Tony laughed. "Sweet. I'm glad you're here too. I just got off the phone with a friend of yours, and I wanted to see what you thought about me bringing another artist around."

There was a still, tense silence around the shop. They had room for one or two more, but it would start encroaching on their business soon if Tony kept bringing people in. And it had taken Felix the better part of a year to learn everyone at the shop. He wasn't sure he had it in him to start over with someone new, and he couldn't imagine who the hell would call themselves Felix's friend who wasn't already at the shop.

"His name is Leif."

Felix sat up, almost knocking Rafe's hand and ruining his lines. "Seriously?"

Tony's smile was soft. "Yeah. Thought you might like to hear that."

Felix fell back with a quiet thump. "I didn't think he was ever going to leave LA."

The silence was punctuated with the sound of a chair scraping, and then Paris's head appeared next to Tony's. "He's good people. My vote is yes."

"If this grumpy asshole's on board, you've got my vote," Rafe said.

"Seconded!" came Jamie's voice from somewhere near the back room.

"Max will say yes," Paris said in his low rumble. "They were pretty close before we left LA."

Tony glanced around, then nodded. "I'm gonna give him a couple weeks' trial to see how he fits. And you and I," Tony said, turning his head to look right at Zeke, "will be having plenty of conversations. I'm not here to step on your toes."

"This is your baby," Zeke said. "I know you need a change of scenery, and…"

"No," Tony said. "Well, I mean, yeah. Kat's desperate to get out of the mountains, and things are a little stale there. We found a really badass school for Jazz here on the islands, and I just…I don't know, man. It feels right. But I have absolutely no fuckin' desire at all to start over with running things. I just hope y'all can find me a spot for a few of my regulars who live down this way."

Zeke stared at him, then burst into laughter. "You think any of us have the balls to tell you to get the fuck out?"

Tony shrugged, rubbing the back of his neck sheepishly. "I don't ever want to be that asshole."

"You are that asshole," Zeke said, cuffing Tony on the shoulder. "But we love it."

Felix couldn't argue. He had been nervous taking up space in the shop, knowing that the name and reputation belonged to someone a few thousand miles away. When Tony had first come around, it almost felt like being observed by their omniscient god who was there to pass judgment.

But it didn't take long for Felix to get the sense that the guy was just there to love the hell out of them all.

"Alright," Rafe said, doing a final pass with the green soap, "you're done. Tell me what you think."

Felix stared down at the silhouette band wrapping his calf. It was a simple design—the ocean surf and a moon in shades of blacks and greys—and to someone else, it might not have meant anything. But to him, it was a small piece of what he'd left behind—one of the few things that he actually missed.

And it lessened any urge to go back.

It allowed this place to fill in those gaps, making it home.

Felix got up and stretched, encouraging some of the blood flow to the rest of his limbs as Rafe cleaned up his station. When he made the second pass around the shop, he caught Tony staring at him, and he offered him as friendly of a smile as he could manage, and Tony took that as immediate permission to walk over and drape an arm over his shoulders.

"I hope you'd have the balls to tell me to fuck off if this was too much for you."

Felix laughed and shook his head. "Do you wish more people hated you?"

Tony laughed. "I'm way less of a people pleaser since marrying Kat, but I think I'd probably shrivel up and die if that happened."

Felix grinned at him. "Well, you can chill. We like you a lot. I think most of us here are pretty damn jealous that the Colorado guys had you for so long." Felix liked the other guys too, but a lot of them had moved on from the shop. They existed on the fringes of the tattoo world—and maybe that would be Felix someday, but he couldn't picture it.

And Tony was a man who could never really leave it behind.

"You doing okay, though?" Tony asked.

Felix still wasn't used to having people give a shit about him that way, but he forced himself to nod because yeah, he was. He really, really was. "Better than I have been in years. And I hope Leif likes it here. I kind of ditched him, and I feel like shit about it."

"You think he fits in?"

"I think he's been searching for a place like this for a long time," Felix admitted. "I should have convinced him to come with us."

"Everyone gets to where they're going. It just takes time." Tony squeezed the back of his neck. "Big plans tonight?"

"Meeting my boyfriend's mom," Felix said and didn't give more details than that. Most of the guys knew about her, so it was likely Tony did too, but Felix appreciated when the older man didn't ask.

"Good luck. I about shit my pants the first time I met Kat's parents. I cussed at her grandma too. But luckily, she still wanted to marry me."

Felix laughed and wished more than anything the meeting was going to be more traditional, only because Dei deserved that happiness, but he'd make the best of it. Tony wandered off, and Felix came back to Rafe to get some Saniderm slapped on his leg, and then he slipped out the back door without any more goodbyes because he knew if he let them distract him anymore, he'd give in to his anxiety.

He made his way across the dark parking lot and eventually stepped through Midnight's front door. There was a small crowd waiting to be sat, but the hostess saw Felix and waved him past, mouthing 'kitchen' at him. He gave her a quick salute, then darted into the server station and through a set of swinging doors.

Felix had once asked if it was breaking some kind of health code, him being back there, but Dei had just rolled his eyes and kissed him. It didn't answer the question at all, but he took it as permission to hang back there when he wasn't disturbing dinner service, and in that moment, the only person behind the line was Dei.

Felix adored watching him move around his space. He didn't want to be a dickhead and say that he couldn't imagine being able to pick back up a career of cooking in a kitchen after losing an arm, a leg, and an eye, but it was true. He could barely function in his shop after losing half his memory and a small chunk of his cognitive abilities.

Felix wouldn't ever say that Dei did it effortlessly. That felt unfair to all the work Dei put in and all the tools Jeremiah had given him so he could do his job without missing too many beats. But he made it look like he was born for it.

And, of course, watching him was addictive because he really was the most attractive man Felix had ever seen, and he couldn't believe he was allowed to love him.

He leaned against the counter and watched as Dei threw together the Noods noodle dish—something Dei had made for him repeatedly since they'd come back from LA. He didn't look up until he finished garnishing the plate, and his face broke out into a huge smile as he slammed the ticket next to the dish and then barreled around the corner.

Felix braced himself to be lifted, pressed into the wall, and kissed within an inch of his life.

"You're early," Dei rumbled against his lips.

Felix nodded. "Rafe finished up faster than we planned, so I thought I'd walk over before I lost my nerve."

Dei sighed and cupped his cheek as Felix's feet hit the floor. "We'll be lucky if she even realizes I'm there."

"It's still your mom. What if she doesn't like me?"

"Then it's probably because she thinks you're a ghost. She's always hated ghosts," Dei told him, giving him another swift kiss. "Give me five, okay? I just need to wipe everything down, and then we can take off."

Felix wanted to tell him not to rush, but he really wanted to get the evening over with. He didn't want to hurry through meeting Dei's mom, but he knew this was a moment of closure for Dei—it wasn't the beginning of what should have been a relationship between him and his boyfriend's mom.

And he knew that was killing Dei.

The man had grown up with almost no family, and he didn't know if he'd ever have a real relationship with his sister, so this was one of the last threads Dei had to hold on to. And there was no way to stop fate from cutting it when it was time.

Felix went back out to the restaurant and found Jeremiah at the bar with one earbud in, his laptop in front of him. Felix approached and tapped him on the shoulder, leaning in to be heard over the slight, buzzing crowd.

"Hey, man."

Jeremiah smiled. "Felix. Dei said you were coming in so you could meet Alexandra."

Felix hopped up on one of the chairs and twisted his fingers in his lap. "Have you met her?"

Jeremiah's face fell a bit, and he reached out, shutting his laptop. Even behind his thick glasses, his blindness prevented him from meeting Felix's gaze, but his expression was piercing. "Yeah. Dei and I used to bring her lunch a few times a week last year, but her stomach stopped tolerating restaurant food."

"I know it's a ridiculous question," Felix said, "but do you think she would have liked me?"

"Fuck yeah," Jeremiah said quickly. He leaned his elbow on the bar top, and his eyes closed. "She was a badass. She had a hard life, and I think there's some resentment Dei's been keeping because he didn't get a mom who was able to care for him the way he wanted. It's shit he's gonna have to deal with eventually, but he loves her. And she loves him."

Felix appreciated the way Jeremiah wasn't using past tense, even if Dei's mom didn't remember her son anymore. And he wanted to believe Jeremiah was right. He waited to see if he felt lingering jealousy that Jeremiah had gotten time with her where he never would, but instead, he was just grateful Dei hadn't been alone for all that time.

"You okay?" Jeremiah asked. "You're quiet."

"Sorry. Bad seizure late last week, so I'm still a little funky."

Jeremiah's brow furrowed. "Dei told me. You feeling okay?"

"A lot better. And he's been more than enough help," Felix said. "Sometimes too much."

Before he could feel guilty for complaining about Dei's mother-henning, Jeremiah burst into laughter and reached for him, squeezing his wrist when he found it. "That fucker is gonna run himself ragged on purpose."

Felix smiled and glanced toward the kitchen. It got annoying from time to time, but he wouldn't trade it for the world. He saw movement a second later, and then Dei appeared in the doorway like some sort of avenging angel on god's mission.

"Stop flirting with my boyfriend."

Jeremiah removed his hand, but only to flip Dei off. "I can't help it. He's adorable."

"I'd threaten to tell Max, but I think he loves Felix as much as he loves you," Dei muttered, walking around the counter and throwing his arm around Felix. He leaned down and kissed his neck. "Hi, baby."

Felix warmed all over. "Hi."

"You ready?"

Felix nodded and felt more secure than ever. "Catch you later?" he said to Jeremiah.

The other man nodded, then went back to his computer as Felix slipped off the stool and took Dei's hand, letting him lean against Felix since he wasn't using his cane. They made their way down the narrow hallway and out the back door, and Dei stopped him just before they reached his truck.

"You sure you're okay doing this?"

Felix frowned at him. "Why wouldn't I be?"

"Because I know it's awkward as fuck, me havin' you meet my momma while she's…you know…"

In hospice. Dei wasn't great at saying that word because he knew what it meant. In the end.

Felix tugged him close and cupped his cheek. "I'd want to meet her under any circumstances, okay? I'm not just doing this for you. I want to know her."

Dei's face went soft, and he leaned in for a kiss. "God, I love you so much."

"I love you too," Felix whispered and let Dei pull him to the truck.

"…AND she caught me with my pants literally around my ankles, and when my granddad found a leech stuck to my ass, she laughed herself until she was blue in the face," Dei said, chuckling along with his story.

Felix grinned, not actually able to picture a tiny Dei with his pants down, half-covered in swamp, but he didn't need to in order to know he was adorable. And trouble. Glancing over at Alexandra, he saw her eyes were open, but there wasn't a whole lot going on in her expression.

From time to time, she'd look over at Dei with a tiny frown like she was trying to figure him out, but she didn't say a word. The nurse had said she'd been talkative in the morning, but usually by dinnertime, she did little besides sit there.

Felix hadn't asked about her treatment plan either. He'd done enough reading to know what happened toward the end, and he didn't need Dei to go through all that with him. He just needed Dei to be open about where he was and what he needed from Felix.

Tonight, it was being here.

Tomorrow, it would be something else.

After a beat, Dei gently slapped the arm of his chair, then stood and bent over his mom, kissing her forehead. "I'll see you later, okay? I love you, Momma."

She didn't react other than to curl her hands into fists, then release them again against her sheets. Felix debated about doing the same, but it felt wrong since she hadn't known him before, and she wouldn't ever really get the chance.

He offered his hand to Dei instead, and they left in silence.

Neither of them was willing to break it either, not even when they pulled into Dei's driveway and got out of the car. Felix still had his place, but more often than not, he stayed in Dei's house—in his bed, wrapped in his arm. And nights like tonight, Felix didn't need to ask if Dei wanted him close.

They undressed together, and then Dei went off to shower, and Felix made himself comfortable in bed as he waited. He heard the shower go on for longer than usual, and his heart ached. Eventually, Dei appeared, hopping on his leg as he made his way across the room, and he collapsed face-first against the sheets, turning his head so he could press his nose against Felix's thigh.

"I wish I knew if she was suffering."

Felix gently carded his fingers through Dei's hair. "My condition is so different than hers," he said, "but I can tell you that from my experience, she probably doesn't know what she's missing most of the time. For me, it's just like blank space. You know? It's like, I don't pay attention to it until I need something that normally exists there."

"And then what?" Dei asked, his voice barely above a whisper.

"And then I search for it. It's like trying to find a word at the tip of your tongue." Felix closed his eyes and breathed through the familiar sensation he always got when he was talking about his memory. "And it really sucks when it doesn't come to me. But it doesn't hurt. Sometimes it's just sad. Like when I try to think of your face during the day."

Dei rolled away just slightly to look up at Felix. "What do you do?"

"Sometimes I look at your photo, but usually, I just think of the way you make me feel."

Dei pushed up on his elbow and crept closer. "How do I make you feel?"

Felix smiled at him and traced a touch over his full lips. "Warm. Safe. Adored. Good."

Dei surged into a kiss, knocking Felix against the headboard. It wasn't a kiss of passion. It was a kiss of possession and in the best way. "You are, my baby. You are so fucking good. You know that, right?"

"I didn't, until you," Felix admitted.

Dei sighed and shook his head, their noses rubbing together. "Then I'm going to make sure you never lose that feeling. Not for one second of a single day for the rest of your life."

"I love you," Felix told him, overwhelmed by the feeling in his chest. "I love you so much."

Dei's eyelids lowered, and their lips brushed together as he said, "And I love you, my whole goddamn world."

AFTERWORD

EM Lindsey does not consent to any Artificial Intelligence (AI), generative AI, large language model, machine learning, chatbot, or other automated analysis, generative process, or replication program to reproduce, mimic, remix, summarize, or otherwise replicate any part of this creative work, via any means: print, graphic, sculpture, multimedia, audio, or other medium.

ALSO BY E.M. LINDSEY

Broken Chains

The Carnal Tower

Hit and Run

Irons and Works

The Sin Bin: West Coast

Malicious Compliance

Collaborations with Other Authors

Foreign Translations

AudioBooks

ABOUT THE AUTHOR

E.M. Lindsey is a non-binary writer who lives in the southeast United States, close to the water where their heart lies.

Join EM Lindsey at their newsletter or join their Ream Stories and get access to ARCs, teasers, free short stories, and more.